W9-BNS-348

VAGABOND
Heart

Ann Roberts

BELLA
B O O K S

Hillsboro Public Library
Hillsboro, OR
A member of Washington County
COOPERATIVE LIBRARY SERVICES

Copyright © 2017 by Ann Roberts

Bella Books, Inc.
P.O. Box 10543
Tallahassee, FL 32302

All rights reserved. No part of this book may be reproduced or transmitted in any form or by any means, electronic or mechanical, including photocopying, without permission in writing from the publisher.

This is a work of fiction. Names, characters, businesses, places, events and incidents are either the products of the author's imagination or used in a fictitious manner. Any resemblance to actual persons, living or dead, or actual events is purely coincidental. The publisher does not have any control over and does not assume any responsibility for author or third-party websites or their content.

Printed in the United States of America on acid-free paper.

First Bella Books Edition 2017

Editor: Katherine V. Forrest
Cover Designer: Judith Fellows

ISBN: 978-1-59493-562-6   **33614080590143**

PUBLISHER'S NOTE

The scanning, uploading, and distribution of this book via the Internet or via any other means without the permission of the publisher is illegal and punishable by law. Please purchase only authorized electronic editions, and do not participate in or encourage electronic piracy of copyrighted materials. Your support of the author's rights is appreciated.

Other Bella Books by Ann Roberts

Romances
Brilliant
Beach Town
Beacon of Love
Root of Passion
Petra's Canvas
Hidden Hearts
The Complete Package
Pleasure of the Chase

The Ari Adams Mystery Series
Paid in Full
White Offerings
Deadly Intersections
Point of Betrayal
A Grand Plan
A Secret to Tell

General Fiction
Furthest from the Gate
Keeping Up Appearances

Acknowledgments

When I first had the idea to set a romance on Route 66, I thought it would be nothing more than just an interesting backdrop. That changed once I began researching the Mother Road (term coined by John Steinbeck) and taking trips along various portions of '66. I fell in love with the great neon signs, the "giants," the stories of the travelers, and the great determination of citizens to preserve and restore a piece of Americana. So this book became a love letter as well as a romance.

I am indebted to Jerry McClellan's *EZ Guide to '66*. It is without a doubt one of the best travel guides available. If my challenged spatial and navigation abilities could find some of these hidden gems, anyone can. If you take a trip on the Mother Road, get this guide.

Thanks to my wife and son for indulging me as we criss-crossed through several states, doubling back when we missed something important and stopping to gaze at piles of rubble that used to be so much more. There was even a ghostly experience at La Posada, which I've included in this book.

As always, a huge thanks to Linda, Jessica, and all of the Bella Books family for their support and industriousness in all things publication that are probably way beyond my understanding. This one is book seventeen. I appreciate you sticking with me.

Finally, without the guidance of my editor, the legendary Katherine V. Forrest, this tale would probably still be meandering somewhere between Flagstaff and Winslow. Of course, as is often the case when I work with Katherine, she's had an experience similar to the plot of my story. So it didn't surprise me to learn she'd traveled Route 66 when she moved across the country. Ah, to be so worldly...and talented. Thank you, Katherine.

Finally, a special shout-out to all the readers who continue to read my books and contact me. Your support is the greatest encouragement to keep writing.

About the Author

A retired high school English teacher and administrator, Ann Roberts lives in Eugene, Oregon, with her wife of nearly twenty-three years and their dog. When she's not writing or editing, Ann can be found at the local wineries or exploring one of Oregon's natural spectacles. A two-time Lammy finalist and Goldie winner, Ann was awarded the Alice B. Medal in 2014. She can be reached through her website, annroberts.net.

Dedication

To Great-Aunt Nell,
a world traveler who wanted to see it all

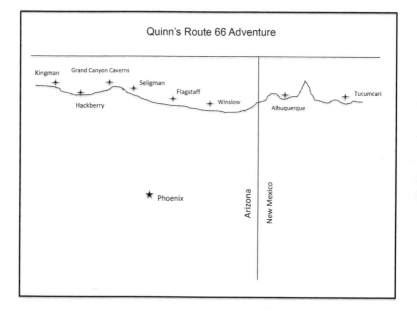

Quinn's Route 66 Adventure

Kingman
Grand Canyon Caverns
Seligman
Flagstaff
Hackberry
Winslow
Albuquerque
Tucumcari

★ Phoenix

Arizona
New Mexico

CHAPTER ONE

"Do it, you damn son of a bitch! Make my wife a rich woman!"

Quinn O'Sullivan charged out of her ground-floor apartment and looked up at the unfolding scene. Her construction foreman, DD, hung over the crumbling second-story railing. The electrical subcontractor, known only as Buzz, hovered over him, ready to shove him off. She raced up the cement stairs. Other members of her crew ran to help.

She reached Buzz first. His small black eyes dared her to do something. While she wasn't a petite woman, Buzz had her by at least a hundred pounds, much of it muscle in his arms. If she tried to attack him, she'd probably wind up over the railing with DD. Emboldened by the appearance of Rod, her drywaller, she grabbed a nearby nail gun. Just as Buzz let go of DD, Rod grabbed DD's hand—and Quinn fired a nail into Buzz's foot.

He wailed in agony and fell to his knees. Quinn and her crew circled DD to make sure he was okay. He nodded and glared at a moaning Buzz.

"What happened?" Quinn shouted.

DD ran his hand through his thick brown hair. He was wiry and muscular, but his soft features betrayed his lack of masculinity. "He asked if I had a real dick. I said I did and I knew my penis was bigger than his because I'd ordered an extra large. Then I compared his to a Little Smokey sausage." Buzz started to shout as the rest of the crew laughed, but DD held up a hand to hold their attention. "Actually, that's not correct. First I compared his to a Vienna sausage, but he didn't know what that was." The crew howled and Quinn couldn't stop the chuckle that burst out of her. While her crew had no problem with DD being a transgender male, some of the subcontractors couldn't get past it.

"My foot! Do something!" Buzz wailed.

"Shut up!" DD ordered. "It doesn't hurt half as much as it will when they pull that nail out," he gloated.

"I got it all on film," Ward said.

"Good," Quinn said. "Send it to me."

"On it, boss."

He was the youngest and most tech savvy of the crew, barely eighteen, with dark Filipino good looks.

Quinn crossed her arms. "All right, Buzz. Time to go to the ER. Since the elevator isn't working yet, you'll have to hobble down these stairs. I imagine it's gonna hurt like hell."

When they lifted him up, he emitted a horrific cry, and the crew scowled at him. Crying was frowned upon by the construction trade in general, but Buzz was crying at a level reserved only for those who accidentally saw off a limb or pierce their lung with a piece of rebar. She followed behind them, checking her Dropbox account for Ward's video footage. They pushed Buzz into the passenger seat of her company truck, ignoring his pleas to be gentle with his foot.

She turned to Rod and said, "Hero man, you come with me. DD, get everybody else back to work. And get Buzz's wife's name from his emergency contact sheet. Call her and tell her we're going to St. Joe's."

"Yes, boss," DD said.

Rod puffed out his chest and smiled before he climbed into the cab's backseat.

Quinn ran back to her apartment for her keys. She glanced at the display on her phone. Her sister Fiona had called as well as Michelle, her funder and sometimes lover. And her Aunt Maura had shared a video in Dropbox.

"Wow." She couldn't believe her seventy-year-old aunt could navigate video sharing. That could wait. Michelle could wait. She hit speed dial and hoped Fiona didn't need her immediately. But since she was calling instead of texting, it probably meant there was a problem.

She piled into the cab just as Fiona answered. Her sister was treated to Buzz's moaning.

"What the hell is that?" Fiona asked in her thick Irish accent.

"Nothing."

"Nothing? Are you crazy?"

"Little accident at work. What's up, Fi?"

"It wasn't little!" Buzz screamed.

"Pipe down," Quinn snapped.

"Just a reminder that you're coming over to stay with the boys tomorrow night, right?"

"Yes. I haven't forgotten."

"I just wanted to check. You get so busy with these flipping projects that you forget a lot."

Quinn didn't disagree. She was deep in an apartment renovation that ate most of her time. She was also her sister's go-to babysitter. Her two pre-teen nephews were always plotting mischief and no sitter had ever agreed to a second visit. The last one had run screaming from the house after Fiona and her husband Steven had returned from a movie and found the sitter bound and gagged in the living room. In true O'Sullivan fashion, the boys were forever making up games. That one had been called Kidnap.

Quinn went over a speed bump and Buzz wailed.

"Oh, my God, Quinn," Fiona exclaimed. "That man sounds like he's dying."

"Not yet," Quinn said mildly.

"Since I have you on the phone, I want to talk about your birthday party."

"No, no birthday party."

"I want to come!" Rod interjected. He leaned forward on the seat and pointed at himself. Quinn shook her head.

"I promise it's not going to be a large party," Fiona clarified. "Just family and a few of your interesting friends."

"Why don't we just keep the party to family?" Quinn whined. Her family disliked several of her close friends and they felt the same about her family. The O'Sullivans were truly an acquired taste. Any new person had to survive an initiation that bordered on hazing.

"I'm not up for an evening of playing referee," Quinn said. "It's my birthday and I should decide."

Fiona sighed. "You really don't want anyone else at your thirtieth?"

"No," she said sharply. "Just tell me when and where."

"Hold a sec," Fiona hissed. Quinn heard her sister's back door open and she pulled the phone away from her ear. Fiona shouted, "Boys! Get Mr. Squeaker out of the pool! You can't teach a guinea pig to swim!" Quinn heard her nephews protest, but Fiona shouted over them. "Right now!" The back door closed again and Fiona said, "Where were we?"

"You'd just canceled my birthday party."

Fiona laughed. "Fat chance." A huge wail blared through the phone from her youngest nephew, baby Donnelly. Fiona cooed at him and eventually said, "Small party. Just family. Fine, I'll get back to you. Please don't forget about babysitting—I mean watching the boys."

Quinn knew her nephews hated that Fiona still used the term babysitting about them. "Of course," she said.

She looked at Rod in her rearview mirror. He'd slumped dejectedly on the seat, pouting. He was the most sensitive of all the guys on her crew, and she suspected he had significant learning disabilities. He never got the jobs that required great thinking, but he was the best drywaller she'd ever seen. "Hey

Rod, don't be mad. The party is just for family. If we have a get-together for friends, you'll be first on the guest list." He nodded. "Are we good?" she asked. He nodded again, but he wouldn't look at her. "C'mon, Rod. Give me a smile. He finally obliged. "Great."

She pulled into the ER parking at St. Joe's and glanced at Buzz. His eyes were closed. She hoped he hadn't passed out—or died. When she squealed into a spot and slammed on the brakes, his foot thumped and his eyes bugged out. *Not dead.*

He turned to her and cried, "You did that on purpose!"

She smiled. "I did. Before we go inside, we need to come to an understanding." She opened Ward's video on her phone and held it up so Buzz could see. "Okay, here's what we've got. A great image of you attempting to kill DD. Look how clear that is!" He watched but his whole face telegraphed agony. "So you need to tell me how you wound up with a nail in your foot."

At first he seemed confused until Quinn waved her phone at him. He hung his head and mumbled, "Accident."

"What, Buzz?"

"It was an accident!"

"That's right. If you don't want DD to call the police, it damn well better be an accident. The fact that you attempted to kill DD because of who he is, makes it a hate crime. That adds time to your sentence. Are we clear?"

She knew what had happened was a gray area. DD might have provoked him, and she doubted Buzz understood the finer points of law. It was better if the whole thing just disappeared. Her insurance would cover the emergency room visit, and she'd never allow him on a project again.

He nodded, and when he looked at her, his face was a puddle of pain. "Please help me."

"Of course," she said sweetly. "Let's go, Rod."

The intake clerk gathered a few basic facts, took one look at Buzz's foot and had a nurse get him into triage immediately. As much as Quinn would've loved to drop him off and resume her day, she wanted to make sure his story about the nail gun remained the agreed upon version. The nurse wheeled him into a room. She took his vitals and was asking him about the accident when the curtain opened and a doctor joined them, reading her iPad. She was petite with dark brown skin and long black hair held back by a gold clip. Despite her stature, her presence was powerful. The room felt as though the air had changed.

"Hello, Leslie," she said to Buzz in a quiet, but commanding tone. "I'm Dr. Singh. Let's take a look at your foot."

Leslie. Quinn immediately understood his need for a nickname. DD would love that piece of information.

He nodded and she gently turned it left and right. "Oh, my." She looked at Quinn for the first time and stumbled over her words. "I'm sorry. Are you Leslie's wife or girlfriend?"

"No!" Buzz shouted, glaring at Quinn.

"No," she said mildly. "He was working on my construction project." She put out her hand. "Quinn O'Sullivan." She gazed into the doctor's rich brown eyes until she introduced herself.

"Dr. Singh."

When their hands met, Quinn grimaced. Dr. Singh's hand was delicate and soft, whereas hers were rough and calloused. "Sorry. Consequence of the trade."

"Nothing wrong with hard work."

"Hey, doc. A little help here," Buzz pleaded.

Dr. Singh had Buzz lie back while she elevated his foot. "How did this happen?"

He glanced at Quinn before he answered, an action not missed by Dr. Singh. Her face grew wary as he said, "Workplace accident."

"I see."

She gave Quinn a hard look before removing his work boot and starting a morphine drip. The staff asked him questions as his treatment proceeded, but Quinn tuned it all out and focused on Dr. Singh. Her movements were fluid and her expression remained focused. The lab coat was slightly too large for her petite frame, and she continually pushed up the three-quarter length sleeves with her long fingers. She wore no rings, only a necklace with a gold emblem and diamond stud earrings. And she smelled lovely, a floral scent that wasn't overpowering or obnoxious.

The examination over, Dr. Singh said, "We're taking you down to x-ray, Leslie. Once we see where the nail lodged, we'll develop a course of treatment. Okay?"

"Great, doc," he slurred. The morphine had taken over.

The nurse and an orderly wheeled him out. He actually waved at Quinn as he departed and she chuckled. Once his gurney disappeared, she felt Dr. Singh's stare. She stood to meet her gaze at eye level. It was a great excuse to be close and study her face, particularly her lips. Sultry was the word that instantly came to Quinn's mind. She wondered what it would be like to kiss her.

"As a doctor," she said slowly, "I must follow up when I notice suspicious behavior."

"I understand."

"Did Leslie's injury—"

"He goes by Buzz, just so you know."

She lost her train of thought and blinked. There was a long pause and only after she took a breath did she continue. "Was Buzz's injury really an accident?"

Quinn hesitated. She wanted to say something cryptic, something that would prolong the conversation and keep the good doctor from floating away to her next patient, because she seemed almost ethereal. She was lovely. Exotic.

She suddenly remembered Dr. Singh was waiting for her to answer. She swallowed and said, "Yeah, it was."

Dr. Singh lifted her chin, debating whether or not to believe her. Quinn sensed she was prolonging their meeting as well. Something was happening. The energy in the room shifted. She leaned toward her...

"Are you Dr. Singh?" a woman blurted as she threw open the curtain.

She immediately stepped away from Quinn and greeted her. "I am."

"I'm Buzz's wife, Shirley," the short, plump woman announced. It was difficult to see her facial expression underneath the red Make America Great Again cap.

Quinn stepped behind Shirley and slipped through the curtain, but not before she took one last look at Dr. Singh. Her beauty was unique, perhaps because Quinn didn't know anyone of Indian descent. She wanted to remember her. For a split second, Dr. Singh glanced at her, as if she were trying to do the same.

Quinn quickly left for the waiting room and reclaimed Rod. Her phone, which she'd set to vibrate, now had five voice mails and three texts. The chance meeting with the beautiful doctor floated away as she plunged back into her chaotic life.

CHAPTER TWO

All Quinn saw was an eyeball. Nothing else. It seemed to jump out from the laptop's screen, and she reflexively leaned back in her desk chair.

"Don't have a damn idea if this fuckin' thing is even working," the eyeball's owner muttered.

She immediately recognized the speaker as her Aunt Maura. After a few more curses, Aunt Maura sat back on the tiny plaid seat of her Airstream camper. Behind her were the familiar bright yellow curtains with smiley faces that Quinn had chosen years ago.

Aunt Maura tucked her shoulder-length gray hair behind her ears and tugged at a chin hair. She'd already forgotten the video was recording her every move. Quinn watched with amusement as her finger and thumb plucked the intruder. She smiled after the victorious pull and wiped her hand on the sleeve of her faded purple sweatshirt.

A mysterious stain that looked like jelly sat above her left breast, and Quinn guessed she hadn't noticed it. Maura was religious about working the crossword puzzle each morning while she had breakfast. Pieces of egg, toast, or pancake routinely dropped en route to her mouth as she analyzed the horizontal and vertical clues. Crosswords were just one type of game Aunt Maura enjoyed. She also loved travel adventures and had passed on that love to Quinn.

"Okay, I'm ready," she announced, smiling into the camera. "Hi, Quinn! It's me, Aunt Maura. You're probably surprised to receive this, but I got this newfangled Mac laptop with a camera." She shook her head in amazement. "Who da thunk you could make a movie with a camera the size of a pinhead on a machine no bigger than a heating pad? I know your generation is all about technology, but for me it's as much a pain-in-the-ass as it is helpful. I'm not sure you'll ever get to see this movie, but what the hell. When I'm done, I'll get it on that Dropkick thing."

Quinn snorted a laugh.

Suddenly the screen went black. Quinn reached for her keyboard, but then she heard Aunt Maura say, "Eleanor Rigby, get your fat ass off the new Mac!"

Quinn laughed heartily. Eleanor Rigby was one of Aunt Maura's three cats that shared the camper with her. Eleanor had a penchant for being the center of attention. When the screen remained covered in fur, Quinn knew Eleanor had stretched across the keyboard, ready for a nap.

"Not now," Aunt Maura scolded. Her liver-spotted hands wrapped around the cat and disengaged her from the laptop. As she vaulted off the table, she howled in protest. Maura sat back and scratched her head. "Where was I?" She looked down and saw the glob of jelly. "Son-of-a-bitch. Hold on," she said, and disappeared from the picture.

Quinn shook her head and used the time to click through several emails, most of them solicitations to volunteer or donate money. She gladly volunteered for multiple organizations, but she didn't have money to contribute to anything except the Fund to Care and Feed Quinn O'Sullivan. Her small construction company, FaceLift, sucked all of her time, money, and energy—

as did her family. She found an email from Fiona. The subject line read *Your Birthday*.

Quinn groaned. Her hyper-responsible sister probably wanted to remind her about the damn party at her parents' house. She deleted Fiona's email without reading it as Aunt Maura returned wearing one of her many Route 66 T-shirts.

Maura made her living driving across the fabled Route 66. She wrote monthly columns for various travel magazines, and every two years she updated her immensely popular travel guide, *Mother Road Travels*. Gift shop owners routinely bestowed clothing and trinkets upon her in hopes of a favorable review. Quinn knew what they did not: Maura O'Sullivan's opinion couldn't be bought.

Maura sighed as she looked into the camera and tucked her hair behind her ears again. She smiled and her face emanated kindness. Her wrinkles were the well-earned result of constant smiling and laughing during her seven decades. She'd told Quinn many times that the secret of life was attitude. Hers was always positive, and her approach, combined with her talent for storytelling, ensured her success as one of the most popular travel guide writers in America.

"Take two," Maura said with a sigh. "So, you're probably wondering why I'm taking the time and trouble to make a movie. Well, I'm not getting any younger. I have to start thinking about what the future holds and the inevitable possibility that I won't live forever. Because I probably won't."

Quinn sat up straighter. Was Aunt Maura making a dying declaration? If the next sentence included the word cancer, she'd scream. Aunt Maura was her favorite relative and the one person in the world who understood her. And, according to Quinn's mother, there was a lot to understand.

"I know you're busy," Maura continued, "and you have your own life, although your father has offered to draw you a map because he doesn't think your life is going anywhere." She quickly held up a surrendering hand and said, "At least not in the direction he would pick."

Quinn automatically rolled her eyes. Aunt Maura frequently broke confidentiality with her brother Shane, Quinn's father, to update Quinn on his comments or plans. He was Maura and Quinn's opposite. While Maura was focused on happiness and freedom, Shane lived for prosperity and success. He was the oldest and remembered the long journey to citizenship he and Maura had endured after they left Ireland.

Aunt Maura folded her hands together and looked solemnly at the screen. "Next week I'm going in for some tests that are probably long overdue. You know me, Quinnie. I don't like doctors. I've never liked anyone telling me what to do, least of all your father. I'm expecting this doctor might give me some bad news," she stated simply. "Regardless, I wanted you to know you'll be getting a package soon. So this video is like a preview. I want you to be on the lookout for it."

Quinn sat up straight, frowning. She rewound the video, having missed several seconds after Aunt Maura announced she was having tests.

Maura smiled and leaned toward the camera. "I love you, Quinn the Mighty."

She left the couch while Quinn wiped tears from her eyes. She knew Maura had a flair for the theatrical, but she really would miss her terribly when she was gone. They were so alike. Maura had dubbed her Quinn the Mighty as there was little Quinn wouldn't try. She'd learned to ride a bike at two and a half, skied at four, eaten chocolate-covered ants at her ninth birthday party, and skydived at eighteen.

A loud bang from the computer screen made Quinn jump. "Oh, my God!" she cried. She never would've imagined her aunt would kill herself. She fumbled with her cell phone. Should she call 911? What good would that do? She'd received the notice of a shared Dropbox video three days before and just hadn't made the time to view it. *I'm a terrible niece!* She pictured the sheriff finding Maura's decayed body. Should she call her father? She stared at the computer screen, stricken with shock and grief.

"Wait, wait!" her aunt shouted as she returned to the couch. "Lousy timing for a car backfire. Had to hit the john. One of life's joys when you get older, stealth pooping. Sorry to scare you, Quinn." She pointed a finger and said, "Don't worry about me. When it's my time, God's gonna have to personally scoop me up, and I promise to be as ornery and prickly about leaving as a jumping cactus." Aunt Maura scanned the keyboard. "Now if I can just figure out which button stops this damn thing…" She flashed one more smile. "Bye, Quinnie."

Neither could know it at the time, but those words would be the last Quinn would hear from Aunt Maura. Until the Indian arrived.

CHAPTER THREE

A knock on Quinn's door woke her. Why didn't she hear saws buzzing and hammers pounding? Then she remembered it was Saturday. Six a.m. The crew came in an hour later. Another knock, this time louder.

"Coming," she called as she poured herself off her futon bed and made sure she was semi-clothed before she opened the door. Standing on the stoop was her best friend Disney, her arms full of stuff. Disney had been conceived on *It's a Small World*. Her parents had been Disneyland employees at the time. Unfortunately their after-hours copulation on one of the little boats had been captured on video. They'd been summarily fired, but not before they'd disproved the title of the ride and enlarged the world by one life.

Disney was the least "Disney-like" person Quinn knew. Her hair was maroon and she had a pierced eyebrow and nose. Today she wore a pro-choice T-shirt emblazoned with Donald Trump's face and the question *Don't you think his mother should've made a different choice?*

"Happy Birthday, Quinn!" she shouted.

And it's my thirtieth birthday.

"Thanks," she said, as Disney pulled her into a bear hug with one arm. Quinn motioned for her to come inside. "What's all this you've brought?"

"A few gifts. First, here's your customary Disney offering." She always gave her something from the Disney store. This year it was a Tigger backscratcher.

"Feels good," she said, testing Tigger's paw on her back.

"And this." Disney handed her a lesbian porn video titled *Lezzies with Lube.*

She nodded. "I don't think I've seen that one."

"Fine filmmaking at its best." Her expression turned serious. And this." She waved a small white flag in Quinn's face before handing it to her.

"What's this for?"

"I'm waving the white flag. I give up," she announced. "I surrender. I've tried to set you up for the last ten years. I admit defeat. As you move into a new decade, you're on your own." She kissed Quinn on the cheek and turned to go. "Don't forget your party tomorrow night at the Stonewall Club. It promises to be a crazy-ass time." She was halfway out the door when she turned to say, "And I hope you survive your family party tonight." She made the sign of the cross. "Go with God." Her face brightened and she said, "Toodles!"

Quinn chuckled. She loved Disney. She stared at the white flag. She didn't blame her for giving up. She wanted a girlfriend, but her relationships usually fizzled within five or six months. The women either couldn't stand her family or the fact that she didn't have a normal career. They always had the same complaint: Quinn and her living space were always under construction.

She was a flipper. She bought run-down places and turned them into profit. With few houses left to flip in Phoenix, Quinn had latched onto a new trend. When the apartment and condo market flourished after the recession, she saw an opportunity to rehab the old apartment complexes in Central Phoenix.

Many had been built in the sixties and seventies, and while they needed a huge makeover, their structure was solid. She'd found two silent partners, her father, who knew how to run a company, and Michelle, a woman with cash and an interest in Quinn—at least some of the time. She'd also found a construction crew of unique rejects, headed by DD, a man who used to be a woman. As a team they'd flipped two complexes successfully and were working on their third.

She always lived in the complex currently under renovation, and she hauled her stuff from one apartment to another as the remodel occurred. She owned little furniture, but stacks of books lined a wall. One day she would own a large house with a vast library, but for now she settled with the stacks. She'd given up on shelves, realizing that hauling the books from place to place was hard enough. She usually read a few books concurrently, and right now that included a book about Gettysburg and a biography of Jane Austen.

The under construction label also meant that any woman who spent the night faced constant hazards traversing to and from the bathroom. Her last real girlfriend had punctured her bare foot on a nail after a rigorous night of lovemaking. The tetanus shot in the ER had ended their relationship.

ER. Dr. Singh. She smiled as she remembered the lovely Indian doctor who'd treated Buzz. She closed her eyes and imagined her graceful movements around the triage room. She was assured and poised, completely at ease in her competence. Quinn felt her heart rate slow. Thinking of her had a calming effect. She was part of a world Quinn knew nothing about.

There was nothing lovely or calming about working in construction with male employees all day. There was belching, too many views of plumber's crack, profanity, and dirt. While she reveled in the daily craftsmanship of her trade, and she loved remodeling buildings that otherwise would be destroyed, Quinn rarely had the time to immerse herself in the finer things life had to offer. She could only read about them in her books.

She sighed. For now it would have to be enough. She scratched her head, thinking about her family party. The only member of her family who was attending her "real" birthday party was her totally cool brother, Ronan, the only person she completely trusted—other than Aunt Maura. She sighed and looked at her computer. She'd meant to call Aunt Maura about her intriguing Dropbox video but hadn't had the chance.

She threw on her work clothes and grabbed her hard hat. She opened her front door just as Bart and Ward approached. They carried a box of donuts. It was a Saturday morning tradition among the crew that someone brought donuts. Since Bart and Ward did everything together, they counted as one person on the rotation.

Ward held out the box to her and she saw that Bart held a dirty piece of notebook paper in his hand. She pointed at it. "What's up?"

Bart cleared his throat and pushed up his glasses. Quinn pictured him in a suit and tie. His appearance screamed geek, and the crew often joked that he looked too smart to work construction. "We used our break yesterday to think of some new names for the apartment complex."

"Great," Quinn said. She'd offered an extra hundred bucks to whoever came up with the best name for the remodeled complex. "Hit me."

Bart looked up and said, "What about the Crystal Met? You know, since we're building a bunch of fountains? The water is like crystal, and met is for metropolitan."

Quinn pursed her lips to keep from laughing and offered a serious look. "I'd worry people might think the name was crystal meth. That probably wouldn't attract tenants, at least not the ones who'd pay their rent."

"Oh," Bart said, recognition on his face. "Gotcha."

Ward pointed at the next one and Bart nodded. "How about The Garden of Eden?"

"Hmm," she nodded. "Possibly too religious, though I know where you were going with that."

They both shrugged, and it seemed they'd already thought she wouldn't like it. Bart looked at her hopefully. "We've saved the best for last. How about Retro?"

Quinn had been prepared to shoot down their last idea but she blinked. "That's pretty good, guys." They turned giddy smiles on her and she laughed. "Let me take that one under consideration. I'll share it with our funders."

"Thanks boss," they said in unison. They handed her the paper and high-fived each other as they headed back to work, almost skipping down the sidewalk.

She really liked the five guys she called her "skeleton crew." Three of them she'd found through friends and the other two had dropped—one literally—into her lap during a drunken party. They didn't have any problems with each other or a female boss. There were only issues with subcontractors like Buzz, and she tried to employ those guys only when necessary. They were often the epitome of the construction stereotype, and they struggled to listen to a female—or DD.

She glanced at her Mickey Mouse watch, a gift from Disney. She'd agreed to pick up a bartending shift at Fiesta South around noontime, not because she needed the money, but because Ronan had asked for her help. His head bartender had a family emergency and Ronan was stuck.

She sighed. It was like that with her family. Since she worked for herself and not in the family business, they assumed she could switch her plans at a moment's notice. And most of the time, like today, she could—because DD was a great supervisor.

Her parents, Shane and Gemma, owned Fiesta Mexican Restaurants, LLC along with their partners, a Hispanic couple they'd met years before through friends. Oscar and Lupe Maríez had dreams of owning a restaurant and had brought several of Lupe's mother's recipes with them when they'd crossed the border. The two couples now owned twelve restaurants throughout Arizona and New Mexico, but Oscar and Lupe had lost interest in the day-to-day operations and were content with reaping profits and allowing Shane and Gemma to make the decisions.

Not bad for two Irish transplants. They'd already passed the baton, or the shillelagh, to Quinn's older brothers, Ronan and Patrick, served as CEO and CFO respectively. Her sister

Fiona periodically stepped up as a fill-in manager when flaky staff abruptly quit, but Shane and Gemma had excused her from daily operations. She was the mother of their grandchildren, a baby and two boys who needed constant supervision.

Quinn was the only O'Sullivan who had not accepted a role in the Fiesta empire. She'd worked at Fiesta West throughout high school as a hostess and busgirl, but the countless evenings she'd spent cleaning salsa spills, interacting with boorish diners and sweeping up tons of complimentary chips had prejudiced her against a career in the food and beverage industry. Also, the smell of jalapeños would forever make her gag.

But they counted on her to help out occasionally, so today she would hang only half of the cabinets in unit nine so she could bartend at Fiesta West in the afternoon.

The morning passed quickly and by eleven she was getting ready for the bartending gig. She threw on her standard uniform of black pants and white button-down shirt. Her short red hair needed a trim, but that would have to wait. She checked her figure in the mirror, as the black pants were a little tighter than they'd been on New Year's Eve, the last time she'd bartended. Nearly four months later it didn't surprise her that she'd put on a few pounds during the winter.

While she wasn't thin, she wasn't really overweight. She had the benefit of a long waist that tended to spread out the extra pounds. Most notable, though, were her large breasts, a genetic gift from her well-endowed Irish ancestors. She'd seen the pictures going all the way back to the 1860s. Her maternal forebears all had an ample bosom, to quote her mother. A few women had been instantly attracted to her boobs, and she strategically unbuttoned an extra button of her shirt. She'd learned the key to big tips from women and men was displaying a bit of cleavage.

She scoured her cluttered desk for her keys. She suddenly remembered Aunt Maura's comment about having tests done. She quietly swore, chastising herself for not following up. Maura would never discuss the results if they were bad, and since Quinn hadn't heard from her recently except in video form, she guessed Maura was avoiding her. She grabbed her copy of *Mother Road Travels*. Maybe she could call her on break. She found her keys under some unopened bills and headed out.

She hurried to her car, a restored VW Thing. Since the complex was a construction area, the chain-link fence wrapped around it. She had a hard rule about company vehicles being the only cars allowed inside the construction zone, so she had to walk to hers just like everybody else.

She usually parked on the street but sometimes was forced to park in the vacant lot on the next block. The neighborhood was still rough, and she was always conscious of her surroundings—even in daylight. There had been a carjacking two blocks away, so she weaved her keys between her fingers like a weapon. As she reached her car, she saw movement to her right. A man emerged from behind a large truck and walked swiftly toward her. He wore jeans, a Western shirt with a bolo tie, an overcoat and a black cowboy hat. She couldn't see his face from such a distance, but she guessed he was Native American.

She jumped in her car and threw it in reverse. She'd seen enough episodes of *Criminal Minds* to know nothing good ever happened with strangers in parking lots. She glanced in her rearview mirror. He stood where her car had just been and watched her leave. She shivered and took a deep breath certain she'd just escaped being kidnapped or chopped into little pieces.

By the time she'd shaken her third martini, she'd forgotten the encounter. It was the NCAA semifinals, and the Fiesta West bar was packed with University of Arizona Wildcat fans. Each time the team made a basket, a cheer erupted. She didn't follow sports regularly, so she had little interest in turning toward the televisions behind the bar. Since her co-bartender Luis was a die-hard basketball fan and had organized the March Madness pool, she found herself doing double duty while he continually swiveled around to follow the game.

It was fine with her. He was a good guy and a great worker. Her extra effort made the time go faster. She'd also expect the bulk of the tips to come her way at the end of the evening. She barely noticed the faces of the patrons, her attention completely focused on the orders and the pours. Her father was a stickler about the alcohol. He knew the bulk of Fiesta's profit depended on alcohol consumption, not on the relatively cheap menu options. Generous pours were not tolerated.

She'd just filled up a tray with drinks and turned back to the bar. The man from the parking lot stood in front of her. He was indeed Native American, and up close she could see the fine turquoise and silver of his bolo tie. His jet-black hair cascaded down his back, and he'd removed his hat as a courtesy. Her eyes widened but she was emboldened by the crowd and the bar separating them.

"Why are you following me?" she asked in a raised voice. He opened his mouth to speak just as the crowd cheered again. He shook his head and pointed to the exit sign.

She mouthed, "No."

He frowned and her level of fear instantly dropped. He wasn't dangerous. Now she was curious. She signaled for him to wait while she crossed the bar and talked to Luis. She whispered that she needed to step away for a bit and pointed at the three people waiting for drinks. He hopped to it, and she motioned for the man to follow her. While the bar was crowded, the dinner rush was over. She found a two-seater table, and he squeezed his long frame into the chair opposite her.

"I'm sorry I scared you in the parking lot. I'm Zeke. I have a last name you wouldn't be able to pronounce," he said in a low but strong voice.

"I'm Quinn, and it's okay about the parking lot," she said with a shrug. "I'm sorry if I rained gravel on you by squealing away."

"You didn't," he said plainly. He withdrew an envelope from his jacket and set it in front of her. Scrawled across the front was her name, written in Aunt Maura's distinct handwriting. "I'm your aunt's attorney in Flagstaff."

"Should I open it?"

He held up his index finger and said, "Before you do, there's something you should know."

Quinn instantly knew. "She's dead."

His stoic expression cracked slightly and revealed his surprise. "Yes."

"She sent me a video about a week ago and mentioned she was having some tests done. She didn't think it would be good news."

He shook his head slightly. "She didn't mention any tests to me. I'm not sure what health issues she may have faced, but she was killed in a car accident two days ago. I'm very sorry."

The bar crowd erupted with a cheer, and she winced. She covered her face and tried not to cry. She couldn't believe it. Aunt Maura was an exceptional driver, logging nearly twenty thousand miles a year.

"What happened exactly?"

"The accident occurred on State Route 24, a two-lane highway between I-40 and the Four Corners. It was past dusk." He paused and asked, "Are you familiar with the road? It has many hills."

She tried to picture it. She and Aunt Maura had traveled most every state road, as well as the roads owned by the various tribes. She remembered a few roads that were quite hilly, and as a teenager she'd loved the drive. "Sort of, maybe," she replied. "I think Aunt Maura and I drove it once or twice."

"When you crest, you have no idea what's on the other side." He angled his hand upward to make his point. "Apparently, there was a drunk driver in Maura's lane. She wouldn't have seen him until she reached the top of the hill."

Quinn closed her eyes, imagining the look on her aunt's face as the drunk driver's headlights suddenly blasted her. "Oh, my gosh."

The bar patrons cheered again, and she almost screamed at them to shut up. She needed to pull it together until the end of the shift.

"I know this is a lot to take in," he said. He gently nudged the envelope toward her. "But she wanted you to have this."

She couldn't touch it. She still had more questions. "What about the drunk driver? Has he been charged?"

He bit his lip. "Unfortunately, no. I'm assuming you're aware that many of the roads in northern Arizona cross tribal land. The driver was a young Hualapai Indian. While he's answering to the elders, they believe there are some mitigating circumstances."

She cocked her head to the side. "Like what?"

Zeke sighed deeply. "His father is on the tribal council."

She threw up her hands. "That's not right," she cried.

"There's more," he said calmly. "The elders actually knew Maura and liked her. The head of the council personally asked me to send you his condolences. However, it seems Maura contributed to her own death. She wasn't wearing her seat belt."

"No," Quinn said, shaking her head vehemently. "Aunt Maura always wore her seat belt. She wouldn't start the car until everyone buckled up."

"I'm guessing she unbuckled it for a reason. Perhaps she was reaching for something, like her Cool Ranch Doritos? She would've unbuckled her belt just for a moment, but that was when she crested the hill."

Quinn wiped her eyes, dissolving the picture of her aunt flying through the windshield of her Dodge Charger like a human cannonball. She nodded, acknowledging that it could've happened that way. Aunt Maura loved to snack on Cool Ranch Doritos and a Mountain Dew while she drove, a combination for which she would compromise her safety. It was her driving fuel.

She glanced into Zeke's steadfast gaze. She saw wisdom in his eyes and it comforted her. She thought about Aunt Maura's video. She'd need to watch it again. Aunt Maura had mentioned dying...and an envelope. She picked it up and opened it. Inside was a note written on a piece of stationery from the Hotel Monte Vista in Flagstaff, one of Maura's favorite places to visit.

Dear Quinn,

I've asked my friend Zeke to deliver this to you. I know you tend to be naturally suspicious of strangers, which I believe is due to your ridiculous consumption of serial killer and murder shows. Anyway, you can trust him. He's one of the finest men I've ever met. He'll help you with what I'm asking you to do.

I want us to have one last adventure. I've put together a little game, following a piece of the Mother Road. All you'll need is time. Zeke will provide the rest.

Take care, Quinn the Mighty. I'll see you on the flipside.

Aunt Maura

P.S. Feel free to bring someone along for the ride. I won't mind.

She read it twice and still couldn't believe her aunt was gone. She noticed a few orange smudges on the paper, which smelled like Doritos. She was ready to bawl, but a thought occurred to her. "Have you spoken with my dad?"

"No, my instructions were to come to you." He looked at her uncomfortably and added, "I understand Maura's relationship with your father was strained."

She nodded. "They haven't spoken in many years. He's always been supportive of us kids knowing her, but he couldn't understand her life choices and she couldn't understand his."

"Families are difficult organisms. There is nothing simple about them."

She'd never thought of a family as an organism, but his definition certainly described the O'Sullivans. Shane had begged and goaded Maura to move to Phoenix and help with the business. She'd paid a secret visit to Fiesta Northeast and was completely underwhelmed. She'd sent Shane an email on the company website explaining that she found the waitstaff rude, the food average and the bathroom conditions deplorable. She'd gone so far as to discuss the pee on the seat. Shane never again suggested Maura join the Fiesta team, but as a good businessman who trusted his sister's judgment, he addressed the concerns she'd surfaced.

Still, Quinn imagined her father would be hurt that Maura had contacted her and not him. "What about her cats?" she asked. "What about Eleanor Rigby, Penny Lane, and Billy Shears?"

"They're fine," Zeke assured her. "My daughter has been taking care of them."

"What about her Airstream?" Although Maura owned a vintage Airstream motorhome, it usually was parked in one place for several months as she drove Route 66 in her Charger and friends took care of her cats.

He shrugged. "I'm not sure. Maybe that's part of the adventure."

She nodded. That would be just like her aunt. Everything was more fun if it was a game or adventure. "And where is Aunt Maura now?"

"Her body was cremated and I have her remains in my office in Kingman."

She cocked her head. "I thought you said you were from Flagstaff?"

"I have several offices," he said succinctly.

The crowd shouted about a bad call, and she remembered poor Luis. She stood up and said, "I have to get back to the bar. I need time to think about all of this."

He pulled out one of his cards and handed it to her. She looked at his last name. *Qoyawayma.* "For when you're ready."

"Thank you," she replied automatically.

He tipped his hat and left.

CHAPTER FOUR

Quinn looked in her rearview mirror at the cloud of dust following her down the winding road to her parents' house. They had bought the ranch after their first restaurant proved highly profitable in the eighties. Gemma had thought Shane was nuts. They were out in the middle of nowhere, had to build their own well, and wild animals routinely showed up on the property. Despite Gemma's objections, Shane had wanted his kids to grow up feeling free. Then in 2002, a homebuilder knocked on their door, asking if they would sell several parcels of their land. They agreed with some very strict conditions, the main one a guarantee that they could tap into the development's water and sewer lines for free—forever. The O'Sullivans were set for life.

She pulled in next to Ronan's BMW and stared out the windshield. She dreaded telling her family that Maura was dead. She'd spent the last twenty-four hours sobbing and laughing as she thought of her aunt. Her father would want to know why Zeke hadn't visited him. She glanced at her copy of *Mother Road Travels* on the passenger seat. She'd been rereading various parts, remembering different trips she'd taken with Aunt Maura. In previous editions she'd been mentioned as "Quinn, my niece and ice cream authority." She flipped to the title page and realized there were six editions of *Mother Road Travels*, with the notice that a seventh edition was planned for summer. She wondered if Aunt Maura had completed it, and if so, where was it now? The last page of the book was always the same headshot Aunt Maura had used for years. It was one of Quinn's favorite photos. Her toothy smile and kind eyes won over strangers, and her trademark river hat was eternally perched on her head.

Laughter drew her attention from the book. Her two oldest nephews ran out of her father's shop, their arms full of tools and supplies. Goran was twelve and Ivan was ten, biological brothers from Croatia who'd been adopted by Fiona and her husband Steven. They loved coming to the ranch and were experts at mischief. When they saw Quinn's car, they immediately ran to her. Often she was their co-conspirator, and they'd heard many stories about her daredevil antics as a child.

Both were lanky towheads with typical Slavic olive complexions and downturned noses. While Fiona and Steven educated them about their Croatian roots, they were proud to be adopted Irishmen. Each year their new teachers got a surprise when they met Goran and Ivan McInerny.

"We're building a zip line in the barn!" Ivan announced as he dropped what he was holding and threw his arms around her.

Goran nodded but offered no hug. He was far more reserved and introverted. Fiona maintained that Goran remembered their early life, which included their parents' murder and a year of living with abusive relatives.

Quinn studied what they had collected for their project, making sure she didn't need to confiscate any of it. Whereas they thought she was their partner in crime, Gemma and Fiona expected her to keep the boys and the family heirlooms safe, especially the antiques Gemma collected on her weekly junking trips. During Quinn's last visit, she'd saved a revolutionary-era bed warmer from being used as a bat during a game of water balloon baseball.

She plucked an antique rolling pin amidst the wire and tools at Ivan's feet. "Nope. Can't use this. Granny will have your heads if you ruin one of her precious treasures."

"But how will we make a handle?" he pouted. "You have to hold on to something when you're going down the line."

"Let me go inside and say hello to everyone. Then I'll come out and help you, okay?"

They nodded and ran off as she climbed the back steps. She turned around and yelled, "Hey!" They automatically stopped when she used the shouting voice, a genetic trait of all the O'Sullivans. "Don't jump off *anything* until I return."

"Okay!" they replied with a giggle and bolted away.

She could hear her family through the door. There were no introverts, except Goran, among the loud O'Sullivan clan. Even those who married into the family held their own in the flowing and fluid dialogue that was like a movie that paused at the end of a gathering, only to resume the next time they met. Her oldest brother Patrick and his wife Eloise were sounding off about a favorite family topic, water conservation.

"Arizona only has a decade of water left," Patrick asserted. "If we don't start rationing like California, we're going to be in trouble." He noticed Quinn and added, "Happy birthday, sis," before his gaze returned to Fiona, his opponent in this debate.

"Happy birthday, Quinn," Fiona said, her finger pointed at Patrick. "Who's going to be in charge of making that happen? Certainly not the legislature. The Corporation Commission? I think not."

Eloise, a curly-haired Protestant, looked at Fiona. "I'm not so sure you're right."

Quinn moved next to Shane, who pulled her into a hug. "Happy Birthday, daughter."

She planned to tell him about Aunt Maura so he could announce it to the family. But as she started to speak, Ronan stated businesses needed to do their fair share, which incited her father to whip his head around and enter the fray.

"That can't happen," he proclaimed, stepping away from Quinn. "Restaurants can't afford any extra taxes or fees. People already complain if we serve them tap water."

"As they should," said Steven. "Phoenix water is the worst. Happy birthday, Quinn."

"Exactly," Shane said.

Quinn navigated toward Gemma, whose corned beef and cabbage, the birthday dinner staple at the O'Sullivan house, demanded her full attention. Ronan grabbed Quinn as she passed and kissed the top of her head before shoving her to Fiona, who did the same. Feeling more like a pinball than a guest of honor, Quinn sidled up to Gemma and Ronan's wife, Maureen, who was testing the cabbage, and handed the spoon to Quinn.

"Not bad," she said and Maureen nodded. She relinquished the spoon to Maureen, and Gemma hugged Quinn fiercely. "Happy birthday, Quinn."

"Thanks, Mom."

"Happy birthday," Maureen offered before she returned to her prep duties.

Gemma eyeballed the rolling pin Quinn held in her hand. "Do I want to know what those boys are doing?"

"They're building a zip line," Quinn reported. "I told them I'd help after I checked in with all of you." She set the rolling pin inside a high cupboard. The boys were known for moments of insolence when they got a wild hair, so any confiscated objects were hidden until the end of a visit. While Quinn had been able to save the antique bed warmer, the horn from Gemma's vintage phonograph had been destroyed when the boys stuck it on their heads as a blindfold during a game of blind tag.

"Did you have a chance to pick up those tile samples for me?" Gemma asked.

"They're in the car. I'll bring them in after supper."

Quinn had agreed to lay new tile in her parents' bathroom. While Shane was a master tinkerer, he didn't relish projects the way Quinn did. Anytime one of the O'Sullivans needed to fix something around the ranch, it was always Quinn to the rescue.

She listened to the continued debate on water conservation, searching for a moment when she could speak to her father. As far as she could tell, Ronan and Eloise were the only two people who favored water regulations. She understood such a governmental shift would be a burden to her family, but it was the right thing to do since they lived in a desert. She'd learned, though, that while she was encouraged to voice her opinion even when it differed from the rest of the family, she inevitably felt like a traitor on the drive home.

After three minutes of unsuccessfully attempting to gain her father's attention, she resorted to the sure-fire method, her mother. She leaned closer to Gemma and said, "I really need to talk to Dad."

"Shane, Quinn needs to speak with you!" Gemma bellowed without ever turning around. The water conservation issue immediately vanished, as if it had been shot dead.

"Oh!" Shane said, clapping his hands. "It's happened!" She was bewildered as he rushed over and threw an arm around her shoulder. "You're thirty and it's time," he said proudly.

Everyone applauded and whistled while Quinn's jaw dropped. Shane was thinking of their deal. He'd agreed to be Quinn's flipping partner if, when she turned thirty, she would reevaluate her life and seriously consider joining the family restaurant business.

"No, no, Dad," she explained.

"It's about time," Patrick said, raising his pint of beer. Everyone joined him, drowning out Quinn's repeated objections. "You can't keep doing all that construction work."

"I say we make her the full-time manager of Fiesta South," Ronan pronounced.

"That's a fabulous idea!" Shane agreed excitedly.

She couldn't decide whom to disagree with first. "No, that's not what I wanted to say. I—"

"She'll have that lackadaisical crew whipped into shape in no time," Fiona added. "And if there's ever a leaky faucet or if a window gets smashed, she can take care of it herself."

"She'll need to be tough, but I think she's up for the challenge," Shane said. He lifted his pint again. "Here's to Quinn!"

"To Quinn!"

"Aunt Maura's dead!"

The room finally went silent. Her mother's spoon clattered as it hit the tile floor. "I'm sorry to spring it on you, but it's too hard to get a word in."

"How do you know this?" Gemma asked. "What happened?"

"Auto accident. Her attorney came down from Flagstaff. He gave me a note she left to be given to me upon her death. She wants us to go on one more adventure. I don't know what that means, but I guess I'll find out."

She looked at her father. His hand rested on the marble countertop as if it were supporting him. His eyes remained downcast. He couldn't look at her.

"Did Aunt Maura leave anything for Dad?" Patrick asked.

"Or the rest of us?" Fiona added, in a hurt tone.

"No, the letter was just for me. I don't know that much about it right now. Her attorney and I only spoke for a few minutes."

Quinn scanned their pained expressions. Despite the friction between Maura and Shane, she'd loved all of them and sent presents on their birthdays, called just to chat and invited them to travel alongside her. Quinn knew, though, as Aunt Maura had, that her siblings didn't enjoy cruising Route 66 as much as Quinn.

She'd always felt one of the greatest things about being Irish was family. Even when she'd told them she was gay, they'd accepted it, despite the opinion of the Catholic Church. It was hard to see them wrestle with the truth now.

Eventually Shane raised his pint. "To Maura," he said solemnly.

"To Maura!"

"I'll go check on the boys," Steven murmured with a look in Quinn's direction.

Everyone else's droopy expressions remained in place. Quinn had tanked her own birthday party. "I'm sorry," she said, "but Dad, I couldn't bear that I knew and you didn't."

He shook his head. "It's not your fault, Quinnie. It's no one's fault." He darted out the back door and she knew he'd disappear into his shop. It was his version of a man cave.

As a child she'd snuck out her window after bedtime and run toward the single light in the shop's window to spend hours with her dad. After several phone calls from Quinn's teacher, who stated Quinn kept falling asleep during class, Gemma had tried to stop her. She told Quinn a story about the Javelote, a mean animal that had the face of a Javelina and a body like a coyote. It ran fast, faster than Quinn, and it would eat her if it found her outside in the dark. For a few nights Quinn remained in bed and fell asleep, too terrified of the Javelote to go outside. When her teacher commended her for staying awake in class, she told her about the Javelote. Mortified, the teacher told Quinn the truth.

She went home and confronted her mother, who shook her head and said, "Can't win for tryin'. Fine, stay up all night."

She'd learned a lot from her father during those evenings, including welding, auto repair, carpentry, and electrical rewiring. Her grades had suffered somewhat, but she became a night owl, a quality that hadn't proved useful in high school or college either. She'd lasted a semester at Glendale Community College but failed most everything because she couldn't wake up early enough for class. She'd also frequented many different beds since women seemed naturally attracted to a red-haired lass. She'd been asked many times if *all* of the hair on her body was red, and she'd allowed a decent percentage of women to find out for themselves. They also loved her inconsistent Irish brogue, which she often practiced on the drive home from her parents' ranch.

She wandered into the living room and Fiona followed her. They dropped onto the couch and Fiona put her head on Quinn's shoulder.

"Tell me more about the accident."

"Head-on collision with a drunk driver on State Route 24."

"Oh, that's awful! When was the last time she talked to you?"

"It's been a while. She sent me a video. It was odd. She said she wasn't going to be around forever and she was overdue for some tests. It's almost like she predicted her time was coming. I didn't think anything of it. You know how she was."

Fiona sat up and crossed her arms. "No, Quinn, I don't."

"Of course you do," she protested. "We each had a game we played with her that she never played with the rest of us. She wanted us each to have a special memory with her." Quinn's game had been Candid Picture. Maura would pull alongside a stranger's car and Quinn would snap a Polaroid. Most people smiled and waved, but a few had flipped her off. The last time they'd played the game had been several years ago, and Maura had ended it when they pulled up next to a good-looking woman who smiled and flashed Quinn.

Fiona looked at her sympathetically. "Honey, we let you believe that. While she tried to play games with us, we weren't interested. Maybe because we're older and you're the baby."

"Oh," Quinn said, feeling a sudden pang of sorrow for Maura.

"You and Maura had a special relationship," Fiona summarized. "It wasn't the same for me, Patrick, or Ronan. You're both free spirits. I don't know," she said, looking at her lap. "You had the same thing with Dad," she murmured. "He never taught me half of the things you know."

"He would've if you'd snuck out with me at night."

She shook her head. "I wasn't going to do that." Their green eyes met and she said, "Truth is, I didn't want to know those things. That's why you can't cook anything and I can't change a tire."

Quinn hugged her. "And you can always call me and I'll change the tire for you."

"And I'll bring you soup when you're sick." She hugged her tighter and the distance between them lessened, at least for the moment. Quinn believed that was the purpose of their talks, to keep building the bridge over the chasm that separated them. She wasn't sure when, if ever, it would be complete, but she kept adding to it, hoping that someday it would be enough, especially after their parents were gone.

"Dinner in twenty!" Gemma announced.

Fiona patted Quinn's leg. "C'mon, let's go save Steven. He'll insist on testing whatever contraption those boys have created, and with his bad back, he'll probably wind up in traction."

"Good point," she affirmed.

They found both Steven and Shane helping the boys run a long cable from the barn's catwalk above the west door to the hay bales that sat across the barn. The rider would crash-land into the bales. Steven was on the catwalk with Goran while Shane and Ivan secured the other end of the line around a post a good distance behind the bales.

"Did you find something to use for a handle?" Quinn asked Ivan.

"Pops did," he said, referring to Shane.

Ivan held up a large C-clamp. The movable jaw had been swiveled all the way up the throat to close the clamp around the line. Her father had pulled the handle off an old scooter and attached it to the clamp with some flexible wire.

Shane checked the line's tension and stood up. He offered a smile in Quinn's direction. "Ivan, I think our birthday guest of honor, Quinn the Mighty, should be the first one to test this." Her father's use of Aunt Maura's special name brought tears to her eyes and extinguished the guilt she felt for being Maura's chosen confidant.

"Will you be first, Aunt Quinn?" Ivan asked.

She ruffled his hair and said, "Sure." She gazed at the line. It looked okay.

She climbed the ladder to the catwalk. Ivan followed but Shane stayed below by the hay bales. She smiled. It had been that way during her youth. Her father had always been on the sidelines for many of her daring escapades. He'd only stopped her once—the time she wanted to attach skis to the back of their four-wheeler. While he'd admired her creation of a new sport, prairie skiing, he wouldn't allow his expensive Rossignol skis to be sacrificed.

Quinn fastened the clamp to the line and checked the handle. It was secure. She glanced at her father. He seemed far away. This was a question of physics, and although he only possessed a high school education, he was a natural physicist. He understood speed, distance, height, force, and thrust. Still, a burst of anxiety overtook her, and she was about to suggest this might not be a good idea when the boys started chanting her name.

"Quinn, Quinn, Quinn!"

Their voices grew louder and she shoved aside the odd feeling. Quinn the Mighty was just that. Without another thought she pushed off the catwalk and sailed across the barn. In the same second she basked in the joy of flying, she also realized she was going too fast. The top of the line was too high. The hay bales loomed in front of her. She pulled up her feet to protect the rest of her body just as she smashed into them. The impact yanked the handle from her hands as her torso flew forward. She landed on her stomach, her right arm pinned beneath her.

Shouts greeted her as everyone rushed to see if she was okay. Dazed and smothered in hay, she didn't feel the pain until she tried to sit up. She cried out and looked at her arm—and the bone slightly protruding through her skin. The pain signaled every cell in her body and she thought she might pass out.

"Oh, my God, Quinn!" Steven shouted. "Are you okay? I mean, I can see you're not okay," he blabbered. Quiet and calm Steven instantly unraveled at the sight of blood or gore.

"Let me see it, Quinn," her father said in a gentle voice.

She held it up for his inspection as her mother wandered into the barn. She took one look at the zip line and then at Quinn's mutilated arm and said, "I guess that went a wee bit arseways, didn't it?"

CHAPTER FIVE

The O'Sullivans traveled as a pack. Despite Quinn's insistence that Fiona and Shane be the only ones to accompany her to the Estrella Hospital ER, the rest of the clan piled into the Suburban, including Gemma with a full pot of corned beef and cabbage. She refused to let her efforts go to waste. Soon the pungent odor required all the windows be rolled down for the fifteen-minute car ride. Quinn inhaled deeply, hoping her olfactory senses would distract her from her throbbing arm. She had a very high tolerance for pain, but each time her father hit a bump or pothole, she'd whimper and her mother would say sharply, "Shane, watch where you're going!" He ignored her, knowing bumps and potholes were unavoidable, and she tended to be shrewish when situations flew out of her control.

He accompanied Quinn to the ER's main desk while her entourage camped out in a corner of the crowded waiting room. The smell that followed them inside gained the attention of the other families and their sick and injured relatives. By the time Quinn returned to the molded plastic chair Ronan had saved for her, most everyone in the lobby was enjoying a bowlful of corned beef and cabbage, including the security guard stationed at the front door and several nurses.

Gemma worked the room, talking to the families and collecting email addresses from those who wanted the recipe. A man in a white tank top looked over at Quinn. She saw the bloody bandage around his right bicep and the cause of the blood, a large piece of metal that protruded from his arm. When their eyes met, he smiled foolishly and swayed in his seat. Quinn was positive he'd already downed a few painkillers. Having heard references to her party, he started singing "Happy Birthday" to her, and by the last line, everyone had joined in.

They applauded as a doctor in a long white coat appeared in the registration area, her back to them. Her straight dark hair was parted in the middle and flowed over her shoulders. She'd probably wandered out from the inner sanctum after hearing the commotion in the lobby. When she glanced over the shoulder of the admitting nurse, Quinn's heart lurched. It was Dr. Singh. She kept pushing up the coat sleeves with those delicate long fingers just as she had in the St. Joe's ER triage room a few days before. The admitting nurse pointed toward Quinn's family and Dr. Singh's gaze landed on Quinn. A slight smile tugged at the corners of her mouth. Then she looked away and returned to the ER.

Quinn frowned. For those few seconds, she'd completely forgotten the excruciating pain in her arm. When she was finally called back half an hour later, the corned beef was gone and Gemma was deep in conversation with the security guard. Her father stood to go in with her, but she waved him off. If Dr. Singh were to be her doctor, she didn't want a chaperone. In the past few days she'd thought of Dr. Singh several times. She'd never seen anyone who projected such self-assuredness. She had a strong presence that Quinn found incredibly attractive.

"It's okay, Dad. I'm fine by myself."

"Are you sure?"

He looked hurt so she leaned toward him and whispered, "The doctor's cute and I think she might've been checking me out."

"Oh," he said and sat back down with a wink.

A nursing student named Lydia led her down a hallway and gushed about Gemma's outstanding dinner and said it was the highlight of her day. Quinn nodded politely, trying to follow her chatter and not focus on her throbbing arm while Lydia took her blood pressure and made notes on her iPad.

"So what level of pain are you currently experiencing? Ten is excruciating, five is some pain and one is little pain."

"I'd say a nine," she answered and glanced at her arm.

"Let me take a look." Lydia glanced, aghast at the bone peeking out from the skin. "Oh. I'm surprised they didn't bring you right back. For someone who's at a nine, you're relatively calm and your blood pressure is in the normal range. That usually only happens with firemen or air traffic controllers. What do you do for a living?"

"Um, not those jobs. I just have a high threshold," she mumbled. The room started to spin. "I think I'm getting a little light-headed," she said. Then everything went black.

"Quinn? Quinn? Open your eyes, Quinn."

The voice had a thick accent and came out of the fog. She did as she was told and stared into Dr. Singh's warm brown eyes. In the harsh lights of the exam room, her black hair shimmered around her face like an aura. *Am I dreaming?*

"Quinn, do you remember me? Dr. Singh?"

Not dreaming. "Uh-huh. I remember you. How could I forget you? What are you doing here? How long was I out?"

She offered an amused smile and said, "That's a lot of questions. I'm subbing here for a friend. You were only out a minute or so. Just long enough for Lydia to come get me. Let's get your arm supported and get you back on the exam table."

She spoke crisply. Lydia handed her a sling, and she carefully slipped Quinn's arm into the pouch and pulled it around her neck. Quinn took a deep breath, inhaling her lovely perfume. She turned and stared into Dr. Singh's dark brown eyes. Their lips were inches apart. Dr. Singh met her gaze as they pulled her upright. She groaned as they set her on the table.

Dr. Singh examined her injured right arm while Quinn offered up her left to Lydia for an IV. "What's in this?" she asked.

"It's propofol, a painkiller," Dr. Singh replied. "The fact that you've gone nearly two hours with a broken arm and no meds is rather unusual. I imagine when you arrived in the ER you were as calm as you are now?"

"Um, yeah. I have a high threshold for pain," she repeated.

Dr. Singh knitted her brow. "While that's admirable, it's also detrimental. One factor that determines how quickly you'll be seen is your pain level. You didn't act like you were hurting so they brought back others before you. Few were as injured as you. Next time, be more dramatic."

Quinn chuckled. "Actually, this ER got me in faster than any other time. I'm thinking it was the corned beef and cabbage."

Dr. Singh cocked her head to the side. "How many times have you been to the ER?"

Quinn had to count. "Nine? Maybe ten? My mother would know."

"Are you prone to accidents?"

"No, just daring."

She said it flirtatiously to see if Dr. Singh noticed. Their eyes met, but when Lydia coughed, Dr. Singh automatically returned to uber professional mode.

"We need to disinfect this wound and she needs to go to X-ray," Dr. Singh said to Lydia, who immediately left to make arrangements. She adjusted her stethoscope and warmed the chest piece on her sleeve before sliding it into the open fold of Quinn's shirt. There was something erotic about Dr. Singh's long fingers nestled under her shirt. Her heart rate quickened, a fact the doctor confirmed when she glanced up at her. She followed her ongoing instructions to breathe as the stethoscope traveled around her chest. She closed her eyes and imagined leaning into her arms.

The fantasy died when Dr. Singh stepped back and pulled the earpieces out. "How did you break your arm?"

"I was the test pilot for a homemade zip line," she replied sheepishly.

"What is that?"

"You hold onto a handle that's attached to a cable and you jump off a platform and fly through the air." Dr. Singh looked at her as if she were nuts, and she realized how stupid she sounded. "It's fun but I'm clearly too old to be a tester."

"Clearly," she chided. "Perhaps you're too old to fly through the air at all."

"Oh, no. Zip-lining is fun and freeing. You should try it sometime."

"I have a fear of heights. I'd be petrified," she said.

"But facing your fears is exhilarating, don't you think?"

Dr. Singh chuckled. "It could be—or not."

"I think if you tried it with the right person…"

"Tried what?" Dr. Singh asked innocently. They left the invitation hanging and Dr. Singh changed the topic. "How is your worker, Buzz?"

"He's not my worker," she corrected. "And I have no idea how he is." Dr. Singh frowned. She felt obligated to explain. "There's more to that story than you know. Minutes before his *accident*, he'd nearly thrown my foreman off a balcony. My foreman is transgender."

Dr. Singh's frown deepened. "That's awful." She shook her head and tapped through Quinn's chart. She looked up, grinning. "It's your birthday."

"It is. I'm thirty."

"Congratulations." Her tone was friendly but not effusive. "I'm sorry you had to spend the first day of your new decade in the ER."

She shrugged. "It's okay. This saved me from an evening of family pressure and expectations."

Dr. Singh gazed at her thoughtfully, as if Quinn had triggered something personal. "And what does that look like in your family?"

"Today was a deadline of sorts. I'd made an agreement with my father that I'd consider going into the family business when I turned thirty. Really, I was stalling."

"What business?"

"We own the Fiesta Mexican restaurants," she managed to say. It felt as if her tongue wasn't in her mouth.

"Ah," Dr. Singh replied. "I've been to one a few times."

"Did you enjoy your dining experience?"

She looked at her as if she might laugh. "I don't remember. I met a blind date there for drinks."

Despite the cloudiness of thought she was experiencing, Quinn boldly asked, "Man or woman?"

Dr. Singh leaned closer and whispered, "Woman," before she returned to her stool and made notes on her iPad.

Quinn couldn't pull her eyes away from the gentle curves of the doctor's face. Her fingers flew across the keyboard without hesitation. Quinn found her seriousness reassuring. She admired the effortless way she flowed in and out of the conversation. She pictured her marching down the hospital corridor while other doctors and nurses approached her, seeking her advice. She'd suddenly yell, "Stat!" at the end of every sentence just because it was cool.

"Has anyone ever you told exotic beauty you are?" She swallowed and realized there was something wrong with that sentence, but she couldn't figure it out.

Dr. Singh pursed her lips and stifled a laugh. "No one has ever said that to me in quite the way you just did."

She wanted to say something witty, but clearly the drugs had staged a hostile takeover of her mind and she needed to be quiet. Luckily Lydia reappeared with a technician and a wheelchair. "Time for X-ray," she said, realigning the energy in the room.

Dr. Singh stood as the tech and Lydia helped Quinn into the wheelchair. "Once I see your films, I'll know how to proceed."

She made the statement with such assurance that Quinn simply nodded. Despite a bone protruding from her skin, she really was calm. She wanted a nap, but she willed herself to stay awake. She pictured herself lying in a field of lilies with Dr. Singh. Suddenly Buzz appeared. He was running...and screaming. DD was chasing him with a spear, threatening to reenact a few scenes from *Deliverance*. She leaned forward to kiss the doctor. She so wanted to taste those lips... But she was already gone.

The X-rays didn't take long, but instead of returning to the exam room, she waited in the corridor. Dr. Singh came around the corner, studying the films as she walked. Twice different nurses stopped her, but Quinn noticed she never yelled, "Stat!"

She offered Quinn a reassuring smile. "Okay," she said, thrusting the films up on a nearby film reader. "You have a compound fracture of your ulna." She said other things but all Quinn could see were her lovely lips moving.

"...the osteopathic surgeon agrees, so we're admitting you for surgery."

"You won't be doing the surgery?"

Dr. Singh seemed pleased by her question. "No, I'm not a surgeon, I'm just an ER doctor, but I promise you'll be in good hands." She glanced at Lydia and added, "Lydia is going to take you upstairs and the floor nurses will get you situated."

"What about my family?"

"I'll go talk to them." She offered a wry smile. "And I'll see if your mother has any corned beef left. I missed dinner."

"Oh, it's wonderful, Dr. Singh," Lydia gushed.

"I'm sure she'd be happy to make some for you if it's all gone," Quinn said, eliciting another smile from the doctor.

"I'll check in on you later." She squeezed her shoulder and left.

She nodded. Dr. Singh didn't need to check on her. She wasn't Dr. Singh's problem anymore, yet she'd promised to see her again. Lydia turned the wheelchair around and headed down the hallway toward some enormous doors. Quinn wasn't sure if it was the drugs or the thought of seeing Dr. Singh again, but after three people smiled at her, she realized a shit-eating grin was plastered to her face.

CHAPTER SIX

Quinn remembered little of the next twelve hours as the pain medication took her to places she'd never been. Her family hovered over her. Goran and Ivan got in trouble for racing wheelchairs down the hall. She was prepped for surgery. Somewhere in there she thought Dr. Singh came by, but that might've been a dream.

When the fog of medication had lifted, she finally opened her eyes and glanced at the enormous purple sheath that stretched the length of her right arm.

A soft knock pulled her attention to the doorway. "May I come in?" Dr. Singh asked.

"Of course," she croaked.

Dr. Singh wore jeans and a long-sleeved Oxford shirt with a backpack slung over her left shoulder. She looked like a college student. Quinn looked down at her flimsy hospital gown. She touched her head and confirmed that her red hair was as spiky as a porcupine's hide. She was a mess.

"I told you I would check on you," she reminded her, and Quinn's heart sank. She wasn't in her room because she was interested. She was just following through with a promise like any good doctor would.

"Thanks," she said, completely embarrassed by her appearance.

"I wanted to stop by before I went home. Has Dr. Galvin come by yet?"

"Uh, I don't think so. I'm still a little out of it, so if he did, I don't remember."

She chuckled and Quinn noticed the laugh lines at the corners of her mouth. "The meds knocked you out," she concluded.

"Yeah, so if I said anything yesterday that was either inappropriate or flirtatious, you'll have to forgive me."

She leaned against the bedframe and her professional demeanor vanished. "Hmm. Last night you claimed I was an exotic beauty, and when I went to update your family, your father told me you thought I was cute. That's not true, then?"

She felt her cheeks burn instantaneously. "No, I mean...yes." She sighed and raked a hand through her awful hair. "Seriously? I can't believe my dad. Dr. Singh, I'm sorry if he embarrassed you."

She slid onto the edge of the bed next to Quinn. "For the record, you're not my patient anymore. I'd never sit on a patient's bed. Please, call me Suda."

"Okay."

"I need clarification. Do you think I'm cute or not?"

Quinn found herself staring at Suda's inviting mouth again. "Cute isn't the right word. That's for cat videos and babies."

"What is the right word?"

"You're elegant."

She smiled and her eyes fluttered as she looked away. "That's quite the compliment. Thank you."

"So, I think it's pretty weird that I've seen you twice in a week."

"It is very weird," Suda agreed. "I only took this extra shift as a favor to a friend. What were the odds we'd see each other again?"

"Don't know. But I'm glad we did."

Suda nodded her agreement.

"So, after I get out of here, could I buy you a cup of coffee?"

"Perhaps, but you should know I'm much older than you."

"What? Like sixty-five?"

She burst out laughing, and Quinn was mesmerized by the sound. It was like falling rain, pleasant and soothing. "No, I'm not sixty-five. I'm forty."

Quinn shrugged. "So you've got a decade on me." Suda's expression shifted as if she'd just thought of something terrible. "What is it?"

"I need to be honest with you. This will not go anywhere or turn into anything serious. I want to be clear with you on that point."

"Not that I'm disagreeing with you, but how do you know?"

"Because I do. It's a story for another time, but I don't want to get your hopes up. If you would like to rescind your offer of coffee, I completely understand."

She snorted and said, "Are you kidding? After that cryptic answer, I'm dying to know the story. So, uh, yes, we're on for coffee." She played flippant and Suda laughed again. She decided Suda had the best laugh she'd ever heard.

A nurse appeared in the doorway. "Dr. Singh, I know you're leaving, but Dr. Nightingale just phoned from the ER. Can you please come speak to him?"

"Of course."

The nurse disappeared and she turned to Quinn. "I'll be back in a few minutes for your contact information."

But she was gone longer than a few minutes. Dr. Galvin came by briefly and assured Quinn the surgery was a success and she would regain full mobility of her arm. Her break was unusual, though, and she'd be wearing the cast for the next two months.

She sighed. She tried not to think about all the things she couldn't do because her arm looked like a Barney the Dinosaur appendage. She wondered if she'd still be able to make the trip to Kingman and see Zeke.

A wave of approaching voices caught her attention, and Quinn distinctly heard her mother say, "I wholeheartedly approve of Quinn dating a doctor. She'd be a great catch."

They herded into the room and fawned over her.

"I want a cast," Ivan announced.

"No, you don't, dummy," Goran scoffed.

"Don't call your brother a dummy," Fiona ordered.

Gemma stepped up to Quinn's bedside and opened a plastic container. "I brought you some fifteens."

Quinn smiled groggily and breathed in the sweet smell. Fifteens were cookies made with marshmallows, cherries, and coconut. The boys immediately surrounded Gemma, knowing they'd get nothing if they reached for a cookie before it was offered. Quinn took a small one and nibbled on it while the container circulated among the family.

"Leave some for Quinn," Gemma warned as the boys each took three cookies.

The lighthearted banter about their favorite Irish snack quickly detoured into a serious conversation about illegal immigration. Such was usually the case when two or more family members were present. The O'Sullivans couldn't engage in banter or small talk, not when there were so many pressing issues of the day that could be solved if only an O'Sullivan were in charge.

Shane said, "It's the people from the Middle East who are the problem," just as Suda entered the room.

She stopped inside the threshold and offered a disturbed look at Shane. His beet-red face disabled his mouth. Gemma wormed her way past her embarrassed family members and held out the container. "Would you like a cookie?" The question pulled Suda's gaze back to Gemma, who added, "Obviously certain people need to eat more and talk less."

Suda smiled. "Thank you." She took a bite and closed her eyes. "Oh, this is delicious."

Gemma grinned at the compliment. "They're fifteens. Quinn's favorite."

Suda glanced at Quinn, whose smirk telegraphed her embarrassment. Suda came to her bedside and said, "Sorry I was gone for so long. I had to consult downstairs. I just wanted to exchange phone numbers." She handed Quinn her phone and asked, "What did Dr. Galvin say?"

"Everything went fine. I get to wear this for two months."

"Are you right-handed?" When Quinn nodded, she asked, "Any chance you're ambidextrous?" They both chuckled and Suda's warm brown eyes drew a curtain around them.

Quinn returned her phone. "So, I'll expect you to call me."

"I'll call you right now," she said, tapping the phone. From somewhere underneath the bed, Quinn's phone vibrated.

She wanted to be witty and charming, but her family had never seen lesbian Quinn put the moves on a woman. She doubted they were ready for her sexually charged banter. She was surprised when Suda's delicate fingers squeezed the short stubby nubs that protruded from the cast. Her face was as red as her hair, knowing her family was glued to the exchange as if they were watching an episode of *The Bachelorette*.

"If you need anything," Suda said cryptically, "please call."

"Dr. Singh," Gemma asked, "I have a question."

Suda turned to her with a pleasant smile, the immigration comment apparently forgotten. "Yes, Mrs. O'Sullivan?"

"Oh, please, call me Gemma," she said. "Dr. Galvin said Quinn would be wearing this thing for two months. Is there anything she should avoid doing, other than zip-lining, of course?"

Suda gazed at Quinn. They engaged in their own unspoken conversation while her family munched on cookies. Quinn knew exactly what *activity* Suda was thinking about when she glanced at Quinn's voluptuous chest.

"Yes, what about making drinks?" Shane asked, ruining the moment and detouring the conversation to the restaurant business.

Goran's hand shot up as if he were in school. "And who'll take us go-cart racing for my birthday?"

Ronan looked at Quinn. "We were going to redo the brakes on my car, remember?"

"I can help you with that," Shane offered.

"Thanks for the offer, Dad, but your back can't take lying on that dolly," he said.

"Hold it," Gemma commanded. The room went silent. "While all of your needs are well and good, the most important question is whether Quinn will be able to sit in the dunk tank at the church carnival in a few weeks."

"Why is that more important than my brakes?" Ronan protested.

"Because it's for charity," Gemma argued. "And Quinn always raises the most money because she's so sharp-tongued with the hotheaded young men who want to show off in front of their girlfriends."

"I don't see how any of that's more important than Goran's birthday," Fiona objected. She looked at Steven and said, "Aren't you going to defend your son?"

They bickered among themselves, and Quinn watched Suda attempt to answer the many questions she'd been asked. When she gave up and looked at Quinn's bemused face, she smiled.

"You have a great smile," Quinn whispered.

"And you have my phone number," Suda replied. Quinn frowned and Suda asked, "Are you already regretting our coffee date?"

"No, I was just thinking about an errand. I need to go to Kingman. I won't be able to drive my old VW because I can't operate the clutch."

Suda gazed at her thoughtfully. She inhaled before she said, "Well, if it wouldn't take more than a day, maybe I could drive you there? I own a car. Do they have coffee in Kingman?"

CHAPTER SEVEN

Suda braced herself for the inevitable confrontation. She could see him out of the corner of her eye as she stood on the platform waiting for the light-rail train. He sauntered closer, swaggering left and right, his hands inside the front pockets of his jeans, his size alone intimidating. He was built like a block with broad shoulders and a square head. He wore black Dickies and a white T-shirt with an indescribable graphic that looked like a Rorschach blot. She continued to ignore him, but she felt his prejudicial eyes assault her as he approached. She could usually tell when a racist comment—or worse—an act of hate was moments from occurring. She'd learned the worst racists and bigots were obvious. There was little subtlety. As he passed, he sneered, "Go home, terrorist bitch," before he continued to the other end of the platform.

She closed her eyes and saw herself pushing him in front of the train. His screams would vanish as the train smothered his oddly shaped body. Of course, he'd need medical assistance. He'd beg for her to help, but she'd insist that he first listen to her. *I'm not a terrorist. I'm not a member of ISIS. I'm not from Iraq or Pakistan. I'm not illegal. I'm a naturalized citizen. I'm not even Muslim. I'm a Buddhist, part of the eastern religion all you white people think is cool.*

"You know, you could report that guy. I've watched him badger you on several occasions. What he's doing is a hate crime, and I'd be happy to make a statement to the police."

She turned to the speaker, a balding, middle-aged white man in an expensive Burberry coat. "Thank you. I appreciate your support. I'll consider it."

He studied her expression. As the train approached, he nodded and turned away. She headed through Door Fourteen and her usual seat next to Horace, a groundskeeper at the Phoenix Art Museum. A lanky man, Horace's limbs seemed too long for his torso, and when he smiled, his white teeth contrasted with his dark black skin. He was on his way to work as she was going home. He always saved her a seat, and during the last year they had become friends. He was from the Sudan and his story was all but unbelievable. He and his brother had lived in a hole for nearly a year before missionaries rescued them. He carried his devotion to them in the Bible that sat on his lap.

"Good morning," he said pleasantly.

"Hello, Horace."

He turned and studied her. "You look different. It's in your eyes."

She felt her cheeks burn. "I met someone recently. She was interesting."

"I see," he said, his tone laden with suggestion. "What happened to Cearra? Is she still around?"

At the mention of her ex, Suda tensed. She'd told Horace a tiny lie, implying she'd dumped Cearra because of drug use, a statement that couldn't have been further from the truth. "As far as I'm concerned, we're done," she said plainly.

He offered a withering look. "Are you sure? Because it wouldn't be fair to catch someone else on the line when the hook is already set in another fish's mouth."

She chuckled at the day's fishing metaphor. He loved to spend his vacations fishing, and at least three times a week he'd use it in a metaphor to teach her a life lesson. He was only in his twenties, but his soul was much older.

"That's a good question. I'll need to think about it."

She hoped the answer ended the topic. She'd never tell Horace the truth: Cearra had dumped her because she wouldn't come out to her parents.

He nodded at her measured response. After a few months of daily exchanges during their morning ride, she'd divulged she was a lesbian, knowing he might rebuke her for it. Instead he'd asked many questions, and one day as they debarked he'd said, "I appreciate your patience with my endless curiosity. I'm glad you are who you are and that we are friends."

Their morning conversation returned to a variety of topics, but once in a while, usually when she had met someone, she used him as a sounding board. He'd steered her away from a few women who only wanted to date a doctor because they thought all doctors were rich. Others wanted free medical advice.

"What's this new woman like?" he pressed.

"Different. She's Irish Catholic. Thirty. On the occupation line of the registration form she put flipper."

His face squished into an odd look. "Flipper? What's that? A burger flipper? Flapjack flipper?"

"I think she means a house flipper. She buys cheap places, fixes them up and then sells them."

"Well if she's got so much money that she can buy a bunch of houses, then she might be a catch."

"Maybe," Suda agreed. "She's also got a large family who care for her, but they are a force."

"She sounds like she's exactly your opposite. Perhaps you should take it slowly," he advised. "Opposites don't always attract."

"That might be difficult," she admitted. "I agreed to go on a day-long road trip with her. She can't drive because she broke her arm, but she needs to get to Kingman to meet with a lawyer about her aunt's estate." She checked his amused expression. "Am I crazy?"

"I don't know. At least you'll have the advantage of two working arms in the event she turns out to be a madwoman and attacks you."

They both laughed as the train pulled up to their stop. They walked to the corner and said their good-byes. He continued toward the museum and she headed into the Willo Historic District. She'd fallen in love with the small homes built around nineteen hundred, and she'd found one that was perfect for her and near public transportation. Although she owned a sporty Mini Cooper, she hated Phoenix traffic. She much preferred the short jaunt on the light-rail and conversing with Horace.

Her phone rang as she turned onto her street. It was her mother. She pressed the silence button and sent her to voice mail. She'd call her when she got home. She wanted to spend the rest of the walk thinking about Quinn O'Sullivan. She believed the injuries people sustained often said something about their personality or character. When a patient made a pass at her, she reminded herself of how they arrived in her ER. Quinn had a daring side, but the fact that she was the zip line test pilot inferred she cared greatly for others and wouldn't allow them to attempt something if it was unsafe.

Suda generally avoided dating patients. Quinn would only be the second, if in fact their drive to Kingman counted as a date. Ironically, Cearra had been the first, arriving in the ER after she'd torn a ligament sliding into third base during a recreation league softball game. They'd started talking and found several common interests. When she'd stopped by Cearra's hospital room the next day, her entire team was there. Most of them were gay—and out. That was a condition Suda couldn't claim for herself, at least not with her parents. Eventually her closeted life caused endless friction with Cearra, who'd walked away and returned twice. This last time, though, her tone and the fierceness of the front door slam told Suda it was probably the end. *But maybe not. Do I want it to be the end?*

She'd decided to take a hiatus from relationships. Dating and casual sex were fine for now, but any future women in her life would need to understand her situation. She was Indian. Her parents were conservative and lived on the other side of the world. Her father's health was failing. There wasn't a need to tell him and she refused to do so. Most women couldn't abide her decision in the enlightened twenty-first century.

"But my parents live in the seventeenth century," she muttered. Her phone rang. Her mother again. "She must be telepathic." She knew she should answer. Something might have happened to her father. She knew a trip home was inevitable, but until then, she kept her family in one box and the rest of her life in another. She rolled her eyes. "Hello, Mother."

"Why don't you answer when I call?" Her mother, Nima, jumped right into the fray without a hello.

"I'm not home yet. I always call back. You know that. I just wanted to get home and shower first. Is something wrong?"

"Not wrong. Your brother?"

She heard the shift in her tone like a CD moving to the next song. She'd gone from accusatory to gossipy in a single breath. "I spoke with Pilar last week."

"No, this would be after."

"After what?"

Her mother had a tendency to voice incomplete thoughts constantly during a conversation. While her English was exceptional, she wasn't compelled to speak in sentences when she felt time was of the essence, which was nearly always.

"After the announcement."

She felt her patience going into cardiac arrest. "What announcement?"

"I really shouldn't say. Your brother…"

She realized she'd walked past her house. She turned around and was grateful no one was out watering the lawn or getting the mail. It wasn't good if the neighborhood doctor forgot where she lived.

She quickly returned to her driveway and took a deep breath as she fumbled with her keys. Once she'd dropped her backpack and deactivated her security system, she said, "Mama, if you're not supposed to tell me whatever it is that you know, then don't. Let Pilar do it. I'm guessing he and Sonan are engaged, but please don't confirm it."

"Fine, I won't confirm it. But I think I just did. Act surprised when he calls and keep August open."

She poured a glass of wine and sat down to take off her sneakers. She knew she was smiling. She loved Sonan, who was the sister she never had—or could've had—even if her parents had birthed another girl. Sonan had very liberal parents. "Which day in August?"

"All of them," she said, exasperated. "Visiting. The wedding. Your father."

She took a big sip of her merlot. Although it was nine in the morning, this was her happy hour. When her mother said, *Your father*, what she meant was her father missed her, or rather, he missed taking her out to visit his friends and bragging about his daughter the doctor in America. Of course that was just his public persona. In private he longed for her to return to India, as her brother had done, but she had no desire to move home. Since she'd never told her parents she was a lesbian, she easily ignored her father's constant bribery attempts. Four months prior he'd offered her a ski chalet in Switzerland if she'd return.

"How's his heart?" she asked as she swirled the fine wine.

"Same. Eats the same. Exercises the same. Smokes the same."

She rubbed her left temple. "In other words, he's not doing anything he's supposed to do."

"Yes."

Her father's bypass surgery was supposed to be a wake-up call for him to change his lifestyle. He refused and she imagined a heart attack loomed in the future.

"Okay, I'll act surprised when Pilar calls, and I'll start working on August. If you know a date before I do, call me. I can't be away from work for an entire month. That's not how vacation works in the United States."

"Wrong," came the curt reply. "Good-bye."

And with that, Nima hung up. Suda tossed her phone on the dining room table. It was a handsome piece of furniture, made from reclaimed barn wood. She glanced about her small historic bungalow with admiration. It was only nine hundred square feet, but she loved the curved archways and the built-in cabinets. On the day she moved in, carrying only a single suitcase, she'd found a piece of wood in the shed that listed the men who'd built the house in 1938. She felt proud to be a part of history. She loved everything she'd added to the place—the eclectic furniture, the antique O'Keefe and Merritt stove, and the claw-foot bathtub.

She heard the shower calling her name as she padded to the small bathroom and stripped off her clothes. She'd take a quick shower, make a cup of soup and fall asleep until two p.m. She'd grown to love the night shift, and she'd finally adapted to sleeping while everyone else carried on with their lives. Her bedroom sat in the southwest corner, and two trees shaded the house and prevented the afternoon sun from shining in her eyes. A NO SOLICITORS sign and the absence of a doorbell ensured she wasn't disturbed often.

Usually sleep came quickly, but not today. She tossed and turned thinking about Quinn. Although they came from different cultures, she saw similarities between the Singhs and the O'Sullivans—a strong maternal role model, a loving father and bickering siblings. It made her a little homesick, although she'd never admit that to her mother.

There was also the issue of coming out to her parents. Pilar knew she was gay, and she suspected her paternal grandmother had guessed as well. Then there was the incident with Hyma. *Your mother knows. Don't forget that.* But her father still believed her career as a doctor accounted for her single status. That was another reason she hated going back to India. It inevitably turned into a dating game, as her mother paraded eligible bachelors through the house. Nima created a ridiculous ruse for each one. The business executive was picking up a book for his mother. The attorney had stopped by to claim his raffle prize from a charity fundraiser she'd organized.

Then there was the doctor who routinely played golf with her father. He'd shown up with his sister, and they conveniently needed a fourth. Suda was prepared to make an excuse, until she'd seen the sister lick her lips. While she'd been stuck partnering with the doctor for eighteen holes at her father's country club, the sister had later licked several of Suda's body parts during a night of passion.

It had been a fling and she'd returned to the states unencumbered. It was how she liked it. Cearra had taught her romance and girlfriends were a hassle, which was why she'd developed her new mantra. Quinn was the first to hear it. Nothing would come of their adventure for a day except maybe some fun and a good fuck.

She thought of that word *fuck*. She didn't swear often and was taught to believe only crude people used foul language. Yet, for her new mantra, fuck seemed appropriate. She closed her eyes and saw Quinn, naked and straddling her on the bed. While they kissed, she fondled Quinn's large breasts. The image made her groan. Then her mother threw open the door, a look of horror on her face.

Her eyes shot open and her heart thumped madly in her chest. She took a deep breath to calm herself. She decided to take as much of August off as the hospital would allow. Family came first.

CHAPTER EIGHT

John Steinbeck gave Route 66 her adopted name of the Mother Road in the classic, *The Grapes of Wrath*. It was a name that stuck because it was indeed the highway of safe passage for those going west. *Mother Road Travels* aims to bring you a memorable and comfortable experience while transporting you back to the heyday of Route 66. I have included all of the exceptional sites to see, as well as explanations about what icons were forever lost—and why.

-Introduction, *Mother Road Travels*

Quinn sat uncomfortably in the Thing's passenger seat as Fiona attempted to downshift to second gear. The horrible noise sounded like a garbage disposal eating a spoon. Her left hand automatically reached for the gearshift knob, but Fiona batted it away. Quinn glared at her casted right arm. There was nothing she could do except grit her teeth as the car stalled for the third time. Behind them several horns honked, calling out Fiona's error. Phoenicians were incredibly impatient. Green lights in Phoenix meant go immediately, just as yellow meant go really fast. Fiona turned over the engine and Quinn closed her eyes.

Suda had texted thirty minutes ago. Her car had fallen victim to the most common car trouble in Arizona: a dead battery. Quinn imagined she fell into the typical female category, which meant she didn't change her Mini Cooper's oil on schedule, didn't check the tires every month, and couldn't change the battery herself. It was probably a blessing they'd take Quinn's car to Kingman. Although it was historic, she kept it in tip-top condition. They would never find themselves sitting on the side of the road waiting for AAA. It pained her to hear Fiona shredding her gears.

"Bugger," Fiona snarled as they jerked forward through the intersection. "Hang on, Quinn," she said breezily. "I know this is killin' you."

She nodded and stared out the passenger window. She hated that she was so helpless. Her hand had been set to keep the fingers equidistant and it was impossible to start the car or shift. She couldn't grasp the keys to turn over the ignition and she couldn't wrap her hand around the clutch. When Suda called about her car trouble, Quinn's heart had sunk in disappointment. She'd grown excited over the past two days, looking forward both to seeing Suda again and satisfying her curiosity about Aunt Maura's cryptic message. When Suda acknowledged she knew how to drive a stick shift, the trip was saved, assuming Fiona could arrive at Suda's doorstep without destroying her car.

They made the last two turns and Fiona easily downshifted. "I think I've got this," she announced. Then they promptly stalled as they pulled up to the curb. "Except maybe for the stoppin' part."

Quinn surveyed the vibrant green lawn that fronted a charming Spanish-style historic home. Seasonal flowers lined the walk from the street to a red door. She pictured Suda kneeling in the dirt, wearing a large floppy hat and planting petunias. They would only last until April when the murderous heat claimed them. She and Fiona had just started up the walk when Suda emerged, purse in hand and a large bag on her shoulder. She waved and locked the door behind her. Quinn's shoulders sagged. She'd hoped to peek inside the historic home.

Suda wore another button-down Oxford-cloth shirt and pressed jeans. She'd chosen loafers over sneakers, and Quinn hoped they would still be comfortable after several hours of driving.

"I feel like such an idiot," she said as she greeted Quinn. "I had no idea there was anything wrong with my car." She smiled warmly at Fiona and said, "It's good to see you again. Thanks for driving over here."

"No problem," she answered. She pointed at Quinn and said, "I thought this one was going to have a heart attack. I'm not really a stick-shift kinda girl."

"Not at all," Quinn confirmed. She smiled at Suda. "Ready?"

"Yeah," she said, motioning to her bag. "I just brought a few things, but we're only going to be gone for the day, right?"

"That's the plan," Quinn said, moving them toward the car. "Let me put your bag in the back."

Suda handed it to her and she nearly dropped it. "Whoa. What's in here?"

"Just some essentials. A woman should never be unprepared."

She wanted to get on the road, and they still had to drive Fiona back home in Friday morning traffic. When Fiona started toward the driver's door, Quinn said to Suda, "Would you mind taking over now?"

Fiona laughed. She opened the door and popped into the backseat. "Don't worry, Quinn, I wasn't planning on driving anymore." Fiona leaned forward as Suda started the Thing. "Quinn's a little possessive about this car. Just so you know."

"I am not," she snapped, already knowing her face was turning red.

"You bought it a birthday present last year," Fiona deadpanned. "And you named it. People who name their car are weird."

Suda smoothly pulled away and headed to the end of the block. Quinn leaned back in the front passenger seat and relaxed, confident that her antique baby was in good hands. Suda cast a sideways glance in Quinn's direction. "So what's its name?"

When she didn't reply immediately, Fiona said, "You're a lot closer than you think." She poked Quinn. "Go ahead and tell her. Tell her you named your car Cousin It." She turned to Suda and said, "Cousin It was a character in *The Addams Family*, a long blond wig with sunglasses and a bowler."

"I think I know who you're talking about, but I'm not very familiar with American television."

Quinn turned to explain before Fiona could interrupt. "This is a 1974 VW Thing. It made me think of *The Addams Family*. You might remember there was another character in the show called Thing, but I thought it would be stupid to name a car Thing Thing, so I named it Cousin It."

"As if that makes more sense," Fiona snorted.

"Do you have siblings?" Quinn asked, completely ignoring Fiona. "And are any of them incredibly annoying?"

Suda chuckled. "I have one brother, Pilar."

"And I imagine he is far less obnoxious than my sister."

This time Suda laughed heartily, throwing back her head, offering Quinn a stunning profile view of her face and long neck. Quinn thought she might dissolve into a puddle.

Once Suda recovered she said, "All sibling relationships are complicated." She wagged a finger between them. "Who's older?"

"I am," Fiona replied. "Older and wiser. It's unfortunate my younger sister doesn't appreciate my sage advice and vast experience. She could learn so much."

"How ironic," Suda said. "I told Pilar exactly the same thing not that long ago."

"Ha!" Fiona spouted.

"Oh, don't encourage her," Quinn moaned. "Please."

They exchanged quips and puns for the remainder of the drive back to Fiona's central Phoenix ranch house, a dark blue stunner with white trim and matching window boxes.

Suda pulled into the driveway and remarked, "What a beautiful house."

"Thank you," Fiona said. "It was a dump when we bought it, so it's been a labor of love. Now we think it's the prettiest house on the block."

Suda nodded her agreement. "It's splendid. I love the window boxes."

"Quinn made those," Fiona said proudly. "She's good for something." She gave Suda's shoulder a squeeze. "It was wonderful to see you again, Doctor. Take care of Quinnie." She turned and planted a kiss on Quinn's cheek and climbed out of Cousin It. "Have a wonderful trip. Drive safely."

Once they were on the road and headed for US 93, Suda blurted, "I think your sister's a riot."

"She is," Quinn admitted. "Despite our bickering, we're all really very close." She glanced at Suda's serious expression. "Are you close to your brother?"

"Oh, yes," she said. "He's two years younger, so I was always the protective big sister. I checked out the girls who liked him, taught him how to cook and convinced him not to succumb to my parents' pressure about a career choice."

Quinn's ears perked up. "What did they want him to do?"

"Attorney," she said disapprovingly. "Having their children be a doctor and a lawyer would make them the ideal cocktail party parents. Everyone would flock to them and want to learn the secret to nurturing both of their children to such prestigious careers."

Quinn heard the disdain in her voice. "I get it. What did Pilar want to do?"

Suda glanced at her with a sexy smile. It was as if a towline pulled Quinn closer to her. "Don't laugh. He wanted to be a TV game show host."

She burst out laughing. "I'm sorry. I couldn't help it. What made him want to be the next Bob Barker?"

Suda looked at her curiously. "Who?"

Her jaw dropped. "You don't know Bob Barker, the legendary game show host who always reminded us to spay and neuter our pets at the end of every telecast?"

She shrugged. "I don't watch television, especially during the day. I'm asleep usually."

"I'm sure Pilar knows who he is. So did you help him reach his goal?"

"I did what I could by sending him money. He moved to Phoenix for a while, just to get his bearings. Then he went to LA. My parents thought he was still with me, exploring law school possibilities. We let them believe that for a long time. Probably too long," she added wistfully. "He did some commercials and some walk-on parts." She glanced at Quinn. "You may not know this, but many American companies are desperate for diverse models and actors to appear in their ads. A handsome Indian man was someone they fought over. Pilar probably could've made an excellent living hocking food products, travel destinations, and over-the-counter medications."

"But that wasn't what he wanted."

"Not in the least. The last commercial he did was for a hemorrhoid cream. We both thought that was symbolic. He still wanted to be a game show host, so his agent started looking around. Ironically, an American company was producing a show to be aired in India called *Answer, Please*. Pilar got the job, moved back home. It's the number one game show in India. He's a star."

"You sound really proud of him," Quinn observed.

"I am, but more importantly, my parents are proud. Now when they go to cocktail parties, they boast about their son the game show host. *Then* they mention their daughter is a doctor," she added with a laugh. "If they even bother to acknowledge I exist. Often they spend the entire evening answering countless questions about Pilar's career."

"So they're happy he didn't become a lawyer?"

Suda bit her lip and adopted a wry smile. "Here's something funny. I mentioned it once when they were entertaining some new friends. They looked shocked and denied ever making such a ridiculous suggestion."

"They edited it out of existence."

"Completely. We've never spoken of it since." They turned onto US 93 and headed northeast toward Kingman. Suda changed the subject. "Tell me more about your family. Are your brothers as colorful as Fiona?"

"Ronan is but not Patrick. He's the straight arrow, probably because he's the oldest. He feels responsible for everything. My father laid out his life for him, and he followed the breadcrumbs exactly where Dad dropped them."

Suda eyed her shrewdly. "You sound a little resentful."

"Ah, no," Quinn scoffed. "Not in the least."

"Maybe resentful isn't the right word. Perhaps disapproving?"

Quinn thought about it as the ribbon of highway stretched before them. Gone were the decrepit strip malls and identical subdivisions that seemed to grow like weeds. Her gaze swept across the pristine landscape, awash in the colors of spring to the point where the sky met the horizon. Her smile widened. She knew if she'd been driving, her foot would have the accelerator to the floor. There was something about driving through the desert that was completely freeing.

"Have I lost you?" Suda asked gently. "I'm sorry if I said something that offended you."

"Oh, no, you didn't offend me, not at all. I was just thinking about your question and I got lost in the scenery. This was one of my favorite drives when I'd go to meet Aunt Maura. My mind veers to different places when I'm out here. I don't know why."

"It's beautiful in a unique way," Suda commented. "Very different from where I've been in India."

"I'm sorry, I don't know much about India," Quinn admitted. "There are deserts there, right?"

"Oh, yes. India is rich in different landscapes, but I've never traveled to the deserts. We live in New Delhi. My parents owned a furniture store before they retired. The hours were long and left little opportunity to vacation. Mostly we visited my relatives who lived a hundred miles away. I didn't have my first real vacation until I moved to the US. When I took Pilar to California, we made a stop at Disneyland."

Quinn grinned. "What did you think?"

Suda seemed unsure of what to say. "I can see why children enjoy it. As an adult, I found it pleasant but not interesting. I didn't understand all of the childless adults running around from ride to ride like they were children."

Quinn laughed as she tried to explain. "Disneyland is one of those places where everyone lets out their inner child. You walk onto Main Street and it's as if you have license to be ten again."

"I wouldn't want to be ten again," Suda said flatly. She glanced at Quinn. "What are you thinking?"

"How do you have fun?"

She bristled at the question as if it were a cut. "Well, I like having dinner with friends or going out for a drink. I appreciate great conversation. I love reading a good book. I'll admit, it's not flying upside down on a roller coaster or spinning in a teacup."

"Hey, you won't get me in those teacups either," Quinn agreed. "What was the last good book you read?"

Suda turned away and Quinn couldn't see her expression. "I'm not sure I should tell you. You'll probably laugh."

"Try me."

She cleared her throat. "Since I'm newer to the United States, I've tried to apprise myself of its history by reading many different accounts of great events and the people who shaped it. I've read all of the books by David McCullough and Howard Zinn."

"Great ones," Quinn encouraged. "Are you reading something by one of them?"

She shook her head. "At the present, I'm reading a lesser-known work. I just wanted you to be aware that I'm literate."

Quinn's lips curled into a grin. "So what are you reading?"

"An unauthorized biography about Marilyn Monroe."

Quinn chuckled. "There's nothing wrong with that. Marilyn was fascinating."

"So tragic," Suda murmured. "It seemed the men in her life totally controlled her."

Quinn gazed at her pensive face, so serious. She remembered what Suda had said about the zip line. "When was the last time you had a really good laugh?"

"This morning. Your sister is very funny."

"True, but I'm talking about an event that made you laugh hysterically, like a funny movie where you almost peed your pants, or a game of charades after everybody's had a few too many drinks. That kind of fun."

Suda's gaze remained on the road. Quinn stared at her, hoping she'd at least offer a quick glance in her direction. When she ignored her for another mile, Quinn said, "I guess it's my turn to apologize. I've obviously offended you and I certainly didn't mean to do so. Will you accept my apology?"

Suda sighed. "You don't need to apologize. You were right about driving in the desert. My mind is freed. Too freed, I guess. When you asked me what makes me laugh and you defined fun, I heard my ex-girlfriend's voice. She didn't think I knew how to have a good time." She paused and added, "That's a part of why she left. She said I was a boring workaholic and I was no fun." She chuckled. "Of course, she was a borderline alcoholic who didn't think there was anything wrong with snorting the occasional line of cocaine."

"Is that why you agreed to this road trip? To prove you could have fun and be spontaneous?"

"Maybe," she said. "I'll admit I've never done anything this impromptu, but…"

Her voice faded away. Quinn didn't look at her, for fear she wouldn't finish the thought. She wanted to know why Suda would join her—virtually a complete stranger—on a daylong road trip. She watched the cacti, the arms of the saguaros turned upward, waving at them as they flew down the road.

Just when she thought the moment had passed, Suda said, "I came with you because it felt right. I'd met your whole family, and your dad told me all about your special relationship with your Aunt Maura."

Quinn turned quickly, completely surprised. "He did? Really?" She'd assumed Shane resented Maura and was putting up a good front.

"Yes, he told me all about her career as a travel guide writer. He pulled up her book on his phone so I could read an excerpt. He credited her as a major reason Route 66 has enjoyed a resurgence of popularity. I went home and bought the e-version."

"What did you think?"

"Her writing is so descriptive and funny. It made me want to visit some of those places, like the Sno Cap and the Hackberry General Store." She took a breath and a dreamy look crossed her face. "And can you imagine a more romantic destination than La Posada?"

"No."

La Posada was now a world-famous inn located on the Santa Fe railroad line in Winslow, Arizona. It had been scheduled for demolition in the nineties until a millionaire and his artist wife decided to buy it and return it to its original glory.

Quinn remembered the first time Maura had taken her to La Posada. She was much younger and didn't appreciate it—yet. She choked up and closed her eyes. She didn't want to cry in front of Suda. Then Suda's hand was gently rubbing her back. The touch, meant to soothe and comfort, did exactly the opposite. She pictured those delicate hands touching her in a much different way. She longed to lean across the few feet that separated them and kiss her neck. She yearned to unbutton her shirt and caress the tender flesh of her cleavage.

"It's okay to cry," Suda said gently.

She felt her face flush in shame and embarrassment. This trip was supposed to be about Maura and Quinn was making it about herself. She needed to stay focused. Then she reminded herself of Suda's proclamation that nothing would come of their dating. Technically they were just meeting for coffee, even if the drive to the coffee shop would take eight times longer than the actual date itself.

CHAPTER NINE

The city of Kingman claims to be The Heart of Historic Route 66, at least in Arizona. In 1880, railroad surveyor Lewis Kingman put the town on the map when he determined the small mining community would be the end point of the Atlantic/Pacific Railroad's latest expansion. The route united northern Arizona and paralleled the Old Trails Highway, which would become the Mother Road in 1926.

-Mother Road Travels

Arrival in Kingman, Arizona, occurred suddenly. The road crested and a wide basin surrounded by basaltic hills appeared. They turned off US 93 at Andy Devine Boulevard, formerly known as US 66.

"This looks like a mining town," Suda commented.

"Actually it was a railroad town named for a surveyor who helped join the eastern and western United States by train."

"And who's Andy Devine?"

"You've never heard of Andy Devine?" Quinn gasped.

Suda looked at her sheepishly. "Should I have? Was he one of your lesser-known presidents? Or a famous inventor?"

She laughed. "I'm surprised you studied our presidents. All I know of India is Gandhi and Benazir Bhutto."

Suda smiled proudly at her. "Well done, Quinn. Most people only know Gandhi and think he defines all of India. Him and Ben Kingsley."

She laughed at the reference to the actor who had played Gandhi in a film. "I didn't know who Andy Devine was either until Aunt Maura made me watch a movie. He was an actor who played cowboy roles in the golden era of westerns. He was born in Flagstaff and lived in Kingman." She checked the address Zeke had given to her as they chugged along at thirty miles an hour. They passed the Route 66 Motel, the Orchard Tree Motel and the Hillcrest Motel.

Suda said, "Isn't there an overabundance of motels for such a small town? Do they have major events that attract droves of tourists on the weekends?"

"No, most are historic relics from the forties and fifties, when Route 66 was the main thoroughfare between Chicago and LA. People would drive all day and look for a place to stay at night. That's why you see so many wonderful neon signs. They were designed to entice travelers. Since there were so many motels, the better the sign, the better the business." She pointed to a faded red one with enormous white letters outlined in hundreds of lights. "That's the famous Hill Top Motel. It has the best view of Kingman."

"Have you stayed there?"

"Actually I have, with Aunt Maura. Once she became known as a Route 66 expert and her travel guide gained success, all of the motel managers and restaurant owners encouraged her to visit at least once a year on their dime."

"So she basically spent her life driving up and down this road eating and lodging for free? That sounds like the life."

"Well, she had her own Airstream, but the older she got, the more she didn't want to drive it so much. She bought a Dodge Charger and used it for a lot of trips. If she stopped somewhere like Seligman, she might stay one night at the Supai Motel and another night at the Romney." Quinn paused. "I wonder what'll happen to her Airstream."

"Maybe it's your Airstream now," Suda mused, coaxing a laugh from Quinn. When they passed the dilapidated El Travatore Motel, Suda said, "It appears many of these places are either closed or decrepit."

"Because of what happened to Route 66. After Interstate 40 opened in the sixties, traffic on Route 66 dwindled to nothing. Then in the eighties, Congress stopped funding it, and it nearly died. The resurgence today is because of historians and travel guide writers like my aunt who demanded each state assume responsibility."

"So Route 66 is no longer a road to travel to get to a destination, but rather it *is* the destination," Suda summarized.

"Well said," Quinn replied. "I should write that down," she added, pantomiming a search for paper and pen. Suda laughed and Quinn smiled. She'd spend the rest of the day coaxing a smile if it meant she'd laugh too.

The road rounded the hill and a giant water tower with a Route 66 emblem welcomed them to Kingman and proclaimed it the Heart of Historic Route 66. Beyond the water tower was the center of the town and the shops and services necessary to keep Kingman's heart beating. Ahead was a cluster of the oldest buildings in Kingman. She pointed and said, "We're going to turn at the next street."

They found a small parking lot in the rear of the office building and some steps leading to a lobby. Zeke Qoyamayma was one of several tenants in what appeared to be an old high school. Each classroom was a different office. Title companies, CPAs, real estate agents, financial advisors, and other services all lived under one roof.

They marveled at the craftsmanship of a grand staircase that led to the second floor. The carved oak banister was definitely original as were the plank steps that shone from a recent varnishing.

"I love this place," Suda whispered as they trekked upstairs to Zeke's office. "I'm a big fan of preservation."

"Me too," Quinn said. "I'm a member of the Phoenix Historical Preservation Society."

Suda raised an eyebrow. "Really?"

"That surprises you?"

They stopped at the top of the stairs and faced each other. "I thought I saw an apartment number on your hospital registration form," Suda said.

"Actually I own those apartments with my dad. It's a post-World War Two place. We're renovating it."

"I'd love to see it sometime."

"Well, I guess we'll have to see how this coffee date goes," Quinn said with a shrug. "Maybe for a second date you could have dinner at my place."

"You cook?"

Quinn scowled. "Do I really project a persona just slightly above town vagrant?"

"No," she said, shaking her head. "I see so many Millenials in the ER who have no maturity or common sense." She touched Quinn's hand and added, "I'm sorry. If anything, I'm projecting a bias against you, or at least people your age."

She'd been in too much pain at the hospital to truly appreciate Suda's long eyelashes, the perfect accessory for her beautiful eyes. And although they'd just spent four hours in a car together, Quinn had thought it an invasion to ogle Suda, whose gaze was locked on the road. This was really the first moment they'd had to size each other up. Quinn liked what she saw. Suda's shirt was tucked into skinny jeans with crisp creases. While she'd opted for Converses, Suda wore leather flats to complete her outfit. Her hair was pulled back with the same gold barrette she wore in the ER, emphasizing her high cheekbones. She'd splashed on a little blush and some eyeliner, but she hadn't bothered with much else. She didn't need to. Quinn felt momentarily uncomfortable and looked away.

"Are you mad at me?" Suda asked.

Footfalls on the steps interrupted their conversation, but Suda made no effort to remove her hand. A cowboy in Wranglers and a Stetson tipped his hat to them as he passed. Quinn hoped he didn't notice they were holding hands. While she was out and proud in Phoenix, acceptance of gays and lesbians in northern Arizona was lukewarm. Proximity to Flagstaff and the Northern Arizona University campus, which hosted the gay pride parade every year, was directly proportional to the amount of harassment LGBTQ people suffered. Considering they were a hundred and fifty miles from Flagstaff and practically standing at the Nevada border, they needed to be somewhat cautious since they were strangers. Ironically, according to Aunt Maura, gay and lesbian community members along Route 66 were welcomed and accepted. She'd explained it to Quinn by saying, "It's the attitude of, 'I'm not big on fags, but you're okay.'"

"Tell me," Suda pressed.

I want to kiss you. Instead she admitted a different truth. "I really can't cook. You were right to be suspicious of my kitchen talents. I only said that to impress you. Fiona cooks. If I ever had you over, I'd make her put together the meal, and then I'd take credit for it."

Suda looked amused. "And what would you have to do for her in return?"

"Probably an oil change. Maybe detail her car."

She nodded. "So that's how you O'Sullivans roll."

"It is."

Suda's gaze flitted up and down the hallway. Many of the office doors were open and a few people chatted in the hallway.

Quinn guessed the tenants knew and depended on one another. A few people glanced at them, and she figured it was only a matter of time before someone strolled down the corridor and greeted them. Aunt Maura had taught her about the ways of small towns. Strangers were confronted and either accepted or rejected. Of course, Aunt Maura had been wholeheartedly accepted.

Clicking heels got their attention, and they turned to see a Native American woman in a plum suit powering toward them. She couldn't have been more than twenty-five, and she wore the suit as if she were its hanger, her posture suggesting she couldn't wait to take it off. She offered a thin smile and faced Quinn. "I'm Louise, Zeke's paralegal."

"Nice to meet you," Quinn said. She motioned toward Suda and introduced her.

Louise offered one serious nod. "Follow me." She turned on her heel and quickly moved back down the hallway as if she desperately needed to return to her work. Suda and Quinn tried to keep up as she charged through an open door. Quinn noticed Zeke's name and *Attorney at Law* stenciled in black on the frosted windowpane.

Louise landed behind a desk covered in papers. An open volume of Arizona statutes, a legal pad and a whirring computer suggested she was deep in research. She motioned to four armchairs against a far wall next to a door marked PRIVATE. Quinn assumed that was Zeke's inner sanctum.

"He's with a client now. He'll be with you shortly."

She returned to her work and they sat down in the spartan waiting area. Unlike some law firms, there weren't magazines to read, refreshing lemon water to enjoy or a brag wall to admire awards and accolades Zeke had accumulated during his decades as an attorney. Quinn shifted in her chair and looked at the only thing in the room worth studying: Suda.

Suda slowly turned and met her gaze. "What?"

"Nothing." Quinn shrugged. "Just admiring the view."

They exchanged a smile. Quinn studied Suda's full lips, which were slightly open. Louise coughed and they both looked in her direction, but her back was to them. She'd put on an expensive pair of headphones. Quinn thought she heard strains of "Highway to Hell" floating across the room, and she guessed Louise's volume control was maxed out. When a sudden burst of profanity erupted from Zeke's office, Quinn understood why Louise needed the headphones to stay focused, although metal music wouldn't have been her choice.

A scratchy voice proclaimed, "That ain't right! Damn it, Zeke!"

Quinn couldn't hear Zeke's response. She remembered his quiet, mild-mannered voice when he'd visited her at the Fiesta South restaurant. Only when a longer stream of profanity permeated the door, did he finally raise his voice.

"Harland, get a grip," he ordered before his voice became inaudible again.

A few more minutes passed. Suda leaned closer, her shoulder momentarily rubbing against Quinn's arm. "I must confess, I would be interested in knowing about your desire for a kiss in the near future."

Quinn's head jerked around. "You want to kiss me?"

Suda shook her head. "I didn't say that. I asked if you wanted to kiss me."

Her mouth went dry. She swallowed before she said, "Yeah."

"I would enjoy that as well," Suda said smoothly, her lips wrapping around the words. "Perhaps we could skip the coffee idea and have a picnic before driving back to Phoenix?"

"That would be awesome," Quinn agreed. "I even have a blanket in the car."

"I'll bet you do," Suda chuckled. She flashed her sexy smile again. "How many women have stretched out on your blanket?"

Quinn felt her body temperature rise. When Suda shifted in the uncomfortable chair, her shoulder again grazed Quinn's arm, only this time she left it pressed against her. "Sorry, this is the most cramped waiting area I've ever seen. And I've seen a lot of them," she added.

"I could move one chair over so you could have some more room?" Quinn offered gallantly.

"In this particular situation, I don't mind at all. But if you would prefer…"

"No," Quinn whispered. "I like it tight."

She heard Suda's intake of breath and cracked a smile. It was definitely tight. Everything felt *tight*. Quinn watched her lips form the words. She realized it wasn't just Suda's accent that fascinated her. It was how her whole mouth engaged with words when she spoke. Whereas Americans mumbled and stumbled through speech, especially after a few drinks, Suda spoke with clarity and eloquence.

She felt herself sweating through her T-shirt. She was about to spring out of the chair when Zeke's door flew open. The man Quinn guessed was Harland stomped out. He whirled to face

Zeke, who stood calmly in the doorway. "This is bullshit, Zeke, and you know it!"

He nodded solemnly.

Harland looked to be a middle-aged rancher with a beer gut that slid over his silver belt buckle. A hefty tuft of chest hair curled out from his open-collared western shirt. When he turned and tipped his hat toward her and Suda, she saw a pistol holstered on his right hip.

"Ladies, I apologize for my foul language." His scratchy voice distracted her from whatever he said next, but he finished with, "—damn fed'ral government."

"Let me make some calls," Zeke offered, "and let's meet next week."

He pulled out a laser pointer and aimed it in Louise's direction. A red dot flashed twice above her computer screen, signaling her to remove the headphones. Quinn caught the chorus of "Cum On, Feel the Noize," before she silenced the song and looked at Zeke attentively.

"Take down the information about Harland's trespasser and set up an appointment for next week." Zeke turned to Quinn and Suda. "Ladies, thank you for waiting."

He pointed at Quinn's cast. "What happened?"

"I had an accident. I couldn't drive my stick-shift car, so my friend Suda was kind enough to drive me up here."

He gazed at Suda for a beat and said, "Let's go to my office."

The large office, which seemed to be two classrooms forged together, was wrapped in dark wood paneling on three sides. Native American paintings, a large, colorful blanket and Zeke's framed diplomas dotted the far wall. The fourth wall, a bank of windows from the building's days as a schoolhouse, provided enough light to counterbalance the somber effect of the paneling. He motioned them toward an old couch under the windows.

He hunted through several stacks of files and books that covered his massive walnut desk. "I wasn't sure when you were coming, so it's buried underneath my other work." After combing through everything, he stepped back and scratched his head. Then he opened several drawers and shut them quickly. Finally he sighed and picked up the handset of his phone and immediately dropped it back into its cradle. Then he did it twice more.

Quinn glanced at Suda, who looked equally confused. It made sense when Louise opened the door. Apparently, it was his way of signaling her from his office.

"Yes."

"Where is the package from Maura?"

"It wasn't a package," she corrected. She strolled through a door that blended with the paneling and into a back room. When she emerged, she carried a bulging manila envelope and wore a colorful sombrero on her head.

"Ah, yes," Zeke said. "How could I forget that?"

She marched over to Quinn. She handed her the envelope and proclaimed, "Ole!" in a voice only slightly less monotone than the one she'd used to greet them. She threw up her right hand with a flourish like a mariachi finishing a song. "Maura instructed me to say that," she deadpanned. "I've honored the dead. I'm sorry for your loss." She dropped the sombrero on Quinn's head and marched out.

Quinn looked at Suda, who had put her hand over her mouth to stifle laughter. "What is this?" she asked as she removed the sombrero.

Zeke pointed at the envelope. "I hope whatever is inside will explain. She explicitly requested that Louise serenade you when she presented the sombrero, but the envelope is all she gave me."

Inside was a train conductor's cap, a thick ring of keys and a folded slip of paper.

"It seems your Aunt Maura favored hats," Suda observed.

"Not really," Quinn replied. "She said hats made her head look pointy." She set the conductor's cap on top of the sombrero and put the keys on her bag. She opened the note and read it aloud. "*Quinn, I've presented you with the first and last clue for our adventure. I want you to visit some of the places we've been before, kinda like a greatest hits. At each stop you'll get another clue that tells you where to go next. This isn't a big mystery and there isn't a big reward at the end. As they say, the journey is the reward.*

I hope Louise serenaded you properly. If not, make her do it again. The conductor's hat will put you on the right track—all the way to the sombrero, six hundred and forty-one miles away. Enjoy!" She doubted she read the last word with the amount of ebullience her aunt had intended.

"What does it mean?" Suda asked.

Quinn glanced at Zeke, who offered a little smile. Most likely he was Maura's accomplice in the adventure. Nevertheless, what caught her attention was the reference to six hundred miles.

"Zeke, is Maura expecting us to travel six hundred and forty-one miles? That would put us…" She tried to do the math in her head.

"Tucumcari," he said. He looked at Suda and added, "The distance between Kingman, Arizona, and Tucumcari, New Mexico, is six hundred and forty-one miles."

Quinn looked at the note and the sombrero. "The last clue is at La Cita," she announced.

Zeke's smile broadened. "I believe you are correct."

Suda shook her head. "What is La Cita?"

Zeke motioned for Quinn to explain. "Route 66 is known for having giant things along the way, like there's a giant replica of Paul Bunyan and a few giant guitars."

"Giant dinosaurs," Zeke offered. "Even a giant head."

Suda looked at him skeptically, one eyebrow raised. "Seriously?"

"Yes," Quinn said, "giant everything. Remember I mentioned all the neon lights along Route 66 were designed to attract customers to the motels? The giants also drew travelers to businesses, shops, and restaurants. La Cita is a Mexican restaurant in Tucumcari. Above its doorway is a giant sombrero." She blinked and turned to him. "Zeke, where is Aunt Maura now? She's supposed to accompany me on this journey."

Zeke sighed and muttered, "It sucks to get old." He reached for a Native American vase displayed on his credenza. With great reverence, he slowly lowered it in front of Quinn. The yellow gold pottery was a trademark of the Hopi Indians. The base, a wide bowl with squares, curved to a high neck with a small opening. In between the grids was a profile of a head with a crown.

Zeke cleared his throat and said, "This vase was given to me by a member of the Nampeyo family, revered for their pottery designs that go all the way back to the early nineteen hundreds. The squares and patterns you see are called the migration design, which was created by the Nampeyos. It honors the tribe's migration, which, according to legend, occurred when the Hopi arrived on Earth, known as the Fourth World. As they spread to new places, they left their mark to indicate where they had traveled. As your aunt is now traveling to another realm, it is a fitting tribute, don't you think?"

Both women nodded, but Quinn's heart felt heavy.

Zeke noticed her despondency and asked, "What's wrong?"

She shook her head and blinked away some tears. "It's nothing. I'm just sad we won't be traveling together."

"Ah, but you will," Zeke explained. "She is with you always, especially on your adventure."

"So, the end of the adventure is in New Mexico?" Suda clarified.

Quinn could hear the anxiety in her voice. A trip across two states wasn't what she'd agreed to. They had driven to Kingman for coffee and to claim whatever Maura had left with Zeke. Then they were driving back.

"I'll have to do this another time," Quinn said to Zeke. She glanced at Suda's somber face then added, "I didn't realize how long this would take. Suda and I are only here for the day. Then we need to get back to Phoenix."

Suda touched Quinn's hand. "I don't want to ruin the adventure." She looked at Zeke. "Do you know how many clues there are between here and the restaurant? If there's only one or two, we might be able to have part of the adventure today?"

Quinn offered a halfhearted smile. She appreciated Suda's flexibility, and it seemed she wanted them to spend more time together. Quinn would've loved to race out of the building toward the first clue since she was rather certain she knew where they needed to go within the Kingman city limits. It would be fun to have Suda alongside her through the entire adventure.

Zeke nodded slowly. Quinn couldn't tell if he was disappointed, angry or merely trying to determine how to rework Maura's plan. The three of them fell silent, listening to Louise madly tapping on her keyboard out in the waiting area.

"How long is the drive to Tucumcari?" Suda blurted.

Quinn's eyes widened. Suda was actually considering the trip. "Probably ten hours with stops." She looked at Zeke who gave an approving nod.

Suda picked up the sombrero. "So, if there were ten clues, do you think we could do this in two or three days? Because if we can, I could probably get Sunday off, and I don't work again until Wednesday."

They both looked at Zeke, relying on whatever else he knew about Aunt Maura's plan. He tented his fingers and looked upward. Quinn wondered if he were seeking divine guidance from her. When he met their eyes with an even stare, he said, "That would work out just fine."

Zeke walked them out to the main hallway. He looked at Suda with sudden concern. "What are you thinking about?"

Suda turned red and her gaze flitted from Zeke to Quinn. "If your Aunt Maura died in an unexpected car crash, when did she arrange for this adventure? More importantly, why would she arrange it?"

Quinn froze. She should've thought of that. Maura's conversation about doctors and tests pricked her memory. She looked at Zeke. His expression was stony. "I don't know. I've been asking myself that same question. She gave this to me just a week before she died. It's almost as if she knew her time was coming."

CHAPTER TEN

MAURA'S MENTION: Mr. D'z Route 66 Diner

We'll forgive the owners the grammar mistake in the name, if for no other reason than their homemade root beer floats. You'll feel like you've time traveled back to the fifties when you sit at the counter for lunch. And if you're lucky, you'll come by on a day when one of the many auto clubs in Kingman shows up in their vintage rides.

-Mother Road Travels

Suda stared into the dressing room mirror and critically assessed the walking shorts she'd chosen. They had stopped at the J.C. Penney's in the Kingman Mall for a few clothes before they headed toward the first clue, the engineer's cap, which Quinn had already solved. She checked her butt and was pleased to see the shorts hugged her curves. She hoped Quinn noticed.

She was still mulling over her split-second decision to miss work and travel the open road with a woman she hardly knew.

She couldn't believe she'd told Quinn she wanted to kiss her. This wasn't like her. Usually she was slow and methodical like her father. Quick and reactive were words she associated with her mother. *I'm behaving like my mother.* She shook her head.

She could be spontaneous sometimes, like when she ordered a caramel macchiato instead of her usual house venti. Or when she joined the rest of the night shift employees for breakfast at five a.m. instead of going straight home. And once in a while she'd spend a day pampering herself. Everything looked better after a mani-pedi, a facial, and a trip to Victoria's Secret.

She grinned at the thought of the hot-pink underwear she'd chosen that morning before Fiona and Quinn arrived. As they'd strolled through the lingerie department, Quinn had held up a zebra-striped thong and asked if she owned anything like it. She hadn't mentioned the three pairs of sexy panties in her large bag. She always had at least one extra with her, and as she prepared for their journey, she'd drifted to a fantasy that ended with her needing some clean underwear. So she stuffed two more pairs in the bag for good measure.

She checked her voice mail in the privacy of the dressing room. She'd texted her supervisor who sounded happy that she was taking a vacation day. She'd only missed a few shifts since she was hired, and she routinely covered for others at various hospitals in their network. She'd never said no when asked to help, so she didn't feel guilty about asking for a day off.

She'd also received a voice mail from Cearra. "Babe, it's me. I've had time to think over the last few weeks. I miss you. I guess I'd rather be persona non grata with your family than persona non grata with you." She chuckled at the end of her joke and said, "Let's try this once more. I promise this is it. Call me. Let's talk. I love you. Bye."

She closed her eyes. It would be easy to fall into a relationship with her again. She thought of the lie she'd told Quinn, the same one she told Horace. She felt bad about portraying Cearra as a drug user. And if Cearra knew how she was besmirching her good name, she certainly wouldn't be calling to reunite. Somehow lying to Quinn bothered her more than deceiving Cearra.

She thought about the way Quinn had looked at her while they waited for Zeke. They had been sitting so close. She shivered, thinking of the moment when Quinn gazed at her lips. She took a deep breath and exhaled. Before she talked again with Cearra, she wanted to see how the weekend with Quinn unfolded.

She changed back into her original clothes and met Quinn at the cashier, Aunt Maura's urn tucked in the crook of her casted arm. Zeke had insisted Aunt Maura pay for their shopping jaunt as well as all of the expenses they incurred. He'd called Louise once more, and when she appeared, she handed Quinn a check for five thousand dollars and an envelope of cash.

Her eyes had widened as she held the check. She mumbled, "I had no idea Aunt Maura had any money."

To which Zeke had replied, "Your aunt was an opportunist, Quinn. She was usually one step ahead of the game. She foresaw the Mother Road regaining its popularity and she made sure she was positioned for a windfall." He'd shrugged and said, "She was right."

Once they were back on the road, Suda turned to her. Quinn still looked shell-shocked. "Are you okay?"

She scratched her head and stared blankly out the windshield. "I thought I knew everything about Aunt Maura. Clearly I was wrong."

"No one really knows anyone," Suda said, thinking of how little her parents knew about her. "Now where are we going?"

"Not far."

Quinn guided them out of the mall parking lot and back onto Andy Devine Boulevard. They followed the curve past the water tower and Zeke's office. More dilapidated or closed motels dotted the roadside and Suda remembered the ghost towns she'd visited when she'd first arrived in Arizona. She'd heard about the state's western roots and had expected to see people on horseback. She quickly learned the antiquated cowboy image was relegated to the rural parts of Arizona.

A neon sign featuring a huge mug of root beer and a large bag of french fries appeared on the right. Sandwiched between the images were the words, *Mr. D'z Route 66 Diner.* The pink and green building was impossible to miss. "That's a great place to eat," Quinn commented, "as diners go."

"We're going there for the clue?"

"Nope, the clue is in the park. Turn into this lot."

She followed Quinn's directions and pulled Cousin It next to a rusty, broken wagon wheel. Behind them sat an enormous multistory brick building called The Powerhouse. Suda drifted to the historic landmark sign and learned from its small print that the Powerhouse had been the hub of Kingman, providing power to the entire town.

They stared at the colossal structure, its long windows spanning the length of entire floors. "When I first saw this building in the early two thousands, Kingman was thinking of destroying it," Quinn explained. "Then a preservation society swooped in and saved it. Now it's a Route 66 museum." She pointed across the street. "Our clue is in the railway park." She pulled out the slip of paper and read the pertinent passage again. "The conductor's hat will put you on the right track."

A black steam engine and a red caboose sat side by side, cloaked by the branches of tall mulberry trees. "So the clue is in one of those cars," Suda said.

"Possibly."

They wandered across the road and stood beside the awesome locomotive engine. Strength emanated from the steel structure. When Suda stepped beside one of the mighty wheels, she realized it was nearly twice her height.

Quinn seemed not to notice the railway cars. She'd set Aunt Maura's urn on the ground and squatted next to an exposed section of track. She cocked her head to the side as if she were reading something. Suda marveled that Quinn could hold the position for as long as she did. Perhaps she was just as limber in bed. A flush washed over her cheeks and she hoped Quinn didn't look up.

"Hmm," Quinn said. "This is interesting." She pulled a penny out. Attached to its surface was a piece of cellophane tape. "This penny was taped to the track."

"Why would your Aunt Maura do that? Are you sure that's the clue? Maybe a child put it there and Aunt Maura's clue is hidden somewhere on the locomotive?"

Quinn glanced about the park. A homeless man lay against a tree near the caboose and a young couple strolled toward the engine, their son running ahead and shouting his joy at discovering the locomotive. She shook her head and held up the penny.

"No, I think this is it. Aunt Maura referred to the right track, not the caboose or the engine. Let's check them to be sure, but there aren't a lot of places to hide things from tourists."

They combed both engine and caboose, navigating around the hyperactive little boy who zipped past them as he explored. Suda didn't mind his presence, but his constant high-pitched sound effects grated on her nerves. They found nothing else that looked like a clue or a place to hide something.

They wandered to a picnic table away from the little boy. "So, if the penny is the clue, what does it mean?" she asked.

Quinn held it up for inspection. It looked like a normal penny. It had been minted in 2011 and looked as worn as would be expected. Suda's gaze shifted from the penny to Quinn's face. She had enticing green eyes and a sprinkling of light freckles across the bridge of her nose Suda hadn't noticed before. They only made her cuter. Her gaze dropped to Quinn's voluptuous chest. She'd never been with a well-endowed lover, and her curiosity demanded answers.

"I think I've got it." She sprang off the picnic bench and quickly strolled out of the park and back to Cousin It. Suda giggled as she followed her. "Are you laughing at me?" Quinn asked while she rummaged under the back seat.

"No, I'm laughing because I'm having a marvelous time. I've never been on an adventure. At least not with someone I find incredibly attractive."

Quinn froze and looked up. "Really?"

"Yes," she admitted.

Suddenly Quinn planted a quick but sensuous kiss on her lips. She blinked and emitted a small gasp. She found herself speechless. Quinn took it as permission. She pulled their lips together, demanding she return the kiss. She imagined Quinn leaning her back on the seat and slowly unzipping her jeans.

When Quinn stepped away to catch her breath, she groaned. "Why did you do that?"

"Which *that*? Kiss you or stop kissing you? Please clarify, and then I'll decide if I'm upset with you," she said, panting.

She couldn't tell if Quinn was joking, so she told the truth. "Both." When Quinn offered a puzzled expression, she crossed her arms. "It was brazen of you to publicly display affection in a town that isn't giving me a great rainbow vibe."

"True," Quinn admitted. "Kingman is incredibly conservative. Aunt Maura said Kingman was one of those places where the restaurant bathrooms didn't say men and women on the door. They said Republicans and Democrats. And most of the time, the Dems' toilet was clogged."

She decided not to tell Quinn the kiss topped her list of best kisses ever. She knew in an instant Quinn was a better kisser than Cearra, who always wore a smug expression afterward as if she knew she was a great kisser. She pointed at the penny and asked, "Moving ahead. What does that mean?"

Quinn picked up her copy of *Mother Road Travels* and found the section on Kingman. "One reason this book is so well-received is Maura's organization of it. She included a lot of extras, like 'A Penny's Worth.' It's an extra tidbit of info about something noteworthy on 66. For Kingman she wrote, 'Check out the famed Hotel Beale sign, which towers over the shuttered hotel. Its neon letters still burn in the night sky.'"

"Didn't we pass that?"

"We did. It's hard to miss."

"So we're supposed to go there next?" Suda was puzzled but the knowing look on Quinn's face told her their adventure was about to take an interesting turn.

"Yes, but I think we'll need some energy first. We should have lunch." She pointed to Mr. D'z and said, "Best burgers in Kingman."

"I'm famished," she said, "although I'm also a little worried, judging from your expression."

Quinn laughed as they started across the street. They'd hit the lunchtime rush and all of the turquoise leather stools at the counter were occupied. They settled into a booth with pink accents. Across from them was a mural of Elvis Presley and somewhere a jukebox played "Love Me Tender."

They studied the predictable menu and Suda immediately took out her phone. "My mother is a huge Presley fan and has all of his albums." She snapped a picture to text to her mother later that night. If she sent it now, her mother would call immediately and ask her to explain why she was near an Elvis Presley cutout on a workday. "My parents have only been to America once," she explained. "My grandfather took them to an Elvis show in Las Vegas in the seventies. My mother still talks about it."

Quinn's face brightened. "I'm a huge Presley fan as well. Your mother and I will have to compare notes."

At the notion of Quinn meeting her parents, her face shifted. Fortunately, a sassy waitress approached to take their order and she was spared the misery of explaining why Quinn would never meet her mother. They both ordered a Cheeseburger Special, but when Quinn learned she'd never had a root beer float, she insisted they include one as dessert.

When the waitress left, Quinn asked, "So do you like Elvis as much as your mother?"

"No. I never developed a huge celebrity crush. But I love music."

Quinn leaned forward and propped her chin on her upturned palm. "Who's your favorite band?"

She exhaled, grateful the conversation shifted from her mother. "I like many artists. I love Indigo Girls, Springsteen, Tegan and Sara, and a bunch from India that I doubt you've heard of."

"Try me," Quinn said. "I once had a girlfriend named Cinquain. She was a poet and a DJ. She had forty thousand songs in her music library from all over the world. She played a lot of Indian weddings. Part of the reason we broke up was the nonstop music that echoed throughout her apartment twenty-four hours a day. So I know a lot of bands."

"Okay, have you heard of the Tetseo Girls or Swarathma?"

Quinn cocked her head to the side. "I don't think I've heard them. But I know Parikrama."

She blinked in surprise. "You know Parikrama? Really?"

"I do. I find it quite interesting that a rock and roll band has a violinist. That's unusual by American standards."

Their food arrived and she said, "Well, I'm impressed. It makes up for not knowing India's topography." She paused before she added, "And for that rather crass comment your father made about Middle Easterners."

Quinn shook her head. "I'm sorry about that. He's really not bigoted." Suda gave her a sharp look and Quinn said, "Okay, he's a bigot in some ways, but aren't we all?"

"Don't do that, Quinn."

"Do what?"

"Marginalize his bigotry by claiming it's just status quo and that somehow it makes it okay. Because it doesn't."

Quinn put up her hands and Suda realized she was pointing at her. "Sorry," she mumbled.

They resumed eating in silence. She didn't understand what was happening. Quinn's earlier comment about the desert freeing her mind had certainly been true. But now that it was freed, it was running around naked and screaming.

Unable to stand the quiet any longer, she said, "Sorry. I've no right to judge."

"It's okay. You're right," Quinn conceded. "I can't imagine what it must be like for you in our xenophobic society."

Her mind drifted to the awful man at the light-rail station. "There are some bad moments when I see ugly Americans," she admitted. "But most people are courteous." She took a sip of her iced tea and said, "Of course, most new people I meet are patients in the ER. Even the worst bigots temper their hostility when it's the difference between excruciating pain or relief."

Quinn chuckled. "Has anyone refused to let you treat them?"

"Only once. A guy came in wearing a confederate flag T-shirt. He'd put his hand through a window during a domestic dispute. Had a huge shard sticking out of his palm. When he saw me he told me that no raghead was going to treat him. I could tell the wound wasn't life threatening and his vitals were good. So I told him I'd go find another doctor, but it might take a while. He said that was okay as long as the new doctor was of his people. I told him that would take even longer, but he said he'd wait."

"So what happened?"

"An intern took him back out to the waiting room, and I told the front desk about his request. Later I heard that he'd sat there for three hours. Finally he went up and demanded to be seen by a white doctor. My friend Aubra was the intake nurse. She's a rather large African-American woman who's got zero tolerance for bigots. She looked him straight in the eye and said, 'Well, you're gonna be waiting forever. After Dr. Singh's shift is over, Dr. Nightingale is on, and he *is* as black as night. Eight hours later comes Dr. Espinoza, a fine Hispanic man, and then you're back to Dr. Singh. So whadda ya want to do?'"

Quinn laughed so hard, she grabbed her side. "Don't keep me in suspense. What did the idiot do?"

"He left."

Quinn slumped back in her chair. "Unbelievable. How sad."

"It is."

The waitress dropped off the root beer float just as Quinn's phone rang. She glanced at the display. "Crap. It's my dad. Go ahead and drink your float. I'll pay at the register and go outside to take the call. I won't be able to hear him over the music. Hi, Dad," she said as she slid out of the booth.

Suda shifted in her seat and her gaze landed on a table across the room. Four middle-aged white men in jeans, flannel shirts, and ball caps were obviously on their lunch break. The one closest to her wore a sneer and said something under his breath to the man next to him. The second man responded and pointed at her. Their tablemates turned and openly gawked. She knew she should look away but she couldn't. Perhaps retelling the story about the bigot in the hospital had emboldened her. She guessed they were mumbling about deportation and illegals stealing American jobs. The sneering ringleader ran his index finger across his throat, drawing laughter from his companions. They went back to their lunches and she focused on her dessert. It really was quite good and it reminded her of the Indian dessert kulfi that her mother served after dinner in the summers.

She glanced through the window and watched Quinn pace and gesture as she talked to her father. Suda could tell she wasn't pleased with the conversation. A commotion drew her attention. Sneering man's friend had pushed his chair away from the table and was gagging.

His friends, dumb as they were, asked questions like, "Are you all right?"

A young man in a tie rushed over from the cash register and joined the circle. The choking man was starting to turn blue. His left hand pounded the table in distress. One of his friends shouted into his cell phone, summoning an ambulance. But she knew he wouldn't last that long. In another minute he'd pass out and a minute after that his brain wouldn't be able to recover, having been deprived of oxygen for too long.

It's not like he's using it for anything. She took a long sip of the root beer float and instantly felt a debilitating brain freeze. Her eyes widened. It was a sign. She was sure of it.

She flew out of the booth and pushed between the men who smelled as bad as they looked. "I'm a doctor," she announced, fearing one of them would haul off and deck her.

She went behind choking man and wrapped her strong arms around his middle. She thrust her fist into his upper abdomen, practically lifting him off the chair. She thought she heard a pop and wondered if she'd fractured one of his ribs. A chunk of hamburger exploded out of his mouth—and hit the sneering man in the eye.

"Ow!" he cried. "Ow! Shit! This hurts. It's burning! I got ketchup in my eye!"

She stepped away, grabbed her purse and hurried out of the diner. She could still hear sneering man wailing, and she imagined his idiot friend would feel his broken rib for several weeks to come. She knew she was smiling when she got into the car.

Quinn looked up from *Mother Road Travels*. "Did you enjoy it that much?"

She realized Quinn was talking about the root beer float. "I did. It was refreshing and an excellent way to end lunch."

CHAPTER ELEVEN

"A Penny's Worth"

Kingman owes much to Lieutenant Fitzgerald Beale. In 1857 he trudged across northern Arizona along the thirty-fifth parallel with the "Camel Corps." He had two assignments: build a wagon road between Fort Defiance and Fort Mojave and test the viability of camels as pack animals in the Arizona desert. How did it turn out? The wagon road eventually became the outline of the Mother Road. As for the camels, well, you won't see anybody riding one down Andy Devine Boulevard.

-Mother Road Travels

The Hotel Beale was located at the corner of Andy Devine Boulevard and Fourth. Quinn had Suda park across the street so they could fully appreciate the sign, which appeared to have fared much better in its one hundred and sixteen years of existence than the decrepit stone and brick building it advertised. Crisscrossing metal supports suspended the enormous yellow letters high above the four-story structure that spelled out

HOTEL BEALE, and underneath, *AIR COOLED*. The building seemed to sag under the sign's weight and Quinn wondered if one day the whole thing would crash to the ground.

"I'll bet it looked fabulous at night," Suda commented.

"Absolutely," Quinn agreed. "If you were a weary traveler on your way to California, and you were looking for a place to spend the night, the Hotel Beale sign would definitely grab your attention. Several famous people stayed here, including Louis L'Amour, Charles Lindbergh, and Amelia Earhart."

They crossed the street and passed the shuttered storefronts that shared the building with the Hotel Beale. Quinn led them down an alley to a small door that blended into the brick. She pulled out Maura's thick ring of keys. There were car keys, safety deposit box keys, a few motel room keys, and several different types of door keys.

"Is there a reason she had so many?"

Quinn nodded. "Over the years Aunt Maura gained the trust of a lot of people along the Mother Road. Remember I said business owners gave her free meals and lodging? Some of them trusted her so much they just gave her a master room key. She'd call ahead and let them know which night she'd arrive, but she never bothered to check in."

"Wow, that's incredible," Suda said. "So one of the keys opens this door?"

Quinn splayed them flat in her palm. "Uh-huh. I just have to remember which one…"

Suda pointed to an old skeleton key. "Try that one."

Quinn smiled. "I believe you are correct, Dr. Singh." She finessed the old lock and heard a pop. The door opened to a steep wooden staircase. "This was the fire exit that doubled as roof access."

"Have you been on the roof?" Suda asked as they started to climb.

"Oh, yeah, several times. Maura loved to look out over Kingman, especially at night when all of the neon signs were lit. It's still quite a sight. Unfortunately, we don't have the time to stick around until dark."

They arrived at another locked door. Quinn used the same key and they wandered onto the roof. They immediately gravitated to the long, sturdy metal rods supporting the huge neon letters. Quinn checked the roof's surface for cracks or damage since the sign was so heavy and the building so decayed, like an old man carrying his adult son.

Suda ventured between the metal rods and stared up through the center of the sign, oblivious to Quinn's concern. "This is amazing," she gushed. "I can't imagine how they got the letters up here."

"Slowly," Quinn joked. "There's a story about the workers misspelling the word 'cooled' and having to fix it, but I don't know if that's really true."

Suda looked around the roof. "Is the sign our clue?"

Quinn shrugged and headed toward the opposite side of the roof. "Not sure. Come look at this." Suda joined her and they stared at the vast expanse of desert beyond Kingman. "When I was a kid, Aunt Maura and I used to come up here to watch the Route 66 parade each year. The family that owned the hotel always had a huge party for an exclusive group. We had the best seats."

She glanced at Suda's stunning profile. A light breeze lifted her dark hair away from her face, beckoning Quinn to kiss her. Never one to disobey Mother Nature, she leaned closer and planted a soft kiss on her jaw. "Do you mind?" she whispered in her ear.

"No."

Suda's raspy voice encouraged Quinn. She trailed kisses along her neck. Suda shuddered and stepped away.

"Quinn, you remember what I told you, right?"

She heard the words but she also heard the quiver in Suda's voice as she fought to believe the words herself. "I remember," Quinn said. Suda smoothed her hair and adjusted her shirt. She looked hot and bothered after just a few suggestive kisses. Quinn imagined the two of them naked, locked together, hips thrusting against each other while Quinn stroked Suda's marvelous bottom, guiding them to climax.

"Oh, that's just great," Suda said, instantaneously dissolving Quinn's fantasy.

"What?"

She gestured over the edge of the roof. Quinn stepped closer and saw a little boy pointing to the roof. His mother held his hand and tried to drag him along. They couldn't see her facial expression, but Quinn surmised it was displeasure. They really needed to get out of Kingman.

Quinn took her hand and led her away from the roof's edge. She could tell Suda was furious.

"I'm sorry. Couldn't help myself," she said lightly.

"I'm not like you, Quinn."

She leaned against an air vent and folded her arms. "What do you mean?"

"I face a lot of judgment every day. About being a female doctor, being Indian, people *thinking* I'm Muslim and harassing me for it, not to mention being a lesbian. I can't handle all of it together. It's not that I want to hide who I am, but lately I feel like a stranger in a strange land, to quote a famous author. And frankly, I haven't felt safe in a long time." She looked around and hugged herself tightly. "Can we just find the clue and get out of here?"

Quinn nodded and her gaze fell. She'd known many lesbians like Suda, women who faced so many barriers that they smothered their lesbianism and denied themselves a relationship because it was one too many curve balls to handle in life. She hoped that wasn't Suda. She hoped she was inappropriately pigeonholing her and Suda would prove her wrong.

With difficulty she thrust her hands in the pockets of her jeans so she wouldn't go off on a famous O'Sullivan rant. "I understand," she said sincerely. "I'll keep it friendly, okay?"

"Thank you," Suda said.

Quinn nodded again and got down to business. She scanned the roof for the clue. She strode toward the southeast corner and saw something dangling from one of the long metal poles.

"There it is," she said.

She held up a T-shirt. On the front in neon letters was a drawing of the giant Hotel Beale sign.

She showed it to Suda who said, "I want one."

Quinn held it out. "You can have it. I already own two of them."

Suda held up the shirt against her front. "Do you think it'll fit?"

Quinn pictured her wearing the V-neck cut spread taut against her small round breasts. She'd look sexy.

"It'll be perfect. We can find a restroom if you want to change," she offered.

Suda looked around. "I'll do it here if you promise to behave yourself."

She heard the flirtatiousness in her voice, but she ignored it and held up her hands in defeat. "Hey, message received loud and clear."

She turned away and strolled toward the stairwell. As much as she wanted to look back at Suda, she stifled her libido, who she'd named Doris. She'd never told anyone about Doris for fear that she'd never have another date or a girlfriend after they learned she named her libido. A friend had given her the idea after the friend's therapist suggested it. She only called upon Doris, who looked a lot like a young Katharine Hepburn, when she needed to temper her feelings of lust and desire. During an evening of hot sex and intense passion, Doris was nowhere to be found. But whenever Quinn needed to dial back her emotions, as she did now with Suda, she pictured Doris stepping onto the gangplank of an Olivia cruise ship and sailing away without her. Such focus usually caused every nerve in her body to run cold, and it didn't hurt that the *Love Boat* theme accompanied the ship's departure. By the time it had drifted out of the harbor, she was usually fine.

"What are you humming?" Suda asked.

Quinn blinked and felt her cheeks burning. Usually she only heard the TV show theme in her head. She glanced at Suda's beautiful yet quizzical face and shrugged. "Nothing. Let's go."

After they climbed back into Cousin It, Suda placed the key in the ignition, but didn't start the car. She turned and faced her. "We're not doing this, either."

Genuinely confused, she asked, "What aren't we doing?"

"The Silent Treatment. I refuse to drive another mile until we're good."

"We're good," she hedged. When Suda looked at her cynically, she added, "I just need a little time to adjust to the fact that you're not interested in me."

Suda took a deep breath and Quinn watched the rise and fall of her lovely shoulders. She closed her eyes, desperately searching for Doris, but apparently Doris was already dancing on the Lido Deck or making small talk with Gopher or Captain Stubing.

"I am interested in you, Quinn," Suda whispered, her gaze on the steering wheel. "But let's pretend for a moment that your aunt hadn't contrived this adventure, or better yet, hadn't died. What if, after we'd met in the ER, we really did just go for coffee? I won't speak for you, but I know I wouldn't have felt you up in the parking lot of the Starbucks as we left. Our date would probably be over by now, and I'd either be back at work or planting my spring flowers."

Quinn stared out the window, contemplating Suda's scenarios and picturing her aunt swerving to miss the drunk driver who'd crossed into her lane. If she'd had her eyes on the road, Quinn was confident she'd still be alive. Aunt Maura had excellent reflexes, but she hadn't had the chance to use them.

Suda stroked her cheek, and only then did she realize she'd been crying. "I wish I'd met your aunt," she said gently.

"I do too." Quinn cleared her throat and said, "You're right. If we'd had coffee, we'd be back in our respective routines by now. And maybe it would've been a rotten date. Perhaps we would've had such a mediocre time we wouldn't have wanted a second date."

Suda shook her head and started Cousin It. "Oh, no. We would've had a second date. I'd have insisted."

Quinn stuck her nose in the air. "Maybe I wouldn't have wanted one."

Though she said nothing, she felt Suda's gaze on her. She glanced at Suda, intending to look away quickly, but couldn't.

Her brown eyes were like a tractor beam, and she felt herself being sucked into Suda's orbit. She desperately tried to summon Doris. But after checking her surroundings, when Suda leaned over and gave her a chaste kiss, a different image appeared: Doris falling overboard as the cruise ship chugged away.

"We both would've wanted a second date," Suda explained, "because if you hadn't kissed me, I would've kissed you. Just like that."

Quinn held Suda's chin with her thumb and index finger. "Why did you offer to come on this trip?"

"I liked the idea of an adventure."

"My point is that you had the choice of coffee, a much easier and safer choice. But you didn't take it. If we'd just had coffee, it would be over now. But we're out here in the desert—alone and carefree. That's what you really wanted." She kissed her again—hard. Suda hesitated for only a second until she gave in, allowing Quinn's tongue deep inside her mouth.

She quickly pulled away and returned to her side of the car. Suda took a deep breath. Quinn noticed her hands were shaking. After a minute had passed, she cleared her throat and checked her mirrors. "So what is the clue from my new T-shirt and where are we headed?"

CHAPTER TWELVE

John Steinbeck was the Mother Road's greatest cheerleader. Route 66 was as much a character in *The Grapes of Wrath* as Tom Joad, the father who leads his family from the dust bowl of Oklahoma to prosperity in California. I won't add any verbiage verbatim, lest I have to get permission from his estate, and I won't attempt a flowery paraphrase and do his writing injustice. Instead, I'd urge you to make a stop at the Powerhouse in Kingman. They've got a great 3-D display that'll make you feel like you're traveling right alongside the Joads with Mr. Steinbeck whispering in your ear."

-Mother Road Travels

They headed east out of Kingman. Andy Devine Boulevard eventually became a two-lane highway, the old Route 66. Suda could still feel Quinn's lips and she was second-guessing her decision to keep Quinn at arm's length. They'd opened Cousin It's windows to enjoy the clean air and beautiful spring day. Perhaps it was the magic of the desert or the sugar rush from the Mr. D'z root beer float that contributed to her unusual mood. Every nerve in her body was alert, ready, but for what she didn't know. She'd felt their passionate kiss down to her very core. If Quinn asked her to pull over so they could make out, she'd do it. She glanced at the speedometer and realized she was doing eighty. She let up on the gas and chuckled to herself. She was trying desperately to hang on to her resolve, but the farther east they traveled, the more difficult it became. She blinked, wondering what the night's sleeping accommodations would look like.

Quinn held up the book and showed Suda a map of western Arizona. "We traveled from Phoenix to the most northwestern city, Kingman, and now we're crossing east toward New Mexico. In about twenty-four miles, we'll come to Hackberry."

Suda vaguely remembered skimming over the name in Maura's book. "What's there?"

"Not much anymore, except the Hackberry General Store. That's where your T-shirt is sold."

"And we'll get the next clue there," Suda concluded, "and then we'll know where to go next."

"That's what I'm thinking. The store is a really cool and unusual place."

"So it's the only attraction in Hackberry?"

Quinn chuckled. "Yes. There's only about a thousand people who live there now. Back in its heyday it was a mining town. There were territorial disputes and the mines shut down in the early twentieth century. The town grew smaller, but it held on until the late sixties. Then in the seventies the last gas station closed and so did the store. But when Route 66 regained its popularity, an artist bought the store. He made it part museum and part store. Now it's owned by the Pritchards."

Suda indicated with her chin the travel guide. "Tell me more about your Aunt Maura. How did she come to be a travel writer?"

"By accident, really."

Quinn leaned back and crossed her legs. Suda felt the tension between them dissipate.

"Did she ever get married or have a partner?"

"Not as far as I know. There were some men in her life who seemed to really like her, but she made sure they knew where they stood." She paused before she said, "Like you."

"Quinn—"

"No, I appreciate your honesty."

Guitars suddenly wailed, interrupting their conversation. "I didn't think I'd get any reception out here," Suda said. "Can you reach in my bag and grab it, please? That's my brother's ringtone. I have to make sure nothing bad has happened to my father. And we're not done with this conversation."

Quinn opened her bag and her jaw dropped. "What the hell did you bring?"

She felt her cheeks burn. "I'm a doctor. I have to be prepared for emergencies."

Quinn chuckled and rummaged through Suda's bag. She withdrew the phone, which had wrapped itself up in one of the three pairs of underwear she'd brought. "Emergencies, huh? This is quite the phone cover," Quinn commented, extracting the phone from a pair of bright red bikini briefs.

Suda clawed the air for her panties instead of the phone, but Quinn shook her head. She stuck the phone in Suda's face and held the underwear out her open window. "Talk to your brother," she said, feigning seriousness, "or the panties meet the highway!"

"Give me those," Suda demanded. She tried to sound serious but she was half-laughing.

"You're gonna miss your call."

She groaned and took the phone. "Hello, Pilar? Is everything all right?"

"It's fine," he replied, the line crackling. "I have news."

"You're breaking up so tell me quickly," she replied. She looked over at Quinn, who was inspecting the red panties. She snapped her fingers and shook her head, but Quinn arched her eyebrows and offered a seductive smile.

"Sonan and I are getting married!"

Even though her mother had already told her, she grinned. "That's wonderful. Tell Sonan congratulations. When's the wedding?"

"August. We're still picking out a weekend, but when I know the exact date, I'll text it to you immediately. I know you important doctors have full schedules."

She knew he was teasing her, and she imagined he was mocking their mother, who undoubtedly suggested to him that Suda would have scheduling difficulties. "I'm so happy for you."

"It will be your turn next," he joked.

She snorted. "I sincerely doubt it." Then she realized where she was and shot a look at Quinn who was wearing her underwear like a cap. Suda burst out laughing.

"What's so funny?" Pilar asked. "Do you really think you'll never get married? I don't find that funny at all."

"No, I'm not laughing at that. I'm traveling right now and my companion just made a funny face."

Still wearing the underwear, Quinn obliged and crossed her eyes while touching her nose with her tongue.

"Traveling companion? Is that what they're calling it these days?" Suda imagined Pilar's impish grin, but she was shocked when he added, "I think you should bring your traveling companion with you to the wedding. I'll make sure Sonan puts you down for a plus-one guest."

"That's not necessary," Suda automatically replied.

"Too bad. I think my wedding would be a perfect time for you to come out to our parents. They'll be so happy about the wedding that your announcement will hardly register. They might say, 'That's nice, Suda. Did you try the pakora? We ordered it special at great cost.'" They both laughed and he asked, "You're not with Cearra, are you?"

"No."

"That's good. What's her name?"

Suda's harsh stare cracked when she said, "Quinn."

Still wearing the underwear, Quinn burrowed further into Suda's bag. She pulled out a stethoscope and put it on. When she attempted to listen to her own heart, Suda chuckled.

"I hear your happiness, sister. I'm definitely adding a plus one."

Before she could disagree he hung up. She handed her phone back to Quinn, who dropped it and the underwear back in her bag.

"I can't believe you just put my underwear on your head."

Quinn sighed heavily. "It's the desert. I always get a little goofy this far away from civilization." She offered a serious look and added, "I should warn you. Anything can happen out here. Why do you think they built Las Vegas out in the middle of the desert?"

"How did your parents wind up in the desert? This is nothing like Ireland, is it?"

"No," Quinn said. "Most of my relatives are still in Ireland."

"How many of your family came to America?"

"Only my parents and Maura. She and Dad were the last of eight kids and the only two who wanted to move here. All the rest of my aunts and uncles are still in Ireland."

"When did they come over?"

"In their twenties during the seventies. They started on visas and applied for citizenship. Took them fourteen years, but they got it legally. That's why my dad doesn't have a lot of tolerance for illegal immigrants. Aunt Maura came to the US to work for the Irish government. She was secretary to a diplomat. He was the one who pushed along her citizenship paperwork. He helped my parents, too, although they had come over before her. Eventually her job ended. My dad and mom had moved to Arizona and started their restaurant. Dad asked Maura to join them, and she agreed, but she decided to take a road trip first."

Suda offered a knowing smile. "When did she get to Arizona?"

"About three years later," Quinn replied. They both laughed. "She fell in love with traveling and that's how she found Route 66. Dad was furious. He thinks everyone should've done it his way, including Maura."

"What's *his* way?"

"He came here with a specific goal, to make a lot of money. He got into the restaurant business and learned everything he could. By the time he became a citizen, he'd already married my mom, had us kids and learned the ins and outs of capitalism. He's wicked smart. My aunt had no interest in it. She'd come for a completely different reason, and I quote, 'I sure as hell didn't want to die in a country so small that I can throw a stone across the whole damn place and hear it plop into the Atlantic on the other side.'" They laughed and Quinn continued. "Both of them wanted to see green, just not the same kind."

Quinn looked at her with a sad face. Suda reflexively reached over and stroked Quinn's cheek while her eyes watched the road. Quinn kissed her palm and took her hand. It was suddenly summer inside the car, almost as warm as Quinn's hands.

"Are you cold?" Quinn asked. "I could give you a jacket I brought."

"I'm okay," she replied. Now that Quinn held her hand she was warm—moving to hot. She needed to change the subject. "How do Irishmen wind up owning a successful Mexican restaurant?"

"Connections," Quinn replied. "They'd thought about opening an Irish pub, but most of them aren't successful. Fortunately, they met a Hispanic couple who became their partners." Quinn leaned back and crossed her arms. "What was it like for you and your brother coming to America?"

"Different," Suda admitted. "We came for the wrong reason."

"Which was?"

"To fulfill our parents' dream. They saw America as many foreigners do, a place of great opportunity where everyone has a fabulous life."

"Yeah, right," Quinn snorted. "We have horrible poverty."

"But many immigrants look at your poverty as a choice. Your government encourages free enterprise and passes laws that give citizens an opportunity at a great future. In most other countries there is no chance to improve your station in life, regardless of how hard you work."

Quinn shifted in her seat uncomfortably. "Well, that's true. We have opportunity in America, but the government also promotes a class system. Most people born into poverty never escape it. So, I don't necessarily agree with you that poverty is a choice."

Suda stiffened and said flatly, "I don't think I used the right word. Working in an ER, I certainly understand what you're suggesting. I treat many people without health insurance. While America may be the land of potential opportunity, when it comes to resources and supporting people who struggle..." She shook her head.

"Your brother went back to India. Are you going back someday?" Quinn asked.

"No," she said quickly.

"Okay, then. In that case, if you're staying here, you're in the boat with us."

She sighed and gripped the steering wheel tightly. "I'm sorry for my abruptness. It has nothing to do with you. I'm just tired of that topic. It's always the main theme of every phone call I have with my mother. She tries to guilt me into returning."

"And you don't want to."

"No, not at all." They fell into a silence, but Suda still felt as though she'd stalled their conversation. "You know, of all the people who've ever asked me that question, you're only the second person who's received my honest answer." When Quinn didn't reply, she glanced at her. She was staring out the passenger window, deep in reflection. "You understand what I'm saying, don't you?"

Quinn turned to her. "I do and I'm flattered. I know we're just beginning a friendship, but I hope you'll always feel you can be honest with me. And I'll do the same."

"Agreed."

Suda felt her good mood return and she loosened her grip on the steering wheel. She realized she'd been holding her breath for those few seconds when she thought Quinn was upset with her. She stared out at the double yellow line of Route 66 that extended as far as she could see. She'd read *The Grapes of Wrath* in school, learning that it was an American classic. She thought about those travelers moving westward, starting a new life, forced to abandon the life they'd known for generations. Hadn't she done much the same thing? She'd left her life in India, one where she was guaranteed a good station as someone's wife, enjoying the luxuries afforded to New Delhi's elite. No one yelled at her, called her names or threatened her. Why was this life better? Could it be that her mother was right?

She blinked and inhaled, drawing Quinn's attention away from the window. "Are you okay? You're not getting too tired, are you?"

"No, I'm fine."

Quinn picked up her casted arm and set it in her lap. "I don't know if I've said thank you, but thank you. I imagine you don't get a lot of time off, and I'm flattered that you're spending it with me and Aunt Maura."

"I'm having a great time. This is quite the adventure so far."

"I'm glad," Quinn said, peering at the passenger mirror.

"What are you looking at?"

"Do you see that banana yellow FJ Cruiser two cars back?"

Suda adjusted the mirror and her gaze flitted from the windshield to the mirror several times. "Maybe, but it's hard to tell."

"I'm probably being a little paranoid, but I think we're being followed."

CHAPTER THIRTEEN

One of the most drivable segments of Route 66 in Arizona stretches from Kingman to Flagstaff. You'll want to be sure to stop at the Hackberry General Store in...wait for it... Hackberry, Arizona, population one thousand. The store sits on the north side of 66, and if you're busy blabbing away on your cell phone or worse, texting, you'll most likely pass it or rear-end the slow moving cars turning off or on 66 from the store's makeshift parking lot. Do yourself a favor and pull over. Stretch your legs, pet Max the Store Dog (who has been featured in a few commercials) and have yourself a tasty Route 66 Root Beer. Dee-licious.

-Mother Road Travels

Quinn watched the FJ Cruiser decelerate to thirty miles an hour along with them as they passed the *Welcome to Hackberry* sign. The state had tried to renegotiate the city speed limit upward several years back when the population dwindled below a thousand. However, the owners of the General Store and other prominent citizens, as well as Aunt Maura, campaigned against changing the speed limit to fifty-five. The Arizona Department of Transportation backed down. While the naysayers publicly decried the speed limit increase in the name of safety, the real reason had been they didn't want tourists racing past the General Store, deliberately or unintentionally.

"Do you really think we're being followed?" Suda asked.

She shrugged. "Honestly, I'm not sure. I know the Cruiser's been with us since Kingman."

"But couldn't that just be another tourist driving Route 66?"

"Sure, but most people pass Cousin It, especially on the hilly portions of the road. The Cruiser had to slow down significantly to stay behind us. Everyone else has sped by when the passing lanes appeared. But not that Cruiser."

"Okay, so why would anyone follow us?"

"No idea," she said. She pointed to six motorcycles turning onto 66. "There it is. Those bikers are leaving the store."

Suda turned in to the parking lot, which was nothing but a patch of cloudy dirt. It seemed visitors used common courtesy and parked their vehicle in such a way that ensured fellow travelers weren't boxed in and many cars could fit at once.

"This place is sure different," she remarked.

"One of a kind. Most every Route 66 tourist stops at the Hackberry General Store. It's the last place for refreshments or restrooms until Peach Springs. Maura called it a not-to-be-missed spectacle." Quinn rustled through *Mother Road Travels* until she found the page she wanted to read. "'Even hurried travelers who initially balk at the idea of stopping, make a U-turn once they see the front of the store and the constant flurry of people entering and exiting.'"

Suda pulled up next to a rusted out roadster. The car's skeleton was intact, minus a roof. They peered inside the holes where windows used to be and stared at the mangled springs, which were all that remained of the seats. A faded aqua blue DeSoto rested next to the roadster. A web of cracks covered the windshield and wide streaks of rust permeated the massive hood. Quinn crouched in front of the DeSoto's nose and admired the steel fender.

"I don't think I'd ever want to be in an accident with this car," Suda noted as she crouched next to Quinn.

"You wouldn't. American cars from the early to mid-nineteen hundreds were quality. They established Detroit as *the* carmaker, and Route 66 was partly responsible. Before all the massive trailers transported eight or ten cars at a time, Detroit got people who were traveling west to drive one of their cars. Many folks who were headed to New Mexico, Arizona and especially California, volunteered to drive. They got a free ride and the auto manufacturer got their vehicle to its destination. A win-win."

They admired the row of old cars that led them to the General Store, a rustic building made of wood scraps and a tin roof. Old signage from Shell, Texaco and Mobil plastered the side of the building and sat against a fence that led to the back of the property. A row of gas pumps lined the front of the store, each one more antiquated than the next.

Quinn pointed to an old Chevy police cruiser parked under a Greyhound bus sign swinging in the light breeze. Tourists patiently waited their turn to be photographed with the old car that looked poised to dash onto Route 66 and catch a speeder. While the rust made it impossible to see the original two-tone colors, the gold, five-point star of the Hackberry Sheriff's Office still decorated the driver's side door.

"You have to see this," Quinn said, taking Suda's hand and leading her under an awning. Another large crowd admired the only car on the property in mint condition, a 1957 convertible Corvette. Its candy apple red and white paint looked new and the bumpers shone in the early afternoon sun. The dashboard sparkled and the white leather seats looked as buttery as the day the car rolled off the assembly line.

"This is beautiful," Suda remarked.

Quinn opened her mouth to explain its significance, but a tall Hispanic gentleman sporting a mustache that curled at each end leaned in and said, "It's a tribute to the old show *Route 66*."

"Um, I'm not familiar with American television," Suda replied courteously. "Was this car in the show?"

The gentlemen crossed his arms and adopted a professorial air. "Not this car specifically. One exactly like it. The show's about the adventures of two young guys cruising across America on Route 66 in a red fifty-seven convertible Corvette. It was regarded as an exceptional drama. Although many of the episodes didn't really occur on 66, the title helped with publicity."

"Let me take your picture," Quinn said to Suda, before the man started another paragraph. If Suda needed or wanted any further information about the Mother Road, she could read her copy of Aunt Maura's book.

"Let me take it and you can both be in it," the gentleman offered.

Quinn nodded at his kindness and chastised herself for being so harsh. She stepped next to Suda and wrapped an arm around her waist. Under the guise of proper picture etiquette, Suda leaned closer and Quinn felt a surge of electricity and sighed quietly. She glanced at Suda, who wore a telling grin.

"Okay, smile," he said, but they were already smiling. He returned the phone to Quinn with a nod. "Should be a good one. You ladies have a nice day."

They joined the herd of people moving toward the front door. Quinn watched their photographer head into the parking lot. That struck her as odd, but she didn't know why. "Let's look around for a bit, and then we'll ask about the shirt."

Once inside, the crowd broke up and headed to different parts of the store. They looked up at the ceiling covered in dollar bills, all donated by visitors who wanted to leave something to prove they'd been there. Conveniently, Bobby Troupe's "Get Your Kicks on Route 66" began to play, overpowering the chatter of the tourists.

Quinn pointed at a large cardboard cutout of a blond-haired girl in a red dress with a sign that said, *School Zone*. It was impossible to absorb everything at once. Pictures, memorabilia and signs covered the walls. Antiques were interspersed with the abundant Route 66 merchandise.

"This is the mother lode of Mother Road memorabilia," Quinn whispered to her. "It's part store and part museum."

"I see that."

They headed through an archway to the malt shop and the jukebox. Set up to look exactly like an ice cream hangout from the fifties, the silver stools with red cushions and the black and white checkerboard linoleum let tourists take a step back to another time, during the heyday of the Mother Road.

Just behind the malt shop was an extensive display of black leather jackets and Harley memorabilia. Quinn was ready to turn away, but Suda gravitated to the women's jackets, pulling Quinn by the arm. She studied each one, stroking the leather with her long, delicate fingers.

"See anything you like?" Quinn asked in a seductive tone.

"I've never owned one," Suda admitted.

"Then try it on. You'll look incredibly hot in leather." She caught herself and said, "But I'm only saying that as a friend."

Suda smirked and pulled a stylish jacket from the rack. It zipped up the front and had zippered pockets. She shrugged it over the Hotel Beale T-shirt and headed to the small mirror. Quinn felt her mouth go dry. Suda was one of those women who could change her look by changing clothes. When Quinn had picked her up at her house, she looked professional in business casual. When she'd changed into the T-shirt, she'd looked cute. But adding the leather jacket made her sultry and sexy. Quinn wanted to yank the gold hairclip away so her black hair flowed over the matching leather.

Suda offered a seductive glance through the mirror. "What do you think?"

"I think you should buy it," Quinn croaked. When Suda nodded and started to take it off, Quinn stepped behind her and put her hands lightly on Suda's shoulders. "No, leave it on," she whispered in her ear.

They gazed at each other through the mirror until a voice said, "Hey, that looks great on you."

They turned and smiled at a biker mama decked out in leather chaps and a leather vest. She'd scooped up her hair inside a blue bandana so the large helmet she held under her left arm would fit over her head.

"Thank you," Suda replied. "It's my first leather jacket."

The biker mama ate Suda with her eyes and said, "Well, honey, don't let it be your last."

Suda nodded sheepishly as a male biker joined them in the cramped space. They headed back to the main room of the store where candy, sundries, and Route 66 memorabilia awaited them. Quinn automatically went to a cold case and pulled out two Route 66 root beers.

"I know you already had a root beer float today, but this is special."

Suda studied the logo on the bottle, the Route 66 highway sign with the word route in place of root. "Who makes this?"

"There's a company in Missouri that sells it to all the stores and shops from Chicago to Long Beach, which is the end of Route 66."

"Well, I'll have to try this. It's a day of new things," she said, stroking the front of the leather jacket.

Quinn groaned her approval and Suda chuckled. Quinn leaned toward her, completely forgetting where they were. When Suda pressed a hand on Quinn's chest, she blinked.

"Sorry," she murmured, walking off toward a display of signs.

Suda followed and they found themselves in an awkward silence, staring at the ball caps, bottle openers, coasters, and belt buckles.

Suda picked up a pair of Route 66 earrings and held them against her earlobe. "Should I get these to go with the jacket?" She batted her eyelashes and offered a coquettish smile.

Quinn played along and said, "No, I think you should get something that brings out the deep brown of your eyes." She grabbed a different pair, a set of jalapenos. "These would work. Everyone should wear vegetables at least once in their life."

Suda stared at Quinn's ears. "I don't see you wearing earrings. Are your ears even pierced?"

"Nope. I hate needles. If I hadn't been in so much pain when I came to the ER, I probably would've fought your nurse when she put that IV in me."

"That bad, huh?"

"Terrible. The last time I had to get a tetanus shot, the doctor had to restrain me."

"Then I guess we got lucky." Suda smiled. "You were just loopy. You told me I had a great ass."

"I did?"

"You did."

Quinn stepped to the left and peered at Suda's backside. "Well, I was right. I may have been forward with you, but I was accurately forward."

"Well, I was equally forward with you. After you told me you liked my ass, I told you I liked your rack."

"You can thank my well-endowed Irish relatives."

They perused the memorabilia until they reached the front of the store where a tall man with a gray beard stood behind the cash register. When he saw Quinn, he smiled broadly.

"Howdy, stranger!" he bellowed. He came around and gave her a crushing hug. She didn't mean to thump him in the chest with her thick cast, but when he stepped away he said, "What happened? Shark attack?"

She laughed. "Something like that."

His grin drooped. "I'm so sorry about Maura."

"Yeah, it's awful."

She introduced Suda to Arlo and felt the gentle thwump of a tail against her leg. She squatted to greet Max, the shop dog. Part terrier, pitbull and cattle dog, Max's soulful eyes had landed him a place in a Harley-Davidson commercial as well as an airline promo.

"Hi, boy," she cooed. Suda crouched and Quinn made the introductions. "This is Max." Suda stroked his ears and Max wagged faster. "I'd say he thinks you're okay," Quinn said.

"I love dogs. If I had more time, I'd own one."

They stood and Arlo pointed at Suda's shirt. "Is that what I think it is?"

"Yes. We are on the adventure collecting clues," Quinn announced. "What do you have for us?"

He laughed knowingly as he rung up their root beers and Suda's new leather jacket. "My clue was easy." He looked at

Quinn and said, "'When Irish Eyes Are Smiling.' That's my clue."

It took Quinn a moment to remember but then she nodded. They popped the caps on their root beers, said their good-byes and maneuvered past the glut of tourists to the exit. She turned left and headed past the gate. They passed the wall of hubcaps and ascended the dusty slope.

"Wait," Suda said. "What is this?"

She pointed to a series of signs along the chicken-wire fence that divided the store from the Pritchard's personal property. Each one was imprinted with a phrase. Together they read: *Big mistake many make is to rely on horn instead of brake. Burma Shave.*

She laughed. "That's really clever."

"This is from one of the greatest ad campaigns ever created," Quinn explained. "Burma Shave preceded shaving cream. It was foamy and came in a jar. The PR team wrote these roadside poems and put them along the highways. Some of them still exist on Route 66."

"The upkeep must have been expensive," Suda noted.

"Yeah, but profitable. People driving across the country liked seeing them along the way. Then the interstates allowed people to drive much faster and people flew rather than drove. With aerosol cans of shaving cream, Burma Shave's campaign became obsolete."

They hiked a little farther to a square metal building surrounded by cacti and tumbleweeds. The words Music Hall were spread across its front in large gold letters. They found a set of stairs and wandered toward an old upright piano tucked in a corner. Judging from the thick coat of dust that had turned the ivory keys tan, Quinn doubted any of Hackberry's musical citizens had used it in years.

"Are you supposed to play 'When Irish Eyes Are Smiling' and something will happen?" Suda suggested.

"Yeah, maybe a hidden wall will appear!"

Suda scowled. "You're making fun of me."

"Only a little," Quinn said playfully. She slid a hand around the leather jacket's lapels and pulled her closer. "We're alone."

Suda glanced down the hill. "For the moment. Won't other tourists venture up this way?"

"Highly unlikely. Few people are naturally curious. Most of the Route 66 tourists just want to hit the highlights and say they've done it."

"Is that something your Aunt Maura said?"

"It is. Nobody loved 66 more than Maura. One of the disappointments in the last ten years was realizing few tourists shared her excitement or her love of history. Nowadays the tourists snap a few pics with the giant dinosaur and the giant head and then bolt back to the interstate."

"There's really a giant head?"

Quinn nodded. "There is. It's right next to the giant aspirin."

Suda only fell for her joke for a split second. Then her eyes narrowed and Quinn laughed. She set their root beers on the piano bench and slid her hands down the sleek leather as their mouths connected. It was a tentative kiss but Quinn grew bolder as she imagined Suda wearing the jacket—and nothing else. Suda accepted her eager tongue. She raked her nails down Quinn's spine and settled her hands in Quinn's back pockets.

The sound of a father calling for his son broke them apart immediately. A few seconds later, a scraggly guy appeared. He asked if they'd seen his son just as a boy with a curly-headed mop came around the corner.

"Where have you been?" the father asked, trying to control his anger.

"Exploring," he said. He pointed at Quinn and Suda. "They were kissing. How come they're not kissing boys?"

Quinn knew she was beet red, but the father was even more embarrassed. He glanced at them and said to his son, "I guess it's time we discuss that it's okay to love whoever you want." He waved to Suda and Quinn and guided his son down the little hill.

When they were out of earshot, Quinn laughed heartily. "Oh, that was funny!" Suda looked mortified. "Didn't you think that was funny?"

"Not really, no. What if he'd been some Trump jerk and went and got his jerk friends?"

She could tell Suda was upset. "I understand your concern—"

"Don't placate me, Quinn. You're the one who said people in northern Arizona tend to be quite conservative."

"Yes, but we were alone. At least, I thought we were. I never would've attempted to kiss you like that if I knew we had an audience."

Suda wagged her finger. "That's not true. You kissed me in Kingman by the train. And then on top of a building."

"And I'm sorry about that." Suda stared at her skeptically. "Okay, sorta sorry, sorta not." Suda threw up her hands and Quinn said quickly, "It's that jacket. I have this image of you wearing *just* that jacket and it won't get out of my head. I don't think I've ever seen a human being look as good in a piece of clothing as you do in that jacket. If you wear that instead of your white lab coat, your patients will fawn all over you. They'll believe anything you told them, women and men. The only thing that could make you even more appealing would be if you let your hair down."

She offered a pitiful look but Suda crossed her arms. "Well, I don't think I'll be doing that right now." She glanced at the piano. "Shouldn't we be focused on the clue? Was 'Irish Eyes are Smiling' your aunt's favorite song?"

Quinn nodded and sat on the piano bench. "It was. She taught me to play it on this very piano during one of our adventures. We got stuck up here one winter for nearly two weeks. It was awesome." She hummed the tune and picked it out. "It's been a long time," she explained. After several attempts she finally remembered the chorus. Surely Aunt Maura wouldn't expect her to remember every verse. She started over several times, but it wasn't until she reached the last line of the chorus that she heard it. She stopped and repeatedly pressed the key.

"It's off," she said.

Suda nodded. "What note is it?"

Quinn shrugged. "I couldn't tell you that. Aunt Maura taught me the song, but I can't read music." Suddenly she chuckled.

"What?"

"I just remembered the word that goes with this note. It's gay. The line says, 'when the world seems bright and gay' and this key," she said, tapping it again, "goes with that note."

"There must be something wrong with that key," Suda suggested. She studied the guts inside. "Play it a few more times." Quinn obliged until Suda said, "Stop. I see what's happening. There's something wrapped around the hammer." She leaned over the top, and it looked to Quinn like she might fall in. "I've got it," she said in a muffled voice. She withdrew a small slip of paper and a rubber band.

Quinn instantly recognized Aunt Maura's distinct handwriting.

Quinn, I've left you a little note on an appropriate note. Get it?
The road to the past
Lies straight ahead
Say 'allo'
And get to bed.

"Okay," Suda said slowly. "I take it this is your aunt's version of a Burma Shave ad?"

"Definitely. I know where we're going." She turned serious and asked, "Do you have any claustrophobia or are you afraid of ghosts?"

Suda turned around suddenly. "What? Where exactly *are* we going?"

Quinn adopted a mysterious look. "I'm rather certain the next clue is underground. And there's one other little detail I probably should've mentioned to you back in Phoenix."

Suda put her hands on her hips and Quinn thought she looked like a total badass. "What little detail?"

"Several of the places on Route 66 purport to be haunted. So I want to make sure you aren't easily creeped out."

Suda scoffed, "No, I don't believe in ghosts."

"Really?"

Suda stopped walking and looked at her skeptically. "You do?"

"Yeah. Aunt Maura and I had a few really weird experiences. Nothing dangerous, but some spirits played a few tricks on us."

"Like what?"

Quinn shrugged and they continued down the hill. "Just simple stuff like knocking a hairbrush off the sink or hearing laughter in an empty hallway. And Aunt Maura swore that the first time she stayed at the Hotel Monte Vista in Flagstaff, a bellboy knocked on her door in the middle of the night and announced that room service had arrived. But when she opened the door, no one was there." She glanced at Suda who seemed deep in thought. "Well, what do you think?"

She shook her head. "Quinn, I'm a doctor, a woman of science. I think much of what people claim is supernatural is really brain science. Some people actually dream, thinking they're awake. And people think they're hearing things when really the sound is something other than what their brain is processing. So I'm not willing to accept the ghost theory so easily."

Quinn knew better than to argue with her as Aunt Maura had with Shane, who was also a nonbeliever. They'd gone through a six-month period where they hadn't spoken because Shane wouldn't believe Maura's story about the Hotel Monte Vista. Quinn hoped a specter might make itself known to them on the trip. Perhaps it would send Suda rushing into her arms.

They reached the parking lot, and Quinn immediately noticed Cousin It's passenger door was slightly ajar. She hurried toward the car, Suda chasing after her.

"What's wrong?"

"I have a bad feeling about this," she said, thinking of the FJ Cruiser that seemed to have disappeared when they pulled into the parking lot.

She flung open the door and stared into the foot well, the place where she'd carefully set the Hopi vase that held Aunt Maura's remains. It was gone and in its place was a note.

She sighed deeply as she opened it. The writer had used stationery from the Hilltop Motel in Kingman. Quinn pointed at the logo and Suda nodded. The message read, *Leave the draft of your aunt's next edition of <u>Mother Road Travels</u> underneath seat D15 in the Winslow Theater by six fifty-eight tomorrow night, and I'll return Maura to you. Otherwise, I'll cast her out into a not-so-nice place—the Phoenix Canal.*

CHAPTER FOURTEEN

Halfway to Seligman you'll come to the Grand Canyon Caverns. Discovered in 1927 by an enterprising young man named Walter, the Grand Canyon Caverns are one of the few dry caverns in the entire world. Such a claim makes it worth a stop, and indeed, they are impressive. Tours cost more than they did in 1927 when Walter only charged a quarter. He'd hand you a lantern and lower you down while those up top would call you a "Dope on a Rope." By 1961 they'd built an elevator. So you'll pay more now, but there won't be a rope involved in your descent. The dope reference will be applicable only to those who earn it.

-Mother Road Travels

"Why would the thief threaten to throw her into the Phoenix Canal?" Suda asked as they headed toward Peach Springs.

"Whoever took her knew her well. He or she knew how much she hated Phoenix."

"And that person thinks you have the latest edition of *Mother Road Travels*." Suda glanced at her. "Do you?"

"No." She wiped a hand down her face. "I might be able to guess where it is, but she didn't send it to me."

"Maybe that's what this adventure is about? Maybe it will be in…what was the odd name of that town in New Mexico?"

"Tucumcari. Yes, it might be there. Or Zeke might have it. Or another one of her friends. She had a lot of friends."

"Who do you think this guy is? Maybe another travel guide writer?"

"Could be, or it could be someone who aspires to be a travel writer and isn't afraid of plagiarizing Aunt Maura." Quinn shifted in her seat to face Suda. "She had her own voice and people liked it. She didn't talk like she was better than anyone else. And she was always brutally honest in her reviews. That's why she was the best."

Quinn lowered her head and tried not to cry. She never should've left the vase alone in the car, but she'd worried she might drop it amid the gaggle of tourists in the general store. She checked the volume on her phone again. She'd left a message for Zeke, urging him to call her immediately.

Suda grabbed her hand and squeezed it. "We'll figure this out and we'll get her back."

Quinn slid her fingers between Suda's and they held hands as they zipped past Peach Springs on their way to the Grand Canyon Caverns, the location of the next clue. Quinn continually checked the rearview mirror, but there was no sign of the FJ Cruiser. She was certain when they'd stopped at the store the Cruiser had pulled off as well, either parking illegally on the shoulder as many tourists did when the lot was full, or turning down one of the few side streets in Hackberry and walking up to the store.

Her phone rang and she jumped. Zeke. "Hi, Zeke. You're on speaker."

"What's wrong?"

She recounted the theft of Aunt Maura and heard him groan. "I was afraid something like this might happen."

"Why didn't you warn us?" Quinn exclaimed.

"Because I didn't want to worry you. If Maura had been here, she would've called me a ridiculous old fart. She never believed anyone was envious or jealous of her success, but plenty were."

"Who would steal her ashes?" Suda asked.

"I'd have to think about that. Most of her competitors wouldn't stoop so low. And anyone who has spent time on the Mother Road would definitely think twice before they'd steal a Hopi vase. That's a great way to anger the gods."

Quinn and Suda exchanged a questioning look before Quinn asked, "Where is the manuscript for the next edition?"

"I don't know," Zeke said quickly. "I thought maybe that was the point of the trip."

Quinn scratched her head and tried to think like Aunt Maura. She wouldn't leave it with just anyone, and she hadn't sent it to anyone in Quinn's family. "Did you search her Airstream?"

"I don't know where that is either," Zeke said, frustration in his voice. "Maura didn't tell me. She came by about three months ago. She gave me the first clue for your adventure and some instructions. I learned later that she'd also stopped by my daughter's house in Flagstaff and left the cats with her. Then she drove off and neither of us saw her again."

"She didn't say anything about her medical tests?" Quinn queried.

"No, but maybe they found something," Zeke said sadly. "That would explain some of her actions."

"Well, we're on our way to the Grand Canyon Caverns, so let me know if you hear anything," Quinn said.

"What sort of tests did they run on your aunt?" Suda asked in her doctor voice.

"She didn't tell me. I thought it was mostly routine stuff she'd been avoiding for a long time." Suda's lips pursed, showing her disapproval. "What are you thinking, Doctor?"

Suda kept her eyes glued to the road and said, "I know when people finally come in to have a routine test they've avoided, or they wait until they're in excruciating pain, we usually find something. Not always," she added, "but usually." She cleared her throat. "I'd like to summarize what we know. Often I do this with patient files. It helps me gain clarity."

Quinn nodded. "We could use clarity."

"You receive a video from your aunt just a few weeks before your thirtieth birthday. She mentions she's having tests and that you'll receive another package in the near future."

"Correct."

"Then, she unexpectedly dies in a car crash. Zeke, her attorney, visits you and tells you about her wishes."

"That's it so far."

She pointed at Quinn's cast. "Since you are injured, I accompanied you to Kingman, where we obtained your aunt's urn and the first of a series of clues that lead to the answer of the puzzle."

"I'm not sure it's a puzzle," Quinn corrected. "I think Aunt Maura just wanted me to visit some of the old stomping grounds. The twist is that someone is following us and that person has stolen her ashes to blackmail us!" Only when she'd finished the sentence did she realize she'd been yelling at Suda. "Sorry," she mumbled.

Suda took her hand. "It's okay. We'll get her back."

They stared out the windshield at one of the flattest portions of Route 66. It would be dozens of miles before they would see the mountains of Flagstaff, and the only scenery on this stretch of desert were tumbleweeds, cacti, and the occasional remnants of a store or motel long since reduced to rubble.

Aunt Maura had told Quinn that a few of the more daring entrepreneurs built their motel in a stretch of nowhere, recognizing that some overly-confident travelers would need a place to stay once they realized they couldn't stay awake long enough to reach Peach Springs. They'd pull over and register at one of the little places, grab their suitcase and hotplate from their car, make a quick bowl of soup and collapse on the bed until sunrise. Of course when I-40 was born, those businesses were the first to fail.

Sitar music burst from Suda's phone and Quinn jumped. "Sorry," Suda said as she answered. "Hello, Mother."

Quinn casually turned her head and checked Suda's stoic expression. Suda pursed her lips and held the steering wheel in a death grip. Her posture had shifted—a mannequin was suddenly driving the car. Quinn reasoned if Suda and her mother ever Skyped, the mother would be horribly offended. Suda looked as if she'd rather eat raw liver than continue the conversation.

"I don't have much time, Mother. I'm out with a friend and I'm driving her car. I can't have any distractions."

Quinn's jaw dropped. If she ever spoke to Gemma like that, she'd get whacked on the side of the head with a shillelagh.

"Yes. Yes. No. No, Mother."

She bit her lip and shook her head. When Quinn thought she heard the words, "a fine young man," in the mother's long monologue, she realized Suda's parents didn't know she was gay.

Quinn exhaled and stared at the scenery through the passenger window. The prospect of a lasting relationship with Suda had just deflated. She didn't have the time or the energy to deal with someone who hadn't yet come out to her parents. Two of Quinn's greatest romantic failures had been with women still in the throes of discovery. Both had ended poorly but made great party stories. The first relationship had fizzled with Quinn standing in a coat closet amid smelly shoes after her girlfriend's parents had dropped by unexpectedly. The second had ended with a one-sentence email in which her girlfriend admitted she was going back to men, which wasn't Quinn's fault.

Right. Sure.

"I'm hanging up now, Mother. We will talk soon."

Suda groaned and Quinn glanced at her with a sympathetic smile. "She doesn't know?"

Suda blushed and said, "My parents live in India. They are older and traditional. Since I have no intention of returning, I'm avoiding an unpleasant conversation. I know you probably think less of me because of it, but Indian customs are as strong as the customs of your Native American peoples. We don't just cast them to the side for principles."

Quinn couldn't help but press the issue. "I understand family customs. I really do," she said slowly. "Irish people have a few as well. But don't you think your parents are missing out? Wouldn't they rather know the real you?"

"No, they wouldn't," Suda said harshly, offering Quinn a quick glance.

"How do you know? How do you know unless you try to explain—"

"Because my mother already told me," Suda interrupted.

"What?"

She sighed before she began. "When I was sixteen, I fell for a girl I'd known most of my life, Hyma. We were best friends. Our parents were best friends. We didn't go to the same school but we lived nearby. My mother came home early one day from the furniture store. She wasn't feeling well. We were in bed when we heard the front door shut. We dressed quickly and hurried down the stairs. She was standing there in the foyer going through the mail. I looked in her eyes and I knew that she knew. It wasn't like we had our clothes on backward or our hair was horribly disheveled. We weren't holding hands. Hyma said hello to my mother as she had a thousand times and left. I asked my mother how her day had been but she didn't answer. She walked away.

"Did she ever actually say anything to you?"

"She did. An hour later she was in the kitchen and I was setting the table. I was so nervous. I worried she was waiting for my father to arrive so it would be two against one. That's often what they did with my brother. They took turns browbeating him into submission. I went back into the kitchen for the napkins and she turned to me and said, 'What happened today will never happen again in this house. We will never speak of it.' Then she went back to making dinner."

"You didn't respond?" Quinn asked incredulously.

"It wasn't a discussion. There wasn't a point to negotiate. I knew what she meant. If I ever brought a woman home again, I wouldn't have a home."

Quinn shook her head. "So your parents knows you're gay but nobody ever talks about it."

"No," she corrected, "my mother knows I'm gay. My father is clueless. She wouldn't tell him because of his poor heart."

"What about your girlfriends? You've been serious with other people, haven't you?"

"Of course. But they don't travel to India with me. Whenever I go, which is usually every summer, I go by myself. My mother finds a suitable man to be my escort to various events, and I'm sure she plays out our marriage in her mind. When I'm packing my suitcase to go home, she always asks if I enjoyed my time with the man and I always say yes. She asks if he's the one and I say no. I pick up my suitcase, kiss her and my father good-bye, and then I head out to the taxi and back to my real life."

Quinn put her head in her hands. "I can't believe it. Seriously? This is your relationship with your parents?"

"It is."

"So, how many girlfriends have left you because of this?"

"Several," she whispered. Quinn could barely hear her answer above the chug of the engine. "The greater amount, though, is the number of women who wouldn't continue to date me when they learned I'm not out to my parents." She looked at Quinn as long as she dared before her gaze settled on the road again. "That's why I told you there wouldn't be anything serious between us. I decided after the last failed relationship not to go down that road, so if you can't handle something casual, then we can't have anything." She paused and added, "And from the look on your face while I spoke to my mother, I could tell you were disturbed. So I know you wouldn't want a relationship with me unless I was completely out and proud."

"So you're doing me a favor and deciding for me."

Suda offered a critical stare. "Am I wrong?"

Quinn didn't reply, which was in itself a reply. They puttered through Peach Springs, constantly stopping for groups of people jaywalking across the town's only road. Quinn wondered what she could say to alleviate the awkwardness wedged between them.

"Why are there so many tourists?" Suda asked, saving Quinn the trouble of reigniting conversation.

"Peach Springs is the only town with lodging that's close to the Havasupai Trail, the second most popular hike into the Grand Canyon. Thousands of people hike to Supai Falls each year."

"I've only seen pictures, but they're unbelievable," Suda agreed. "My brother and I tried to get on the list, but they were booked a year in advance."

"Yes," Quinn said. "Only so many people are permitted to travel down on any given day. There are accommodations at the bottom, but Peach Springs is the only place to receive people at the start or end of their trip."

"Have you ever been down?" Suda asked.

"A few times." She opened her mouth to suggest they plan another trip, but she caught herself. There was obviously no future relationship with Suda. At least there couldn't be an honest one, and Quinn would never again hide in a closet.

As Cousin It chugged up the steep hill that would take them out of Peach Springs, Quinn realized that at thirty, she was tired of the games. She wanted a solid and steady relationship. Yet again, another sign that the desert freed her mind.

As they crested the hill, she pointed north and said, "If you look quickly, you'll see the Grand Canyon in the distance."

Suda peered out the driver's side window and nodded. It wasn't much further before Route 66 flattened out and the oversized signs for the Grand Canyon Caverns appeared. They passed the Caverns Inn, an old motel that struggled to keep a good reputation. Aunt Maura had been critical of the place in more than one edition of *Mother Road Travels.*

"Is that a dinosaur?" Suda asked, leaning forward over the steering wheel.

"It is," Quinn affirmed. "Aunt Maura used to say the caverns were part natural spectacle and part tourist attraction. After the interstate was built, they added some cheesy stuff since coming to see a dry cavern just wasn't reason enough to make the trip. Remember how I said there's a lot of giants on Route 66?"

"Uh-huh," Suda said as they pulled around to the cavern entrance.

"This allosaurus is their giant."

"How do you know it's an allosaurus?"

"It's three fingers," Quinn said.

They parked Cousin It and strolled over to the green dinosaur with the shiny white teeth and yellow belly.

"This is what your aunt's poem was referring to, right? When it said 'say allo,' like hello?"

"Part of it." Quinn grew uncomfortable. The last line of Maura's jingle had said, *Get to bed.* She had a sinking feeling she knew which bed Maura meant—the one in the suite located twenty stories below ground.

CHAPTER FIFTEEN

In 2010 the owners of the Grand Canyon Caverns opened one of the greatest gimmicks I've ever seen: a motel suite in the caverns. You can actually stay overnight surrounded by the crystals and mummified bobcat. This isn't cheap. Unless you've had a windfall from a wealthy loved one, this opportunity is reserved for those who possess big bucks, use words like *hoi polloi*, and have a serious adventurous streak. Only the strong-willed spend the entire night in the largest, deepest, oldest, quietest, and driest motel room in the world.

-Mother Road Travels

They pulled up to the long one-story building that housed the entrance to the caverns and the curio shop. Since it was nearly four p.m., only a dozen cars dotted the parking area. The last tour went out at four thirty, and Quinn guessed Zeke or her Aunt Maura had planned for her—and now Suda—to be on that tour. The only difference would be that they weren't coming out with the rest of the group.

"Do you think the clue is in the allosaurus?" Suda suggested.

Quinn shook her head. "No, I think Aunt Maura just included that reference so I'd know where to go."

Suda reread the clue. Quinn took a deep breath and prepared to answer her obvious question.

"What does the part about going to bed mean?" Suda asked cautiously.

Quinn put on her cutest face and said, "I think Maura has arranged for us to stay here for the night. She knew by the time we arrived it would be late in the day."

Suda pivoted and looked behind them at the Caverns Inn. "That place looks okay. Are we taking a tour first?" Quinn held her breath and Suda narrowed her eyes. "What aren't you telling me?"

Quinn pointed at a large sign across the parking lot that read, SPEND A NIGHT IN THE CAVERNS! THE GREATEST ADVENTURE IN ARIZONA!

Suda whipped her head to face Quinn. "No! Are you kidding me? Your aunt expects us to spend the night in a *cave*!"

"Technically it's a cavern. Caves are any opening—"

"I don't care what you call it!" Suda cried. "I can't sleep in a cavern. That's like camping. I don't do creepy crawlies or bears…or anything like that. I'm a city girl, Quinn. And I'm not even an American city girl."

Quinn raised her index finger to make a point. "This isn't the same. These caverns are different from anything you've ever read about. They're completely dry. There is nothing that can live down there. No bugs. No creepy crawlies, but that's kinda the same as bugs, really. No animals. There's no water, which is why they have to tote a hundred gallons of water down for guests. It's a really nice place. I've stayed there a few times and it's life-changing." She paused and when Suda didn't comment, she said, "I'll make you a deal. Let's take the tour. It goes past the suite. If you don't want to stay after you've seen it, then fine. I'll sleep down there alone, and you can get a room at the Caverns Inn."

"Okay," Suda said, climbing out of Cousin It.

They headed into the curio shop to buy their tickets. Quinn glanced at the cashier's station and saw Pearl, one of the guides. Quinn had met her five years prior when she and Aunt Maura stayed in the cavern for an entry in the fifth edition of *Mother Road Travels*. Pearl looked exactly the same. She was tiny and thin. Her bobbed brown hair framed her round face, and she wore jeans and a polo shirt, the typical uniform for guides. When Pearl saw Quinn, her face lit up and she ran to her, offering a strong hug.

"You made it!" she squealed.

"Yes," Quinn managed before Pearl's hug cut off her oxygen. She might've been tiny, but Quinn knew few women who were as strong as Pearl. Her small stature allowed her to crawl through the slivers between the cavern's prehistoric rocks.

Several of the people in the shop turned to see the commotion. Fortunately Pearl released Quinn quickly and turned to Suda. Before Quinn could introduce her, Pearl had clamped onto her. "I don't know you," Pearl exclaimed, "but if you're with Quinn, I know you're special."

"Thank you," Suda croaked.

Pearl stepped away and put her hands on her hips. "All right, so you found the clue that got you here. Are you both ready for your night in the cavern?"

Quinn smiled at Pearl but it quickly faded when she glanced at Suda's serious expression. "Actually, Pearl, Suda's not sure about staying in the suite."

Pearl's smile instantly evaporated and her eyes turned to slits. "I see," she said curtly.

"I just have a fear of enclosed spaces," Suda offered. "And I'm not outdoorsy."

Pearl turned to Quinn as if to say, *What the hell were you thinkin' getting together with this woman?*

"We're going to take the tour," Quinn said. "If Suda feels comfortable after she sees the suite, then we'll both stay down, but if not, she'll come topside and go back to the Inn. I'll be down there by myself."

Pearl nodded slowly, still not happy with Quinn's decision. "Go ahead and get your tickets," she said, waving to Mr. Packer, the cashier. "Willow's your guide." She threw Suda a cold look and said to Quinn, "I'm sure she'd be more than willing to give you an extra tour this evening if you're going to be free." She gave a sly smile before she headed to the restroom.

"I'm not sure she likes me," Suda murmured.

"It's fine. She's just protective of this place."

They got in line behind three other couples and watched as Mr. Packer counted out change to a customer. His slow speech and movements were almost hypnotic. The gentleman receiving the change grew impatient and shifted his weight from one foot to the other. It took so long that soon everyone in line watched. Finally he handed him the tickets.

"How old is that cashier?" Suda whispered.

"One hundred and four."

Suda gasped. "No, seriously?" Quinn nodded. "Does he go down in the cavern?"

"He does."

"Is that safe?"

Quinn smiled and gazed at Mr. Packer with admiration. His skin was pasty white and the deep wrinkles in his face reminded her of the rugged rocks in the caverns. Aunt Maura had said he blended into the cavern walls unless he wore a dark T-shirt.

"It's perfectly safe," Quinn said. "He knows the caverns better than anyone."

Suda looked at her skeptically. "Is he really a hundred and four?"

Quinn shrugged. "Well, I haven't seen his birth certificate, but Aunt Maura said he was born on Arizona's statehood day, February 14, 1912. And he has some great stories. One time she fact-checked his detailed account of attending FDR's second inauguration, and she concluded he was really there."

The line moved forward and they were next.

"As a doctor I'd be worried about someone that elderly having a heart attack down there," Suda continued. "I hope he gets regular checkups."

"I have no idea."

"It's not as if there's a ton of doctors racing to work in the rural areas," she pressed.

"True," Quinn agreed.

They exchanged a grin and the message was clear: they were back on track and the awkwardness was gone. They stepped up to the counter and he smiled at Quinn. "I was quite sorry to hear about Maura."

"Thank you."

His pale blue eyes seemed to shine as his gaze flitted between them. "Going down today as part of the adventure Maura had planned?"

"Yes." Quinn gestured toward Suda. "My friend, Suda, is accompanying me."

He offered a slight bow and leaned toward Suda. He whispered in her ear and her cheeks turned bright red. She mouthed, "Thank you," as he stepped away to retrieve their tickets. She stared at the ground, embarrassed.

"What did he say to you?" Quinn asked.

"Well, there's nothing wrong with his hearing. He heard all of my concerns, which he appreciates, but he told me I don't need to worry about his health. He sees a physician on a regular basis, but I am correct that there aren't enough doctors up here. He said he'd be delighted to be a reference for me if I ever wanted to move."

A tour group of six, including Quinn and Suda, took the elevator down with their guide, Willow. Young and rather soft-spoken, she wore a striking beaded clip in her long, braided hair, and one of the women on the tour quickly commented on it. Her denim shirt bore the Grand Canyon Caverns logo, and it tucked into faded jeans that had seen hard work. She explained she'd recently graduated from Northern Arizona University, but she wanted to return and be near her people, the Hualapai. While she loved giving tours, she was a trained paramedic who spent most of her days driving the one ambulance in the area.

As they exited the elevator, she shared the standard pitch about the caverns. They were among the few dry caverns in the world. There was no water, no humidity, no wind, and consequently, nothing could live in the caverns. That meant there was also no sound or noise of any kind.

As they stepped off the elevator, Quinn glanced up just in time to see Willow whip her gaze away. She'd been staring at her. They meandered through a few of the various rooms, marveling at the craggy limestone rock formations created three-hundred-forty-five million years earlier when the Southwest was completely engulfed by an ocean.

"When was the last time water was present here?" Suda asked.

"Over six million years ago," Willow replied. "That might seem like a long time, but it's really not when you're talking about the lifespan of a cavern." While she'd initially looked at Suda to answer her question, she ended up gazing at Quinn. They exchanged a look that Quinn had always associated with opportunity. She knew that usually the last guide of the day acted as the host for the tourists staying in the cavern suite. Perhaps if Suda wasn't interested in staying below ground, she could persuade Willow to go exploring with her. Extensive touring was usually a part of the suite package, if the guests were interested.

Quinn watched Suda. Was she enjoying the tour? Did she hate being underground? Quinn couldn't tell. They came upon the cavern suite, which was a two hundred by four hundred platform with a layout similar to a one-story tiny house.

"This is our latest addition to the Grand Canyon Caverns," Willow said. "Up to six people can spend the night here in our version of a motel suite. It has all the amenities you'd find in a regular motel room, including a shower, a flat-screen TV and a small refrigerator. We serve you dinner and breakfast prepared by our chef, and there's the opportunity to have an extended, behind-the-scenes tour. I can guarantee you won't be disturbed by anything. Some guests have said it was the most peaceful sleep they've ever had."

She locked eyes with Quinn. They were definitely on the same page. Quinn casually glanced at Suda, who was craning her neck to study all aspects of the floor plan.

A young guy who'd spent most of the tour hanging on his girlfriend asked, "How much does this cost?"

Without blinking an eye, Willow replied, "Eight hundred dollars for two people and an additional hundred for each extra person up to six."

Audible gasps circulated through the group, but Quinn's eyes remained on Suda. She could tell Suda was deliberating their sleeping arrangements. The fact that there were two beds should've reassured her that she didn't have to sleep with Quinn. And she'd meant what she'd told her. The first time she'd stayed in the suite with Aunt Maura had changed her life. It was the night she'd told Maura she was gay.

Willow fielded a few more questions about the suite before leading the group back to the elevators. Once they had disbanded in the curio shop, and Suda had bolted for the restroom, Willow approached Quinn.

"I hear you're staying underground tonight."

"Yeah, it's part of my aunt's adventure."

"I only met Maura once, but she was amazing. Such a good, honest person. My tribe tends to be naturally suspicious of white people, but Maura was an exception." She bit her lip and added, "I don't know if I should tell you this, but it was my cousin behind the wheel of the car that hit her."

Quinn blinked and felt her insides knot. "I see."

"He's beside himself in grief," she explained. "It was his first time drinking and driving. I know that's not an excuse, but he really will live with this for the rest of his life. The elders will never let him forget."

Quinn heard the sincerity in her voice. When her eyes welled with tears, she automatically pulled Willow into a hug. She knew Aunt Maura would never harbor a grudge against a young person who made a mistake, even if it was a terrible life-altering mistake. She'd forgive and would expect others to do the same.

"I've made my decision."

Quinn and Willow stepped apart and looked at a stony-faced Suda. She stared at Willow and said, "I'll be staying in the cavern tonight."

CHAPTER SIXTEEN

During the tour Suda had found herself waffling over her quick decision to boycott the suite. Perhaps Quinn and Willow's furtive glances at each other were the reason, or maybe she'd changed her mind because the suite didn't look so bad. She'd envisioned a tent and camp chairs with an outhouse in a dark corner. So she'd been pleasantly surprised to see the amenities. Most important, the ceiling of the suite was seventy feet high. Her claustrophobia wouldn't surface in a room the size of a skyscraper lobby.

Now, seeing the hug brought forth an image of Quinn and Willow taking an after-hours hike while she sat in the Caverns Inn watching cheesy cable movies. On their hike they would suddenly become sandwiched by two gigantic boulders. Before they called for help on Willow's radio, they'd find a way to unbuckle and unfasten whatever stood in the way of a mutual orgasm. She pictured Willow's face buried between Quinn's breasts, kissing her cleavage and tasting her nipples. The thought made Suda's heart race and her jealous streak surface.

If anyone got to suck on Quinn's glorious breasts, it was going to be her!

Before she could talk herself out of what she was sure would prove to be the most ridiculous thing she'd ever done, she marched over to them and announced her decision. Darkness settled over Willow's face that Suda found pleasing. Quinn's eyes widened and seemed to smolder, but perhaps Suda was reading too much into it.

"That's great," Quinn said. "Let's get our stuff out of the car."

"I'll be your host for the evening," Willow said in a less than enthusiastic voice. "After you get your things, let's check in with the chef before we ride down again."

As they headed out to Cousin It, Quinn asked, "What made you change your mind?"

She decided to share a partial truth. "You were right. It looked like a nice place to stay." Quinn smiled as they pulled out their few possessions. They started back and Suda felt the awkwardness returning. All of the other cars were gone. They were alone, as they would be for the next fourteen hours. "You're not expecting us to sleep together, are you?" she blurted.

Quinn stopped and turned to her. "Uh, no. You've made it clear that you're not interested in pursuing a relationship. And now that I've heard you on the phone with your mother, I understand. I don't agree with your choice, but I understand." She offered a wry grin. "But if you change your mind, let me know."

Suda blinked, too stunned to respond. Quinn hiked up her backpack and kept walking. "As far as I'm concerned," she said over her shoulder, "you're just helping me fulfill my aunt's dying wish."

Suda quickly caught up, trying to juggle her bag and the clothes she'd purchased. She didn't want to miss whatever Quinn said next. "And you're helping me get my aunt back," she continued, "since I so carelessly left her in a parking lot."

Suda heard the angst in her voice. She longed to give her a hug as Willow had done, but their arms were weighted down.

She offered a sympathetic look instead. "Hey, we'll get her back." She looked around at the empty lot. "I haven't noticed the FJ Cruiser since Hackberry. Maybe it wasn't following us?" she suggested.

"Could be," Quinn said. "But I'm almost positive it was."

Willow led them to the kitchen and they met Chef Matt. Suda sensed that in the time it took for them to get their things, Willow had extinguished her torch for Quinn. Gone were the sideways glances at Quinn and the cold stares at her. They chose vegetarian lasagna for dinner with a decent bottle of wine. It pleased Suda to see that Quinn tolerated meatless food. Suda's borderline vegetarianism had been another issue for Cearra, who believed meat was essential to a good meal. While Suda occasionally enjoyed meat, like the great burger from Mr. D'z, she mostly abstained.

On the elevator ride down, Willow outlined some of the hikes they could take later that evening. "We could go back to the Mystery Room, or try the Theater Room or the Crystal Room. If you want a romantic place, I'd suggest Chapel of the Ages. We've actually married couples there."

"I'd love to see that," Suda offered. "And I'd really like to see the Crystal Room."

"It's cool," Quinn agreed.

"We'll get to as much of it as we can," Willow said with a chuckle. She pointed to Quinn's arm. "There might be a few places that are out since your arm might get in the way. I'd hate for you to get stuck down here."

Quinn's cheeks turned red as they exited the elevator.

"Here's one of the light switches," Willow said. "You can turn off most of the cavern lights here or in the suite." They took a short path to the platform stairs. Suda took a deep breath of the dry air. It was difficult to define. She smelled…nothing. And she certainly heard nothing except their footsteps.

They dropped their bags onto their respective beds. Suda admired the comforter, a roadmap of Route 66. Two couches separated the bedroom from the living area and their fabric matched the comforter. Willow showed them how to operate the TV and the selection of movies or TV shows, which included every genre imaginable.

"You've got *Route 66*," Quinn noticed. "We stopped at Hackberry today and saw the Corvette."

"That's a great car," Willow said. She showed them the record player, CD player, and minifridge. "It's stocked with all kinds of soda, and there are snacks and popcorn in the drawers." She crossed the platform and they followed her around a wall. Tucked away in the corner was a tiny bathroom with a shower. "The key is to remember you only get five flushes between the two of you. Make 'em count. After that, you need to call me on the phone, because you'll have to come topside to pee. Showers are two minutes, so go fast."

While the shower offered privacy from the rest of the suite, the bather had a full view of a beautiful cavern wall. The showerhead was ten feet above them, preventing guests from wasting precious time and water adjusting the nozzle or the pressure. It reminded her of the one summer camp her parents had forced her to attend. Her fear and dislike of the outdoors began then.

"Okay, I'll be back in an hour with your dinner."

She disappeared and once the sound of the elevator dissipated, a silence like Suda had never experienced settled upon her. There was always noise, even in the quiet. Birds chirping, cars humming, wind blowing. It was the way the world spoke. She closed her eyes and stood perfectly still just to enjoy it. Quinn must have been doing the same because there was complete silence. While she imagined it would eventually drive her nuts, she thought about how great it would be to have fifteen minutes a day where she heard nothing. She opened her eyes to find Quinn staring at her.

"Caught me," Quinn said jokingly. "I may not touch, but I'm gonna look."

Suda lowered her gaze to the bedspread and busied herself by emptying their Penney's bags while Quinn scoped out the drinks in the minifridge.

"Want anything?" Quinn called. "There's sodas and seltzer water."

"Water, please," Suda replied. She rummaged through her handbag and when she came across the sexy red underwear, she remembered how cute Quinn looked with it on her head. She quietly chuckled, but in the soundless room it seemed as if she were shouting.

"What's so funny?" Quinn asked as she handed her a seltzer. Suda automatically shut her purse, but Quinn smiled. "I know what you're thinking about."

"I was not." But since she couldn't keep a straight face, they both wound up giggling. "Where will the next clue be? Do you think it's in this room?"

"Possibly," Quinn said. "We should make a search before dinner if we want to take a hike. Knowing Maura, if it's not somewhere in the suite, then it's somewhere in the cavern."

They split the suite in half. Quinn searched the area behind the living room and Suda searched in front. When they met in the middle, they were still clueless.

"Nothing," Quinn said.

Suda wandered to the shelves holding the records, DVDs, CDs, and books. "Do you think she'd put it inside a record sleeve or a DVD box?"

Quinn joined her and began reading the spines. "Um, maybe, but it wouldn't be random. She's not trying to make us crazy. It would have significance to me or it's important to the rest of our trip."

Suda began pulling titles. "Okay, so I'm guessing that eliminates Judith Kranz's *I'll Take Manhattan*, the movie *Reefer Madness*, and a complete season of *Family Affair*."

Quinn made a face at the mention of the ridiculous 60's comedy. "Definitely not the show, but you should pull out *Reefer Madness*." Suda raised an eyebrow and Quinn explained. "Aunt Maura was a proponent of legalizing marijuana. Living in northern Arizona where many Native Americans regard herbs and plants as medicinal, she couldn't understand the ridiculous and hypocritical laws that protect alcohol and opiates but ostracize one of the greatest plants ever known." She made air quotes at the end. "Her words, not mine."

Suda pulled out the *Reefer Madness* DVD and set it on the coffee table. "Noted."

As they continued to hunt for the clue, Quinn said, "I'm curious to know what you think about legalizing medicinal marijuana. As a doctor, have you ever had patients ask you to prescribe it?"

"A few, but since I work in a hospital, I'm bound by their policies, whether or not I agree with them. And they say no to pot for several reasons, number one being that it cuts into the profits of the drug companies. Of course, they don't advertise that reason."

"Ah," Quinn said, understanding. She pulled two books about Route 66 from the shelf, as well as the complete series of *Route 66*. "So what's your personal opinion, Dr. Singh?"

She paused and chose her words carefully. "Keeping in mind that America has some of the most ridiculous drug laws in the world, I think we have enough evidence to suggest there are great benefits to marijuana and more research should be done; however, the same old white men who continue to control women's vaginas will keep marijuana illegal so the pharmaceutical lobby will be happy."

"So you're for legalizing Mary Jane?" Quinn pressed.

"Yes, but I'm telling that to you in confidence. If I ever said it at the hospital, I could lose my job."

Quinn gestured at the cavern walls. "Well, you couldn't have picked a better place to tell a secret."

They finished combing through the shelves and returned to the couch. There were now more books, DVDs, and CDs on the coffee table than there were on the shelves. Suda picked up a large book filled with pictures of the Route 66 neon signs. She flipped through the pages, admiring the creativity of yesterday's artists, not really sure what she was looking for. Her progress slowed when she found an enormous neon guitar.

"That's the Museum Club in Flagstaff," Quinn commented. "It's a country and western place."

When Suda turned the page, she automatically said, "Wow." A two-page spread depicted Central Avenue in Albuquerque, which boasted more neon than anywhere else on Route 66. "Does it look like this today?"

"Somewhat. The historical society worked really hard, but neon signs are difficult to restore. They're made of tubes and are very fragile. It takes time and a lot of money. Unfortunately, many got destroyed before the historical societies formed."

Realizing she had a responsibility to help find the clue, Suda set aside the book and started opening DVDs. Quinn picked up a paperback and showed her the cover, *The Verse by the Side of the Road.*

"Oh, does that have all the Burma Shave rhymes?" Suda asked, distracted again.

"It does."

They chuckled through several, and Suda realized their laughter in the cavern sounded different, more authentic and full. She suddenly felt invigorated. A piece of paper slid out of the book and onto the coffee table.

Quinn scooped it up and smiled. "Now, what's this?" She opened the note so they could both see it. Aunt Maura had written another one of her own Burma Shave verses.

Put a little spice
Into your drive east
Just stop in
And have some dead chicken.
Okay, so it's not my best work, but you know where to go, don't you,
Quinn the Mighty?

"You're Quinn the Mighty?" Suda asked playfully.

"Only in my family. I'm known for taking risks. Sometimes they don't work out despite my planning."

"Yes, your zip line adventure was unfortunate," Suda said.

"I don't think so," Quinn replied.

Their eyes met. Quinn was asking permission. Suda knew if she didn't fill the deafening silence immediately, she'd be offering herself up. "Was Aunt Maura as much a daredevil as you?"

Quinn blinked and looked away. "No, she was more adventurous. I'm a risk-taker."

"I don't understand the difference."

"I'll do stuff like fly down a zip line. Ride the roller coaster that has a vomit-inducing plunge. Eat chocolate-covered ants on a dare."

Suda made a face. "Really?

"Yeah. They're actually pretty good, but I like a dollop of whipped cream with them." They laughed and she said, "Maura wouldn't do any of those things, but she spent her whole life traveling Route 66 alone. She went to unknown places and met some rather crazy individuals along the way. One guy pulled a knife and mugged her in a rest area."

Suda gasped. "That would've scared me enough to stop traveling alone."

"Not Maura. She bought a gun, took a safety class and got a permit. Never happened again."

"She wasn't alone all of the time," Suda noted. "From what I read in *Mother Road Travels,* you were along on several adventures."

"That's true. She liked having a kid with her because it gave her more insight into what really happened at these businesses and how tourists were treated."

"What was your role?"

Quinn laughed. "Often I would play a bratty kid or later, a stuck-up teenager. I'd be acting like an airplane in the lobby, or I'd throw a fit at the restaurant to see how the staff and management reacted. One time I pretended to shoplift. At first the gift shop manager was furious, but when Maura appeared and introduced herself, she completely changed."

"Sounds like you have some great memories."

"Oh, yeah. What kid wouldn't like a license to be obnoxious?"

They both laughed and Suda pointed at the last line of the poem. "Dead chicken?"

"There's a place in Seligman that's known for its dead chicken."

Suda cocked her head to the left. "As opposed to live chickens?"

"Sort of. I'm just glad we found the clue." Quinn folded the note and stuffed it into her back pocket.

"Me too." Suda gazed at the ancient walls and pictured the ocean sweeping over the land. "I see what you mean about this place. It's fascinating but it's…more. I can't explain it."

"Try."

Suda stared at her amused face. She'd propped her chin on an upturned palm. Suda imagined her discoveries were things Quinn already knew. She took a deep breath and said, "It feels like I'm in the middle of a big secret." She made a face. "That sounds stupid."

"No, it doesn't. Close your eyes. I want to show you something."

She hesitated but her curiosity wouldn't let her protest, even if Quinn's request seemed like a come-on line. She closed her eyes and felt Quinn's nearness. She knew her mouth, her breasts, and her sweet lips were millimeters away.

"Stay perfectly still. Listen."

Quinn's breath caressed her cheek. Then she heard it. A heartbeat. Pounding. Racing. She couldn't tell if it was hers or Quinn's, but it was loud. Another joined. It was the sound of life, of connectivity. When Quinn's lips found hers, it seemed completely natural. Tongues touched and she gently lowered Quinn on the couch. Their legs tangled as she pressed against her. She wanted their hearts to beat in time together, but she couldn't stay focused. Quinn's breasts demanded attention and the burning between her legs intensified with every kiss.

She knew they should stop. Quinn's green eyes shone brightly in the dim lighting of the cavern, drenched in longing. This meant something entirely different to her. But Suda knew if she reminded Quinn again that this moment was all there could be, Quinn would sit up and push her away. She wanted a relationship. Honestly, Suda just wanted a good fuck twenty-two stories underground. *Do I? Is that what I really want?*

This seduction was unlike any she'd ever experienced. Even when two lovers snuck off to be alone, they took parts of the world with them. Wind still tapped at their windows. The air conditioner or furnace rumbled and mumbled to adjust the temperature. Plane engines roared as they ascended or descended from the nearby airport. Birds chirped and dogs barked. But not in the cavern. Suda and Quinn made the only sounds, and at this moment, their heartbeats and every nerve they possessed were focused on one task—pleasure.

Unzipping Quinn's jeans sounded like a buzz saw in a room devoid of life. The couch springs creaked slightly every time their bodies shifted. Her hand slid down Quinn's smooth belly and played with the seam of her underwear. She struggled to focus on her task and fully enjoy the tantalizing experience inside her mouth. Quinn's kiss was exquisite.

When Quinn broke it, she groaned her displeasure—until Quinn unsnapped her bra with her one good hand and her lips wandered between Suda's breasts. Suda rolled onto her side and closed her eyes as Quinn separated her from her clothes. Her nipples turned to pebbles once they were exposed to the chilly temperature. She longed for Quinn to suck on them, and it was as if she could read her mind—and deliberately ignored her desires. Quinn fondled her breasts, and kissed everything else—while her nipples ached.

Two can play this game.

Her hand returned to its work between Quinn's legs. She pushed her jeans down and slid two fingers inside of her. Quinn gasped.

"Look at me," Suda commanded. Quinn struggled to do as she was told. "Open your eyes, Quinn," Suda said firmly, but softly.

She obeyed, but then Suda saw her vulnerability, her passion, and the indescribable effect she had on Quinn. It was intoxicating. "Do you want me?" she asked innocently.

Quinn managed, "Yes, please."

"Even if it's just for now?"

When Quinn closed her eyes and nodded, Suda plunged deep inside her and pushed up Quinn's T-shirt with her free hand. She wanted—needed—to see her voluptuous chest.

Quinn sighed. Suda felt Quinn's passion tighten around her fingers. She was close.

Suda pushed up Quinn's bra and fastened her lips onto Quinn's left nipple. She sucked and stroked, Quinn's hips matching her rhythm. When Quinn came, Suda was certain they heard her cry up in the gift shop. She stayed pressed against Quinn, content to suckle on each nipple and enjoy the tender valley between her large breasts until one orgasm rolled into two.

"I need to move my arm," Quinn whimpered.

Suda slid off the couch and headed for the bathroom. As she emerged, she heard the rattle of the approaching dinner cart. For a reason she couldn't explain, she wanted Willow to know what they'd been doing, in the event she hadn't heard at least one of Quinn's exquisite orgasms. Suda unbuttoned the shirt she'd just rebuttoned before she appeared in the living room. Quinn had managed to reassemble her clothes somewhat, but when Suda appeared, both Quinn and Willow turned to stare, their gazes never rising above her exposed cleavage.

Willow recovered first and said, "Dinner is served."

CHAPTER SEVENTEEN

Interstate 40 murdered Route 66. Established stores, motels, and restaurants that had served travelers for decades closed their doors permanently when the Mother Road no longer proved prosperous. People wanted to get where they were going in a hurry. There are many points where Route 66 and Interstate 40 are within spittin' distance of each other, and some politicos couldn't see paying for both. Route 66 was decertified as a US Highway in 1984 and seemed destined to fade into history—until several towns started campaigns to reinvent and resurrect the Mother Road.

-Introduction, *Mother Road Travels*

Quinn had always thought what a woman wore to bed said a lot about her. When Suda emerged from the tiny bathroom in a tank top and flowing black yoga pants that rode low on her hips, Quinn's gaze raked over every spot of her exposed skin. And she'd finally undone her hair. It wasn't an attempt to look sexy. It was understated and Quinn found it sexy as hell.

Suda seemed oblivious to her effect on Quinn as she continued her bedtime preparations, putting toiletries in her bag, retrieving a book and setting up her phone charger. She continually swept her hair out of her face in a graceful, hypnotic motion. Quinn found it impossible to follow her Jane Austen biography. Why would she concentrate on a fascinating, but deceased woman, when an equally fascinating live one was just a few feet away? A woman who, a few hours ago, had touched her heart and her soul and taken control of her entire being.

While the sex had been unbelievable, hearing their heartbeats together had been a life-changing moment for Quinn. If Willow hadn't interrupted, she was certain she would've taken Suda. As it was now, she was too tired to move.

Their vegetarian lasagna had been delicious and the conversation fascinating. Quinn learned much about Indian culture and the customs of Suda's family. "We are very old-fashioned," she explained. "The women stay home and the men work. My mother wanted more for me, and she figured out how to get it and drag my father along." She waved a finger as she said, "I never would've been a doctor had my father not agreed."

"Our families sound a lot alike. I'm surprised you got to America."

"Me too. I owe that to my grandparents. They took my parents to Las Vegas for a vacation. Not that the Las Vegas strip represents the idyllic American life, but my mother saw the incredible opportunity for women."

"But your father doesn't know you're gay and your mother doesn't want to talk about it," Quinn summarized. "I don't want to start a fight, but I just can't believe they wouldn't accept you. You're brilliant, you're highly accomplished, and you're a beautiful person inside and out. So what if you're a lesbian?"

Suda seemed to bask in the compliments. She stroked Quinn's cheek. "Thank you for saying that. It means a lot." She returned to her dinner. "But what you have to understand is, those very reasons you mentioned are exactly why I can't come out. My parents' entire understanding of who I am would crumble. My father is a heart patient who refuses to follow his doctor's directives." She set her fork down and sat up straighter. "If I came out to them, and then my father had a heart attack, I'd blame myself. Even though there are many factors that can contribute to heart disease, stress is one that cannot be perfectly quantified."

She looked at Quinn as if waiting for her response. Quinn decided to let it drop. "Understood." Her gaze settled on the cavern walls. She asked, "Why don't you tell me about your most interesting patients, and I'll tell you about some of the crazy things I've found in condemned apartments?"

They were still laughing about a woman who'd managed to swallow her own engagement ring when Willow returned carrying flashlights and hard hats. They strapped on the gear and followed her underneath the red tension cables that had corralled the day's tour groups. Quinn had forgotten how dark the caverns became just a few turns past the installed tour lights. The openings narrowed, as if the spelunker was headed through a funnel.

In several places, Quinn took Suda's hand as the trail grew rockier. It was hard for their feet to find purchase, even with hiking boots. When they came upon two giant kissing boulders, Willow said, "There's a great path just beyond this point, but we'll have to earn it." She pointed to Quinn's cast. "Are you really up for this?"

"Yeah, no problem," Quinn said. She certainly wasn't going to back out and ramp up Suda's anxieties even if she was a little concerned about how to fit the bulky cast around some of the paper-thin openings.

"Okay," Willow said. "You'll need to get down on your back and slide under the rocks. On the other side is a narrow sill that leads to another set of rocks. We climb over those to reach our reward." She looked at both of them with a wry smile. "Are you game or should we go to another path?"

Suda glanced at the small opening between the rocks. Quinn slid her arm around Suda's waist and said, "I won't let anything happen to you."

Suda gauged her sincerity and nodded. "Okay, let's do this."

It had taken nearly thirty minutes to get through the opening, but Suda had been a trooper, and managed her claustrophobia while Quinn had been forced to contort herself like a Cirque du Soleil performer at certain points. But it was worth it. The Crystal Room was a reward. They marveled at the white mineral that covered the walls and ceiling. It was as if they were surrounded by glass. The sight had been breathtaking, enough so that the return trip through the narrow boulders didn't seem as challenging.

They'd returned to shower and prepare for bed. Awkwardness crowded the room as if it were another guest. While she'd hoped they would reclaim the amorous mood before dinner, she knew when they returned from the hike that the only other evening activity would be sleep. She wondered if Willow had pushed them hard to deliberately thwart a night of passion.

Quinn wondered how Suda would fare once the suite's lights went off. Some people couldn't make it in the blackest darkness they'd ever seen. That's why there was a phone. Quinn knew the cavern employees took bets on which suite guests would be phoning to come topside and stay at the Caverns Inn for the rest of the night.

Suda slid into her bed and faced Quinn. "Thank you for today, and thank you for inviting me on this adventure. I'm having a good time."

Quinn abandoned her book and faced her. "I'm glad. Aunt Maura would've really liked you."

Suda blushed. "Really?"

"Yes. She would've liked your flexibility and willingness to face your fears. One of her favorite words was gumption."

"I don't know that one."

"It's old-school. Hardly anyone uses it now, but it's a word that means a whole lot of words put together—resourcefulness, initiative, courage, and bravery. Those are a part of gumption."

"Do you really think I'm brave?"

Quinn knew what she was asking. They weren't talking about the hike in the caverns anymore. "Yeah, I think you are."

Suda smiled then yawned. "I'm exhausted. This has been a busy day." Her expression hardened and she asked, "Do you think we'll get your aunt's remains back tomorrow?"

"I hope so. I have a plan, but we're going to need a little help. Luckily, the blackmailer picked Winslow. Aunt Maura has a lot of friends there."

"Do you think we're in danger, Quinn?"

Her concern was obvious and truthfully Quinn was a little worried. But now wasn't the time to discuss it. "I don't think so," she hedged, "but I can't know for sure. Aunt Maura kept a lot of secrets. We might be dealing with someone who doesn't want one of them revealed."

Suda weighed the idea and looked at the picturesque ceiling. "Could it be something to do with the next version of *Mother Road Travels*?"

"Possibly." Quinn sighed. Her limbs grew heavy. "Are you ready for the darkness?" she asked, her hand poised on the light switch next to her bed.

"I think so," Suda said hesitantly.

Quinn flipped the switch and a whoosh deactivated every light in the suite and the ones that illuminated the walls. Neither of them said anything as they adjusted to the pitch-black cavern. Quinn held up her hand, but couldn't see it at all.

"This is incredibly odd," Suda proclaimed. "I don't know if I like it."

"It takes a few minutes to adapt," she said optimistically.

"I feel like the dark is wrapped around me."

"Do you feel claustrophobic?" Quinn asked seriously. "I can turn on one of the soft lights by the entertainment center."

"No," she replied. "I want to try. Since I work the graveyard shift, I've learned how to sleep in the day. I block out the noise and the light. This is the opposite."

Quinn remained perfectly still while Suda rustled the sheets and cleared her throat. She could hear her breathing. She imagined Suda's warm breath tickling her ear. She shivered. Suda's bed creaked as she sat up. Quinn waited to see if she'd say anything. She hoped Suda wasn't giving up and going topside.

Suda sighed in defeat and Quinn bit her lip. *Here it comes.* "Quinn, would you mind if I slept in bed with you?"

Quinn smiled and pumped her fist, knowing Suda couldn't see it. The glory of sleeping in pitch dark was just that. "I don't mind at all," she said coolly. She moved over on the bed. "Just crawl in."

Suda slid between the sheets. Did she smell Quinn's shampoo on the pillow? She must have felt her warmth on the sheets. Quinn imagined Suda's tank top riding up, revealing more than she intended. She longed to reach across Suda's backside and slide her hand along Suda's cool belly. She'd cup her breasts and stroke the soft, delicate skin. In the most intimate darkness either of them would ever experience, every sound would fuel their passion. The sounds in the darkness would tell her when to gently push Suda onto her back and slide on top of her. Every moment would be a mystery, a surprise to the other. Blindness would free their imagination and their anticipation.

"Quinn?" Suda asked breathily.

"Uh-huh?"

"What are you thinking about? I can feel your heart racing. I swear I can."

She believed her. "Honestly, I'm imagining what it would be like to make love to you in this darkness." She chuckled and added, "But don't worry. Willow wore me out. I'm too tired for anything now."

"I'm exhausted as well." She paused before she asked, "Can you hold me, please? Can you *just* hold me?"

Quinn gritted her teeth. "Yes, I can."

But before she wrapped her arms around Suda's gentle curves, before she felt her luxurious hair against her cheek, and before she inhaled the lovely scent made lovelier in the lifeless cavern, she made a gun out of her index finger and thumb—and pantomimed shooting herself in the temple.

The next morning they were up early and out of the cavern by eight. While guests could stay until eleven, they were forewarned that tours started at nine, and groups of strangers with cameras would be strolling past the suite. Aunt Maura had shared some great stories of couples caught in compromising positions, an unsuspecting woman walking out of the bathroom naked and two brothers fist-fighting. The tour guide and a tourist who worked security separated them, but not before the tourist sustained a black eye.

Neither Quinn nor Suda wished to be ogled. So after a wonderful breakfast of waffles and bacon, they took the elevator to ground level.

Then they hit the road for Seligman, the destination of the next clue. Suda's phone buzzed for the third time. She looked at the display and disconnected the call.

"Are you sure you don't need to answer some of those?" Quinn asked. "We could pull over." Before they'd left the caverns, Suda had spent fifteen minutes listening to messages and deleting texts. Someone or several people were desperately trying to reach her.

"No, it's fine," she said. "I have colleagues who constantly text throughout the shift, asking for a consult or wanting to discuss the bizarre cases that come in. I'm getting the texts even though I'm not there." She glanced at Quinn who nodded and smiled. But she knew Suda was hiding something. "Tell me about your friends or your work," Suda said. "What's it like to remodel apartment complexes? I don't do any home repairs. I feel completely helpless."

Quinn snorted. "You and my sister. She can't drive a nail, but she makes a seriously good tiramisu."

Suda smiled. "Is that your favorite dessert?"

"No, I like tiramisu, but fifteens are my favorite."

"The cookies your mom had after your surgery?" When Quinn nodded, she said, "Those were delicious."

Suda's phone buzzed again. She glanced at the sender, shook her head and tossed it into the console. Quinn's gaze flitted to the glowing display before it shut down. The messages, or at least the most recent one, weren't from anyone at work. The caller was her mother.

Quinn was about to say something but her own phone rang. *Her* mother. "Hi, Mom. How's it going?"

"Not well," Gemma replied in a clipped tone. "*Your* brother-in-law came over yesterday to help *your* father put up a fence to keep the wild horses off the property. You know, old Soupy won't stand up for herself."

"I know."

Soupy was the family mule. Her food was constantly poached by a pack of wild horses that roamed the west valley desert and had discovered the O'Sullivan ranch. Everyone had chased them away, including Quinn. All it took was a loud noise, like beating a metal pot with a spatula, but the horses came around so often that Gemma finally donated her oldest copper-bottomed pot and a wooden spoon to the cause.

"Did they finish the fence?"

"Ah, did they finish the fence," Gemma repeated. "No, they barely started on it. Shane packed a cooler of Guinness for when they got thirsty. So what do you think happened?"

Quinn pulled the phone from her ear. She glanced at Suda who was quietly giggling. Gemma's strong Irish voice filled the little car. When Suda offered an embarrassed look, Quinn rolled her eyes.

"I hope you didn't let Steven drive home," Quinn said.

"Oh, no, of course not. He stayed on the couch and went home this morning to deal with Fiona, who wasn't happy at all. They were supposed to go out last night to celebrate their wedding anniversary. It's not good when you spend your anniversary sacked out on your in-laws' couch, too scuttered to move. The only one who kissed Steven last night was the dog!"

Suda laughed and quickly covered her mouth so Gemma wouldn't hear. Quinn shook her head. "Is that why you called me? You wanted to tell me about Steven?"

"No, of course not. I want you to come fix the fence. Can you be here by ten?"

"Mom, I'm out of town, remember? I'm on the adventure with Aunt Maura?" Suda frowned and Quinn pictured a faceless creep pouring the contents of the beautiful vase into the stinky Phoenix canal.

"Oh, that's right. The pretty doctor went with you, didn't she?" Gemma's words dripped in sugar. "How's that going?"

Quinn knew she was blushing. "We're having a very nice time getting to know each other." She felt Suda watching her, but she didn't dare look up. If she looked at the woman who'd given her one of the greatest orgasms she'd ever experienced while she talked to her mother, she might combust into a pile of ashes.

"Well," Gemma continued, "can you put it on your calendar for when you return? Poor Soupy's hardly had anything to eat in the last week. Those damn horses wander in here like they own the place. It's obvious your father and brother-in-law can't be trusted to get the job done!" Whenever Gemma was angry, she completely disassociated herself from whichever family member had drawn her ire.

"Sure, Mom. I'll do it as soon as I get home."

"That's my good girl. Thank you, love. Say hi to the doctor for me."

"I will," Quinn promised.

"So how are you going to build a fence one-handed?" Suda asked in her stern doctor voice. Her stony face matched her tone.

"I promise, Dr. Singh, that I will be extremely careful. I'll recruit my able-bodied, non-alcohol imbibing nephews to help me."

"Good. It sounds like your family relies on you a lot."

Quinn bristled at the statement. She wasn't sure if Suda approved or not, but it wasn't her business. "I don't think my family's much different from any other, except what they ask me to do is usually done by a male child. That's the difference. I could build and weld better than most of my peers in school." She shifted in her seat and rubbed an itchy spot under her cast. "Of course, I never went to college like you did, at least not for very long. It just wasn't my thing."

"It's not for everyone," Suda said quickly. "There are different kinds of intelligence and most have nothing to do with a university."

They fell into silence as they approached Seligman. Quinn worried she'd stalled the conversation until Suda noticed a series of Burma Shave signs.

"Look!" She read each sign, which were placed a half-mile apart. "Drinking drivers...Enhance their...Chance...To highball home...In an ambulance."

They laughed until the predictable last sign appeared. "Burma Shave!" they proclaimed together.

"Did they have any women's products?" Suda asked.

"Not specifically. Their soap was for men, but I'm sure many women used it on their legs." She pointed at the speed limit sign. "You'll want to slow down. Like a lot of the Route 66 towns, Seligman is big on speed traps."

They chugged along at thirty miles per hour. On the left was an enormous gift shop covered in Route 66 memorabilia. They passed the Roadkill Café and West Side Lilo's, two of the handful of restaurants that served the tiny community. Interspersed between the smattering of decrepit brick houses and old motels were condemned structures from long ago.

"Why don't they tear down some of these eyesores?" Suda asked. "It would seem they could use the land to build more attractions." She glanced at Quinn and asked warily, "Or am I being disrespectful to history?"

"You're not," Quinn assured her. "I asked Aunt Maura the same thing." She reached for her copy of *Mother Road Travels* and soon found the page she was looking for. "Maura wrote, 'Think of the remains of old trading posts and abandoned motels and their destroyed neon signs as historic monuments. While I applaud the renovated and reborn on Route 66, at least some of the decayed structures tell an important story and remind us of 66's true roots—a pathway to opportunity. Whether you were a young woman yearning for adventure as a Harvey Girl, a family trudging west to escape the dustbowl, or a businessman seeking his fortune, there was something on the Mother Road for everyone.'"

She peered over the book at Suda, who wore an odd expression on her face. She wasn't sure she'd been listening, or perhaps she'd been listening closely and was deep in thought.

Eventually she said, "I see what she means. What's a Harvey Girl?"

"The Harvey Girls were women hired by Fred Harvey, the railroad executive who established restaurants and lodging along the rail line. If you were young and adventurous, it was a thrill to come west and work."

"Sounds like he was a liberated man for the time," Suda commented.

"He was."

Three blocks later they reached the center of town. Three motels in a row, Supai, Romney, and Aztec were still in business because of the Annual Fun Run, which brought visitors from around the globe. A series of old buildings, some from Seligman's mining days, also remained. Their exteriors had received makeovers that attracted tourists and telegraphed Seligman's celebratory nature. Seligman Sundries' aqua colored paint was eye-catching, but so was the pink Rambler that sat outside the Route 66 Motoporium next to a rusted-out Model A.

Suda automatically slowed to glance at the interesting shops. Two blocks later she pulled up next to the most unusual structure in all of Seligman, Delgadillo's Snow Cap. Hordes of people gathered in the front patio that faced Route 66.

"This is it, right?" she asked proudly. "I found the clue, didn't I?"

Quinn chuckled and nodded. "How did you know?"

Suda pointed at the small white building. The main menu items were listed in multicolored paint across the top like a banner. "It says they serve malts, tacos, burritos...and dead chicken."

CHAPTER EIGHTEEN

There are two Arizona towns that have my permission to wallow in the sour grapes created by Interstate 40. Those towns are Seligman and Winslow. We'll get to Winslow later, but if ever there was a town worthy of a place on a map, it's Seligman. Nestled in northern Yavapai County, Seligman was a hot spot on the Mother Road, but prosperity vanished quickly once the interstate appeared. Seligman nearly died. The Delgadillo family and their like-minded friends saved the small community by starting Arizona's first Route 66 Historical Society. They still own the pool hall, barbershop, and the famous Snow Cap, the town's weird and quirky version of a Dairy Queen.

-Mother Road Travels

Suda tried to take in everything there was to see at the Snow Cap, but according to Quinn, it was like an ongoing sixty-year-old school project. A collection of outdoor furniture was crowded together under an awning that wrapped around the little white building, ensuring that winter visitors would have a place to sit, free of snow.

"Let me show you the back before we go in to order," Quinn suggested.

She led Suda to a group of onlookers staring at a white car unlike any she'd ever seen. The top was gone and the sides were cut low, exposing silver bench seats in the front and back that displayed Route 66 highway signs. The white exterior was an advertisement. The car doors said *Snow Cap* and the words *Dead Chicken* were written in red along the fenders. Colorful plastic flowers adorned the windshield and a red speaker sat in the center of the dashboard.

She gave Quinn a questioning look and pointed at the speaker. "Is this their version of an ice cream truck?"

"No, they don't need to drive around. Everyone in Seligman knows the Delgadillos and the Snow Cap. This is their Fourth of July parade car."

"Oh," Suda said. "It's certainly eye-catching."

Beyond the parade car was an array of old jalopies and gas pumps, giving the appearance that customers from several different decades were currently dining at the Snow Cap. An old black Chevy Deluxe, a green Ford truck and a red Chevy Impala reminded Suda of the front of the Hackberry General Store. An outhouse sat next to a fenced area titled *Juan's Garden*.

"Who's Juan?" Suda asked.

"Juan Delgadillo was the person who built the Snow Cap. He kept a lot of quirky stuff in the garden area. Now, it's an extra place for customers to enjoy their food or ice cream."

Air Conditioned was scrawled across the top in yellow letters. A collection of signs covered the splintering wood, so much so that it was impossible to see the entrance. A little girl sat on the only seat nearby—a toilet. Her legs bopped up and down, as if she were waiting her turn.

"This is a very unusual place," Suda murmured.

"It is, and it's one of the most popular tourist attractions on Route 66. Juan built the original structure in the fifties from scrap lumber, and the family continues to add and change the décor every year. Let's wander through the garden."

Picnic benches lined both sides. Large plywood signs advertised the burgers, tacos, and ice cream. She saw little that reminded her of a garden except the plastic flowers and vines woven through the chain-link fence.

They walked back to the entrance and followed a small group of senior citizens through the front door. Quinn pointed to a large neon sign in the window that proclaimed *Sorry, we're open.* Two doorknobs greeted them, and after trying the customary right one, which drew a chuckle from Quinn, Suda opened the door with the left.

"The Delgadillos are known for their jokes and pranks."

Suda blinked and her eyes grew wide. Every surface, save the floor, was covered in posters, flyers, decals, stickers, and signs. As they waited in line, she glanced at a poster for a missing dog lost in 1986.

"That would be one old dog," Quinn said, reading the same poster.

"They don't take down anything, do they?"

The line moved forward and Quinn pointed to three different flyers, all of which advertised an upcoming edition of *Mother Road Travels.* "Aunt Maura put those up every time a new version of the guide became available. The Snow Cap was one of her favorite places." Quinn checked the line and said, "I'm running to the restroom. Be right back."

She shimmied past the food line of people to join a few others across the room in the bathroom line. When the woman ahead of Quinn chatted her up, Suda immediately reached in her purse for her phone. It had vibrated several times since they left the caverns. She knew it was her mother, and she felt bad for lying to Quinn. She had no right to suggest Quinn's family relied too heavily on her, since her own mother couldn't stop calling and texting.

She had twelve new texts, each one slightly shorter than the one before. She'd glanced at the first one before they left the caverns, just to be certain nothing had happened to her father. Once she realized his condition hadn't changed, she ignored the further texts. Her mother wanted to chat or nag at her, and she wasn't in the mood for either. The gist of the messages was the same: call her. Since neither the food line nor the bathroom line was moving quickly, she placed the call.

"Is everything okay?" she asked when Nima answered.

"For me, yes. Where are you?"

Knowing her mother would realize she was in a noisy place, she said, "I'm at work, Mother. I'm out on the floor and it's very busy. I only have a few seconds."

"Work. I see. We have a date. August eighth. Can you make it?"

"I'm certain I can arrange for the time off this far in advance. Thank you for getting me an exact date. I have to go."

"When are you through today?"

Suda stared at the phone. It was an odd question from someone who was thousands of miles away. "The usual time," she said. "Why are you asking?"

"No reason." Then Suda heard the click.

She shook her head and tossed the phone back into her purse. Something was going on with her family, but she couldn't imagine what it could be. Her mother's strong desire to control her life was increasing, not decreasing. Part of the reason Suda stayed in America was to keep her independence. Yet, in moments like these, she could feel her mother's fingers wrapped around her upper arm, guiding her through life's maze, just as she had when they shopped at the busy outdoor bazaar when Suda was little.

Her gaze wandered back to the posters Aunt Maura had tacked up on the wall. The closest one advertised the current edition of *Mother Road Travels*. In addition to the title and the logo, thought bubbles surrounded the edges with testimonials from Route 66 patrons and travel guide readers who praised Maura's ability to find the best, the cheapest, and the most entertaining adventures on Route 66.

She blinked at the top thought bubble. She'd skimmed the words, but she leaned forward to read it again. It wasn't part of the original flyer. Someone had typewritten the text on a different sheet of white paper and carefully pasted the new words over the bubble. Suda imagined that person was Maura and she believed she'd just found their next clue. It was an ingenious hiding spot. Hundreds of flyers surrounded it, and it was unlikely someone would realize the text didn't belong.

She read the words again in the bubble. This time Aunt Maura hadn't bothered to make a jingle. *Nobody swings like a lumberjack.*

Quinn returned to the line and Suda showed her the clue. "That could be a double entendre," Quinn said dryly, "but I'm rather certain she's referencing the giant lumberjack at Northern Arizona University. We're about seventy-five miles away, so why don't we get something to go since we're already in line?"

Suda peered at the simplistic menu above the counter. It was old-fashioned, the kind that had the black letters pressed into a small white marquee. It didn't look as if the menu or the sign had changed in decades. "Do they have a salad?"

"Right. You're more of a fruit and vegetable girl."

"I detest cooking, and since I live alone, it's much easier to have an apple and yogurt for dinner. Same with lunch. What about you?"

"I agree. I cook a little, probably because I'm Irish and it's a skill we're taught in the womb. Fiona's the real cook. She's the one who learned from Mom while I was out in the shop with Dad."

"So you're handy," Suda concluded.

A sexy smile crossed Quinn's face. "I am. Do you have something that needs my hands?"

Suda chuckled. "That was a terrible come-on line. You know that, right?"

Quinn feigned offense. "Well, I don't think it was so bad."

"It's actually worked on a woman?"

"Several."

"Hmm. Well, I do have a few things in my historic home that need fixing, but I hate to impose."

"It wouldn't be an imposition."

They both seemed pleased at the prospect of having another reason to get together after the adventure. When the counter clerk cleared his throat, they both turned red. They ordered a to-go bag and went to the waiting area outside. Other customers milled about, easily striking up conversations with complete strangers. Suda checked her phone and Quinn closed her eyes to eavesdrop on other visitors.

Suda noticed and asked, "Are you okay?"

"I'm fine. When I traveled with Maura, we would often sidle up next to a group of people to hear what they thought about the attractions they were visiting on Route 66. Maura said she learned much more from casual conversation than she ever could from the testimonials guests and customers left on websites. Apparently many owners paid or offered incentives to travelers in return for excellent reviews."

"I can believe that," Suda murmured.

Quinn stepped away to listen to another group of tourists while Suda continued to delete messages and texts, all of which were from her mother. Except for the one from Cearra. The woman wouldn't leave her alone. Yet Suda wasn't entirely sure she wanted to be left alone. She glanced at Quinn, who was leaning against a pole, her thumbs stuck in the front pockets of her jeans. She appeared relaxed but Suda thought it was an act. She was on guard all the time. When Suda had climbed into bed with her the night before, she'd tensed. Suda had longed to touch her, but being near her proved much more frustrating than lying alone in the dry, soundless cave. She'd slid her hand slowly along the pillow, hoping to feel Quinn's wiry red hair against the tips of her fingers.

"John, come get your order before we sell it again to the highest bidder!"

She chuckled and most of the waiting crowd joined her. She had no idea how far behind John their order was, but if her stomach growled any louder, other customers would turn around and point.

She yawned. She'd had little sleep, constantly tossing and turning. Every time Quinn changed position, despite making only the quietest noise, Suda heard it and was pulled from sleep. Around three a.m. she'd considered returning to her own bed, but she guessed that would wake Quinn. Then Quinn would've asked why she was swapping beds for a second time that night, and she wouldn't be able to explain. She struggled with any changes to her routine. She wished she had Quinn's sense of adventure, but she actually liked predictability. She liked being able to accurately guess what came next, especially when she was treating a patient. Surprises were not welcome in the ER.

Her phone vibrated again. This time it wasn't her mother, but a colleague in the ER. He asked her to call him as soon as possible.

"Quinn, come get your order and nobody gets hurt!" the loudspeaker blared.

When Suda looked up, Quinn was no longer leaning against the pole. She scanned the crowd under the awning, but Quinn wasn't among the waiting customers. Her heart fluttered. "She better not have left me," she muttered. She doubted Quinn would do such a thing, but she couldn't be sure. They hardly knew each other.

She walked to the back past the row of jalopies and into Juan's Garden. Quinn was hiding behind a tree, gazing across the street. Two motorcycles faced each other, their rear wheels buried in the dirt, their front wheels suspended in the air, leaning against each other. They were painted red, white and blue and matched the patriotic wall behind them, which also included a large Route 66 sign. The building signage indicated it was the Route 66 Motoporium.

Quinn motioned her to join her behind the tree. "What are we doing?" she asked.

"Look behind that green VW microbus in the parking lot."

The microbus was covered in Sharpie marker signatures, a piece of art from the 90th Annual Seligman Fun Run. The yellow FJ Cruiser hid behind the bus.

"It's him!" she cried. "Should we go confront him? If it's unlocked, maybe we could steal the ashes back?"

Before Quinn could answer, the loudspeaker sounded again. "Quinn O'Sullivan, I'm eating your food!" Loud chomping sounds caused everyone listening to laugh.

Quinn groaned. "Dang it, Reg," she said, referring to the cashier.

Suda grabbed her arm and pointed. "Look!" A man in a green and yellow John Deere cap hurried from the Motoporium to the FJ Cruiser carrying a cup of coffee. "It's the guy from the Hackberry General Store! The guy who spoke to us when we were looking at the Corvette."

"It certainly is," Quinn said.

CHAPTER NINETEEN

If you want to see Tall Paul holding his wiener, plan a stop in Atlanta, Illinois. He's one of only four remaining original "Muffler Men," made popular in the mid-twentieth century as a giant way (literally) to promote a business. These thirty-foot fiberglass guys traditionally held the product they advertised in their arms. Car mufflers were one example, but Tall Paul was owned by a café that served great hot dogs. Muffler Men fell out of favor in 1973. It had always been expensive to transport these hulking figures, but when the oil crisis happened, the cost of fiberglass skyrocketed and killed yet another unique attraction on the Mother Road.

-Mother Road Travels

By the time they'd returned to Cousin It with their lunches, the FJ Cruiser was long gone. Quinn guessed their sighting in Seligman was happenstance. It wasn't surprising their paths had crossed. There were only so many places to stop on the Mother Road for refreshments or a bathroom.

As they drove out of Seligman, they saw another set of Burma Shave signs. Suda read them out loud. "He tried…To cross…As fast train neared…Death didn't draft him…He volunteered…Burma Shave." She chuckled and said, "So it seems some of the signs were public service announcements."

"Uh-huh, when the company realized how powerful the campaign was, they made several sets of signs promoting safe driving. It was one of the first anti-drunk driving messages in America."

Suda's phone exploded with the cannons from the *1812 Overture*, and Quinn jumped in her seat.

"Sorry," Suda said. "Hospital gets a special ringtone." She tucked her hair behind her ear before she answered. "Dr. Singh."

Quinn turned and watched her in doctor mode. She listened intently. Quinn could tell she wanted to say something, but she waited patiently.

"Okay, yes. Good call. Bring in Dr. Anwar for a consult. Bye." She tossed her phone on her bag.

"Was that a nurse?"

"Yes."

"So the nurses call you when you're not working?"

"Sometimes. This might be hard to believe, but some doctors are difficult to work with. They don't inspire respect and loyalty from their staff. I've told my colleagues they can call me any time. Peoples' lives are at stake, and we can't have personality conflicts stand in the way of treatment."

She looked at Suda with an apprising smile. "I'll bet you're a great leader."

Suda shook her head humbly. "No, I just do what makes sense." She glanced at her. "How do you deal with your crew? They're all men and you're a woman. Do they follow your direction?"

Quinn nodded. "Yeah, they do."

"How do you get them to respect you?"

"I don't know, really. I try to be fair. Consider their ideas. I value their contributions to the project."

"That's leadership," Suda concluded. She licked her lips. "I'd love to see you in your tool belt."

Quinn raised an eyebrow. "Really?" Her phone rang. "We will continue this conversation," she said, offering Suda a wicked smile.

She'd have known the caller was Fiona even without Caller ID because her hello was greeted with a bloodcurdling scream from her teething nephew Donnelly. She pulled the phone away from her ear and put it on speaker. Suda's eyes widened and she offered a look of concern when his shrieks grew louder. He sounded like he was being tortured.

His screams faded as Fiona passed him off to someone else. Then she bellowed, "And Ivan, you better not use your brother for home plate!" They heard an unintelligible reply from Ivan, to which Fiona shouted, "No, third base isn't any better!" A door closed and Quinn knew Fiona had locked herself in the only room where she got any peace and quiet—the bathroom.

"You have me on speaker? How's the trip?" she asked. "Suda, are you enjoying the Mother Road?"

"I am," she replied with a grin. "Quinn is an excellent tour guide."

"How was your night in the caverns? I hope Quinn didn't scare you with one of her famous ghost stories, or worse, a recounting of a previous visit with her girlfriend of the moment."

"No, Fi. There was neither. And Suda made it through the whole night."

"Good for you!" Fiona cried. "I think you're the first one. Isn't she the first, Quinnie?"

Quinn shifted in the bucket seat, her cheeks growing hot. "Yes, that's correct."

"Well, then, she's the keeper. Congratulations, Suda."

"Thank you," Suda said, touching her own flushed cheek. "But I think I'd like to hear about some of the other girlfriends." She winked at Quinn who shook her head. Fiona didn't need any encouragement when it came to her love life.

"Oh, my, there're too many to count. And it doesn't matter now. You're the keeper."

"Unfortunately, Fi, Suda doesn't want a relationship. We're just friends." Quinn smiled innocently at Suda, who scowled.

Fiona chuckled. "Well, I always say the line between lovers and friends is constantly redrawn. It was like that with me and Steven. He—"

"Did you need something, Fi? We're approaching Flagstaff and I need to navigate."

"Oh, of course. I'll be quick. First, I wanted to make sure your arm was doing okay."

"It is."

"And I wanted to know if you'd be home by next Friday. We've finally got Donny's baptism scheduled for Saturday morning. I told Father Boyle's secretary that if she didn't squeeze him in before May first, we were switching parishes. That lit a fire under her."

Quinn bit her lip so she wouldn't laugh. She pitied anyone who was on the other end of Fiona's anger. "Yes, I'm sure we'll be back by then. Did you find some godparents?"

"You're the godparent," Fiona spat.

Quinn fell back in her seat. "Fi, we've been over this. I'm not a practicing Catholic and I'm a lesbian. The church thinks I'm going to hell."

"Well, they don't know everything, and the pope's left some latitude on that one."

"Okay, but I'm not standing on their altar and swearing I'll make sure Donny has a Catholic education and abides by the faith. If anything, I'm liable to bolt for the door and take him to the Unitarians."

Fiona gasped. "You wouldn't!"

"Find another godmother. Love you."

She hung up and rubbed her temple. She felt obliged to explain. "I love my sister, but she has a very narrow focus. She wants what she wants, and if it means bending a rule to suit her purpose, so be it."

"Sounds like my mother. The world revolves around her."

"Are you close?"

Suda mulled the question before she said, "Not really, I guess. When I decided to stay in America, I physically distanced myself from my family. A byproduct of that decision was that I mentally distanced myself from them as well, especially my mother. When I go home, it's like I enter a fictional world she's created. I pretend to date men. I do and say things that suggest I might move home. I talk about my career as if it's nothing important. Then I leave and go back to my real life."

Quinn scratched her head. She had something to say, but she knew it would offend Suda. She opened and then closed her mouth.

"Say it," Suda insisted.

"Say what?"

"Whatever it is that you're thinking."

She took a deep breath. "I know respect is important to your culture. Isn't truth a huge part of respect? How can you respect your parents if you won't be honest with them?" Suda's gaze never left the road but she watched her jaw set and her fingers clench the steering wheel. "I shouldn't have said that," she backtracked. "I'm sorry."

"Are you?"

She sighed. "Okay, I'm not." She cleared her throat and turned to face her. "Here's what I think. You are a beautiful, intelligent, and caring person. The fact that you like women is incidental. I know that's not how your parents see it," she quickly added, "but if they're ever going to see you any differently, it's up to you." She paused before she finished with, "I really hope that someday they can see what I see."

Suda's expression softened and her death grip on the steering wheel loosened. "Would it help if I told you I agree with you?" she asked, her voice barely audible above the VW's old engine.

"Then why—"

"Because it's not about me!" she cried. She gazed at Quinn for as long as she dared, her eyes on fire. "This is about my father. Knowing I'm gay might kill him."

"Have you ever thought he might already know?"

"He doesn't know," she said automatically.

"How can you be sure?"

"I am."

Quinn turned away and looked out the passenger window. It was like arguing with a child, she thought. She'd known other women as smart and beautiful as Suda, who resisted coming out to their families. She'd learned through heartbreak that she couldn't hurry along their coming out process. She also knew she wouldn't ever be serious again with someone who wasn't out to their family. The emotional currency spent on hiding, lying, and avoiding the issue drained the relationship of everything good.

"You still haven't explained the next clue," Suda said casually. "Nobody swings like a lumberjack. What does that mean?"

"The lumberjack we're looking for stands outside Walkup Stadium at Northern Arizona University. NAU. Originally he was located a few blocks away at the Lumberjack Café on Route 66. Back in the forties, one of the gimmicks used by businesses was to have a giant statue everyone could see."

"Like the neon signs," Suda commented.

"Yes, this was another way to attract customers. They were all called Muffler Men because one of the first ones commissioned was for a muffler shop. Most of them have been destroyed, but four are left. Three are in Illinois and one is in Flagstaff."

"The lumberjack," Suda clarified.

"Yes, his name is Louie."

Suda looked puzzled. "Why Louie?"

"It's from the song, 'Louie, Louie' that was popular in the sixties."

"I don't know that one."

"Neither does anyone else, really," Quinn said sarcastically. "The words are horribly difficult to understand, which is why I always make up my own version."

"Well, sing it," she asked playfully and with a coy smile.

Quinn felt the electricity between them. She tapped the dashboard and started the beat as she sang. "Louie, Lou-I, oh, oh. I say, we gotta go. Na, na, na, na, na, na. It's down the road that we gonna go…looking for clues…we are so amused… Louie, Lou-I, oh, oh, we gotta go."

Suda laughed and joined her for another verse. They were off-key and the lyrics were terrible, but Suda laughed and flashed her dazzling smile. It was enough to keep Quinn singing all the way to the outskirts of Flagstaff. When they pulled up to a stoplight, she ended the song and leaned back before other motorists noticed her.

"Why aren't you singing anymore?" Suda teased. "I like your singing."

"Then you're the only one." She pointed to the top of the Skydome. That's where we're headed."

Within a few more blocks they merged with the slow-moving campus traffic. Even though it was a Saturday, cars, pedestrians, and cyclists crowded each stoplight. They turned off Milton Road and headed east on McConnell. They passed several buildings cloistered in the forest.

"This is a beautiful campus," Suda remarked.

"It is," Quinn agreed. "NAU prides itself on its commitment to preserving the landscape. The university refuses to ravage the greenery to expand their programs."

They made the final turn onto San Francisco Street and headed for the entrance to Walkup Skydome. Suda peered over the steering wheel as Louie came into view. "I see him. Wow, he's big."

"He is indeed."

The twenty-foot high lumberjack wore bright blue pants, a yellow shirt, and red beanie. He held his ax in both hands, and his stance suggested he was ready to swing. His lopsided, thin-lipped smile and enormous eyebrows suggested a menacing expression, which seemed appropriate for a mascot standing outside his home turf.

"Pull up here," Quinn directed. "We should only be here a minute."

They parked in front of the box office and trekked across the grass recently released from its snowy prison. April signaled the end of winter in Arizona, and ski season was over. They made a complete circle around Louie's base but found nothing that looked like a clue.

Quinn's eyes scanned the landscape. "I don't see it, do you?"

Suda held her hand at her forehead as a makeshift visor. "There's nothing out of the ordinary, but this looks like a heavy traffic area. Do you think someone might have taken it?"

Quinn shrugged. "It's possible, I guess."

"Excuse me," a voice said.

A chubby young man with wavy brown hair approached with a raised finger, as if he were making a point in a class. He wore tan khakis and a shirt that matched Louie the Lumberjack's yellow shirt. Across the breast in NAU blue were the words *Activity Services*.

"Excuse me, but you can't park there. That's a loading zone."

"We're only going to be here for a minute," Quinn explained. "We just need to check out the statue."

His eyes narrowed. "Why? You're not going to prank Louie, are you? Or steal him? Or deface him?" With each question his agitation grew.

"No," Suda said soothingly. "We wouldn't do anything like that."

He relaxed as he stared at Suda. Quinn couldn't blame him. Suda had that effect. "I'd get in trouble if anything happened to Louie," he explained. "Whoever works in the box office is supposed to keep one eye on him at all times. They made that abundantly clear in the training."

Quinn noticed he wore a nametag. *Dean.* "We understand, Dean. Have you seen anyone else lately who might have seemed suspicious, perhaps in the last week?"

Dean scratched his head while he thought. "Well, there was a guy here this morning. I had to lecture him about the same thing. He parked where you parked and then he came over here and squatted like he was doing something to the grass. I couldn't see him from my ticket window so I came outside. It wouldn't be the first time somebody stuck a penis on Louie or put him in a giant diaper. By the time I got outside, he was leaving, and it didn't look like he'd done any harm to our mascot." He patted Louie's bulging fiberglass elbow, and Quinn thought she saw a tear in his eye.

They checked the area Dean indicated. The grass had been flattened, but it was hard to tell by what. Quinn squatted and stared at the base of the statue, a map of northern Arizona. Suda joined her and she pointed at the map.

"I'm wondering if Maura left the clue here on the ground. Maybe it pointed to where we're supposed to go."

"Or maybe she tied a note to a small rock and put it against the base."

"Could be," Quinn agreed. "Whoever got here first might have taken something or destroyed the clue."

"Excuse me, but I have to get back to my post," Dean said. "Can you please move your car?"

They nodded and Dean headed back. Quinn pulled out her phone.

"Who are you calling?" Suda asked.

"Zeke."

He answered immediately and she tapped the speaker so Suda could hear. She explained about the man Dean had seen and the missing clue.

"Hmm," he said. "I'm not sure what's going on, but the person who stole Maura's ashes expects you to meet him at the Winslow Theater this evening, correct?"

"Yes," Quinn said.

"Then I guess that's where you need to go. If in fact the same man who took Maura also took Louie's clue, then perhaps you'll get both back tonight."

"But we don't have anything to exchange," Suda exclaimed. "We don't have the next edition of *Mother Road Travels*."

"Understood," Zeke said evenly. "But I imagine you'll get some help from the gods tonight." Suda and Quinn exchanged a doubtful look. "Go to Winslow. Go to La Posada," he said and hung up.

"I guess we go to Winslow," Quinn said.

"What is La Posada?"

Quinn smiled at the question. "It's one of the most amazing resorts you'll ever see."

Suda stroked her shoulder and pressed against her. "Is it romantic?"

"Very."

Quinn pulled her into a lingering, sizzling kiss. When Suda's hands caressed her bottom she whimpered. Then she stepped back. "We need to stay focused," she said, as much for her own benefit as Suda's. She took Suda's hand and headed toward the car.

"Do you get the feeling Zeke knows more than he's saying?" Suda asked.

Quinn nodded. "The thought has occurred to me." They headed back to the car but Quinn suddenly stopped. "Wait. I've got one more question for Dean."

They walked to the box office where he perched on a stool. "We're about to move our car, Dean," she offered before he repeated his request, "but we had one more question about the man who came by earlier. Did you notice what kind of car he drove?"

"No."

"Could you describe him," Suda asked.

Dean's gaze flew upward as he tried to remember. "About six feet tall, long hair, Native American."

Suda and Quinn exchanged a look. "Did he have a black hat?" Quinn asked.

Dean nodded. "Yup."

"Interesting," Suda said.

"He a friend of yours?" Dean asked.

"Sort of," Quinn replied.

Suda asked, "Do you have a restroom?"

Dean's expression conveyed his predicament. "I do, but it's for employees only."

"Could you make an exception?"

Quinn bit her lip. She wasn't surprised when Dean's cheeks reddened and he opened the door. Suda hurried inside and Quinn returned to Cousin It. Zeke was controlling the adventure, and while it made sense that things had to be altered because of Maura's untimely death, Quinn didn't like it. She didn't like losing control. *But you didn't seem to mind it yesterday when Suda made you come. Twice.* The thought made her cheeks burn.

Suda's phone chimed. She'd received another text. Quinn glanced at the box office door. Suda was still inside. She knew she shouldn't, but she couldn't help herself. She picked up the phone from the top of Suda's bag and read: *I know we'll make it this time. One more chance is all we need. C.*

Quinn groaned and tossed the phone back on top of Suda's purse. Maura was gone and Zeke and Suda were lying to her. She felt completely alone.

CHAPTER TWENTY

The La Posada Resort is the story of how a painter and a millionaire, having no experience as hoteliers, turned one of the most epic lodging tragedies of all time into the Southwest's crowning gem. They revived the dream of Mary Jane Colter, one of the few female architects in the 1920s. They restored the hotel, which had closed in the late 50s and been turned into business offices (Ack! Gag! Barf!) for the Santa Fe Railroad. Were it not for the tenacity of these current owners and their collaboration with the city of Winslow, Arizona, La Posada would be gone and the land probably turned into a Walmart. I'll tell you straight: there is no finer lodging on Route 66.

-Mother Road Travels

Suda didn't realize Quinn was upset until they turned off I-40 for Winslow. Quinn had seemed okay for much of the drive out of Flagstaff, explaining that parts of the original Route 66 were no longer traversable and even the diehards had to cruise I-40 for certain stretches. She'd laughed at one of Suda's jokes and asked Suda about her hand surgery. But when they turned off, she didn't launch into her usual explanation of the town's importance to Route 66. Suda felt like she was prying information out of her as they cruised down Kinsley Avenue, Winslow's main thoroughfare.

It looked like Winslow was thriving. Most of the historic buildings were occupied by local businesses providing services to the community or goods to tourists. She wanted to cruise around the other streets, but Quinn pointed east and told her to go up the hill and prepare to turn into La Posada.

"What's the history?" she asked.

"It's one of the most famous hotels on Route 66."

"Why?" Suda asked, sensing an opening for conversation.

"I think that'll be self-explanatory when you see it." A silver sedan made a right turn and Quinn said, "Follow them."

It was indeed obvious as she slowly motored through the busy parking lot. She glanced through Quinn's window at the four-story, Spanish Revival building, complete with clay-tiled roofs, large wooden shutters and tan stucco exterior. A beautiful garden fronted the entrance, as well as a decorative wrought-iron arch with the La Posada sign.

"This looks lovely," Suda murmured as she looked for a parking space. "What does La Posada mean?"

"The Resting Place," Quinn replied.

Suda glanced at her, but her gaze remained on the resort. They parked and silently removed their few bags. Quinn said nothing as they passed through the arch and entered the garden, which was really a series of small gardens joined together by brick walkways and short walls covered in festive Mexican tile.

To her left was a pond with a large vase in the center. Water flowed gently out of the top and over the vase's ridges. It was incredibly soothing. Over to her right was a small niche. A metal donkey brayed, his head turned upward while the head of a second donkey leaned over the wall, as if he were listening. She looked up and realized Quinn was nowhere in sight. She'd obviously marched through the French doors at the end of the path, ignoring Suda and the garden.

She shook her head and decided Quinn could wait. She wanted to indulge her first impressions. Next to the entrance was a large metal plaque proclaiming La Posada as a historic monument. She looked over her shoulder once more at the elaborate gardens, wishing they had time to sit on one of the benches scattered throughout and talk about whatever was bothering Quinn.

"But I guess we'll skip it."

She stepped through the entryway and found herself in a small lobby. A few unmarked doors stood on the right, and a beautiful metal divider blocked her path. Symmetrical zigzag patterns, diamond cutouts and Gila monsters made it a functional work of art.

Her only choice was to enter the gift shop on her left. Quinn stood at the front of a long counter that doubled as registration. Suda headed inside but suddenly stopped when a young woman emerged from a room behind the counter. She threw her arms around Quinn. Their hug quickly turned into a tender kiss. Quinn, whose arms were full of bags, couldn't stop the woman from demonstrating affection, but judging by the way she kissed her back, Suda didn't think Quinn minded at all.

The woman wore tight jeans, a plaid western shirt, and shiny cowboy boots. Her straight blond hair was tied back in a ponytail. A fancy black cowboy hat at the end of the counter looked like it fit the woman. She defined what Suda had always assumed all Arizona women looked like before she'd moved to Phoenix—a cowgirl.

Quinn seemed to have forgotten all about Suda as they continued to chat. The cowgirl's left hand remained on Quinn's shoulder, gently massaging it. She whispered in Quinn's ear and they both laughed. Quinn's gaze flitted across the room, finally remembering she had a travel companion. She thrust her chin in Suda's direction, and the cowgirl looked her way as well, as if she were sizing her up. When the cowgirl's eyes narrowed, Suda realized she wasn't smiling. She'd inadvertently given the woman a death stare, one that was meant solely for Quinn.

She took a breath and approached them as if she were entering a treatment room for the first time and meeting a new patient. "Hello, I'm Suda."

The woman nodded in lieu of a handshake and said, "I'm Rain, just like the weather. Suda is a lovely name."

Suda couldn't help but notice her deep blue eyes. She felt her cheeks redden and she stumbled over her words. "Thank you, Rain." She looked at Quinn and said, "Did you check us in?"

"No need," Rain said. "Maura took care of everything. When Zeke called us, we made sure we reserved the rooms she requested." She held up two keys, each attached to a La Posada brass keychain. Suda noticed the room numbers were different. "Suda, you'll be staying in the Mary Pickford room and of course, Quinn, you'll stay in your usual room, the Amelia Earhart."

"Did Amelia Earhart stay at La Posada?" Suda asked.

"She did," Rain answered, "along with many celebrities. John Wayne was a frequent guest whenever he made a western up here in northern Arizona. Charles Lindbergh and his wife Anne had their honeymoon here."

"Oh, my," Suda said, surprised. "Well, my father will be very impressed that I'm staying at a hotel frequented by John Wayne. He's a huge fan." Rain flashed a wide smile that was contagious. Suda returned it, and for a brief moment she forgot Quinn was there and they were fighting. "I would love a tour, if you or someone else is available to show me around."

Rain glanced at Quinn. She'd pulled out her phone and appeared to be engrossed in email. "Quinn can give a tour better than most people, including me."

Without looking up, she replied, "That's not true. You should be the one to give the tour." She looked at Suda and said, "I need to check in with a few of the employees who knew my aunt. Why don't you spend the next few hours with Rain? I'll text you before dinner. We need to get to the theater around six forty-five."

"Okay," Suda said, hoping the smile she offered Rain hid her disappointment.

Something had happened. She wanted to confront Quinn, but not in front of Rain. The kiss between them had been more than friendly. It was intimate, a reminder of the past—or perhaps a license for the future.

Quinn raced out of the gift shop, and Rain donned her cowboy hat. The gift shop exited to a small foyer. Rain pointed at an immense set of doors on their left. "That's the legendary Turquoise Room. Chef John is amazing. He's won several awards and reservations are hard to get. Lucky for you and Quinn, Maura already took care of it."

They continued through an enormous space with tables, high-back chairs and overstuffed couches. A chess set with hand-carved pieces sat on a table imprinted with checkerboard squares. Books were scattered on the various sofa tables and end tables, inviting guests to partake in leisurely activities—to rest.

"This was the original lobby," Rain said. "You'll see these large rooms throughout the resort. They're known as arcades and they're a common feature of the Spanish Revival style. Unlike a lot of hotels that are compartmentalized with meeting rooms, La Posada is nothing like that. The architect was a woman—"

Suda whirled around. "Seriously? In the early nineteen hundreds?"

"Yes. Her name was Mary Jane Colter. She was hired by Fred Harvey, the gentleman who convinced the Santa Fe Railroad to build this hotel." She pointed to another set of doors. "That was the original entrance, and beyond those doors is the Winslow train stop. The arrival of new guests was always a celebration."

Suda nodded but said nothing. She was too busy immersing herself in the feel of the hotel. It felt like a friend taking her hand. Rain guided her to a long hallway with high beams. Windows opened to the gardens that surrounded every side and Suda heard a waterfall somewhere. Paintings and tapestries were displayed on large wooden dividers cut into Southwestern patterns. Between each divider was a comfortable chair and table for guests who wanted a little privacy while they worked or read. She also noticed many signs and pictures that told the story of La Posada. At the end of the hallway was a grand staircase leading up to the second floor. Its dark wrought iron banister accentuated the rich red Mexican tile steps.

Rain put her hand on the end of the banister and said, "This staircase is about the only thing that's endured all of La Posada's history without change or remodel."

"What happened exactly?" Suda asked.

"La Posada opened in 1930, right after the crash."

"That's unfortunate," Suda commented.

"True, but Fred Harvey didn't know it was coming when he lobbied to have the hotel built. He had high hopes that Winslow would be the major hub of northern Arizona. That didn't happen because the feds built I-40, and cut off the town. Still, the hotel thrived for twenty-seven years because of the railroad stop, entertaining celebrities, hosting hundreds of weddings, and setting the bar for hoteliers around the country. When it started to fail in the sixties, the railroad executives turned it into offices. Try picturing cubicles everywhere, HVAC systems, and popcorn ceilings taking over this place."

Suda stared down the hallways from where they had just come and shook her head. "I can't picture it but it sounds horrible."

"It was. Fred Harvey had built La Posada for two million dollars, the equivalent of forty million today. They sold off all of the original furniture, painted over the incredible murals, except for two of 'em, and gutted the rooms. They destroyed everything Fred Harvey and Mary Jane Colter had built." She motioned to the staircase and added, "This is the only thing they left alone. Everything else had to be rebuilt by the new owners."

Suda followed Rain up the stairs. Another sitting area greeted them. Chairs, sofas, a buffet with a filled water pitcher, and a table with magazines invited guests to enjoy the view from the top of the stairs. Resting place is an apt name, Suda thought. There were opportunities to sit down everywhere.

As they continued down the hallway, Suda noticed the tile room numbers on each of the dark wooden doors and a framed article on the celebrity for whom the room was named. She lagged behind Rain, skimming many of the articles.

"I'm sorry I'm so slow," she said. "But as an immigrant to America, I don't know most of these people."

"Take your time," Rain said easily. "I've worked here for over a decade, and I still learn new things about this place every day. That's the reason guests frequently return." She paused and said, "For most resorts or hotels to make it, they either need lots of services like massages and eyebrow waxes, or they're merely a place to drop your head for a few hours before you run out to do whatever else is on your itinerary. Not this place. This place *is* the adventure."

Suda heard the passion in her voice and understood why Quinn would find her so attractive. Rain gestured to a door and Suda saw it was the Mary Pickford room. She skimmed the article on the hallway wall and learned Pickford was a silent film star. Rain opened her door and she walked into a hotel room, unique to any she'd ever seen.

Her gaze was pulled to the giant headboard that covered most of the back wall. Long black planks with cutouts shaped to form a Southwestern desert scene were framed by varnished pinewood. The red comforter added to the dramatic effect. An emerald green nightstand and a small light sat on each side. In the corner was a tall wicker bookcase filled with hardcover and paperback books. Whereas the bed and nightstands shared a Southwestern flavor, the dark dresser was from a different period. She thought it might be mission style, but it didn't matter because the entire front was covered in an intricate design of flowers and leaves.

"Did someone paint this?"

"Yes. Each room is distinctly different because one of the owners is a world-renowned artist. She acted as the interior designer, putting her own touch on everything."

Suda peeked into the bathroom and smiled at the claw-foot bathtub surrounded by subway tile. A white pedestal sink and black and white checkerboard tile struck her as retro. It was pristine and reminded her of her own historic home.

Rain moved to the door. "I'll leave you to unpack and explore. I've got some things I need to do, but I'll catch you later and gladly answer any questions."

She tipped her hat and headed down the hall while Suda enjoyed the view of her backside. The woman was alluring. She frowned, remembering Rain's kiss with Quinn. She emptied her bags while she pondered what to do. Quinn was angry with her and she had a history with Rain, probably a sexual one.

"Their relationship isn't my business," Suda muttered. But it still bothered her.

She flopped down on the comforter and closed her eyes. Why had she ever agreed to this road trip? She'd had fun up until they reached Flagstaff. That was true. Her phone rang. She glanced at the display. Her mother again. She wasn't in the mood. She sat up and looked around. "You're in one of the most beautiful places you've ever visited. Enjoy it," she admonished herself.

Determined to do just that, she shoved her phone into her purse and headed out. She'd give herself a tour. Quinn be damned. She headed down the hallway, wondering where the Amelia Earhart room was located. She strolled past the grand staircase to the other wing. She glanced at the articles next to each room. Some of the names she knew but most she didn't. She found Amelia Earhart's room at the end of the hall.

She held her fist up, ready to knock, but quickly jammed her hands into her pockets. She could hear Quinn on the phone, but the thick doors made it impossible to hear the conversation. She debated what to do. Usually she was all about confronting issues. She just needed to knock on the door and force Quinn to tell her what was wrong. But she couldn't do it. Perhaps she didn't want to know the truth. Perhaps a convenient problem had separated them emotionally—and that was a good thing. She felt as though she'd been fighting Quinn off. Now it was done for her. *Except when you took control and made love to her.*

She quickly headed back to the grand staircase and down to the first floor. She and Rain had passed a small staircase on their initial walk down the long hallway. She decided to check it out and the gardens as well. It was only two o'clock, so she might venture down the street to some of the shops and stand on the famous corner in Winslow, Arizona. If Quinn weren't interested in showing her the town, she'd turn to *Mother Road Travels*. After all, Aunt Maura was the true expert.

CHAPTER TWENTY-ONE

MAURA'S MENTION: Standin' on the Corner Park–Winslow, Arizona

In 1999 the Standin' on the Corner Park was christened in tribute to the song, "Take it Easy" by the Eagles. You'll never see another park like this one. A bronze statue, a mural on a brick wall, and a flatbed Ford sitting at that corner is all it contains. What's more important is what the park symbolizes: the renewal of Winslow, Arizona, after I-40 crushed it. And that statue of a guy who looks like Glenn Frey, the co-writer of the song? Well, if we're splittin' hairs, the statue should look more like Jackson Browne, Glenn Frey's co-writer who actually wrote the lyric when his car broke down in Winslow, Arizona. But who wants to split hairs?

-Mother Road Travels

Quinn winced and opened her eyes. Her shoulder was killing her. She glanced at her reflection in the mirror. Her right arm had somehow twisted behind her back and she looked like a circus contortionist. She slowly sat up and shifted her casted arm. A pulsating pain radiated throughout her right side. *If this is what I can expect in my thirties, I'm in real trouble.*

She checked the time on her phone. Four fifteen. She had several text messages. Fiona had asked how things were going with the doctor. "Not well," she murmured. Rain wanted to take a walk later that night. She chuckled. Every time she and Rain took a walk, they wound up back in the Amelia Earhart room. The last three texts were from Suda. She'd gone down to the Standin' on the Corner Park and a friendly tourist had taken her picture with the Glenn Frey statue. She looked amazing in the sunlight. The second text was a selfie of her sitting on the west patio, and the third was a simple message: *I'm exploring downstairs on my own self-guided tour.*

Quinn smiled, pleased that Suda was alone. She was still pissed. Suda had played her and been dishonest about her relationship status. If she was involved, why didn't she say that, rather than telling Quinn she didn't want to be with anyone?

"Unless it's me," she muttered.

It sounded like Suda's relationship with "C" was complicated—about breaking up and reuniting. It was drama. Quinn could do without that. She imagined their problems related to Suda's refusal to come out to her parents. But if C was in love with Suda, she probably kept trying to make it work.

She rubbed her temple. "I just need to confront her," she whispered to the empty room. "Easier said than done."

Confrontation wasn't her strong suit. She was amenable. That's the word Fiona and her mother used to describe her. She rescued everyone and often solved problems. Even when she hated a decision by a family member, she found it was much easier to just help the person through it rather than disagree. She wasn't a discusser, a debater, or a watcher. She was a doer. A smile surfaced. She'd make some woman a damn fine husbutch.

She tapped replies to the texts. She told Fiona things were fine, said maybe to Rain as she had no idea what would happen at the Winslow Theater that night, and told Suda she'd meet her in the lobby soon.

She took a shower, keeping her cast outside the curtain. It proved ridiculously comical. All she could do was slap some soap on her body, so it was a sorry shower at best. The image of Suda joining her crept into her mind. The curtain would rustle as she slipped behind her. Most likely Suda's breasts would caress her back as she drew nearer. She'd quiver with anticipation when her delicate fingers massaged her shoulders, sculpting her, tracing the droplets of water that fell on her large breasts until her nipples stood erect. No doubt she'd moan when Suda's hands roamed over her belly, traveling lower into her bush. Suda would whisper in her ear, asking for permission. She'd spread her legs in reply. *The first time had been so good.*

Suddenly the water went cold and Quinn gasped. She automatically reached for the handle with her right arm and gave her cast a shower.

"Damn!"

She managed to get out and shake off the water, wondering if it was possible to grow mold inside a cast. Fortunately, she was traveling with a doctor who would know the answer. She dressed and headed downstairs. Suda wasn't in the large room with the chess pieces nor was she in front of the Turquoise Room.

There was a small art exhibition off the main room, and she found Suda standing in front of a rather disturbing portrait of Jackie Kennedy dressed in her historic pink suit with matching pill hat. She held a king of hearts playing card in front of her; however, President Kennedy was the king of hearts. The disturbing part was a bullet had ripped through it and was headed out of the picture while the top half of the card flew in the opposite direction.

Suda was so engrossed in the painting that she jumped when Quinn touched her shoulder.

"Sorry," Quinn said. "I didn't mean to scare you."

"This picture...it's tragic." She gestured to the other paintings in the room and said, "They're all very unusual."

"That's one way to describe them."

Every painting had macabre overtones, but often featured bright, vibrant colors in a complete contradiction that added to the complexity. "They're by the same artist," Quinn said. "Tina

Mion is the designer who decorated the rooms. She's one of the owners, married to the millionaire who bought La Posada. That's why her work is prominently featured." She checked her watch. "We need to get to dinner so we can make it to the theater early. We stand a better chance of catching this guy before the lights go down."

They headed to the Turquoise Room in silence and Quinn sensed their relationship had shifted. Although Suda's eyes darted about the lobby, she didn't ask any questions as she had throughout the trip. Quinn frowned. She didn't like the change.

The hostess immediately seated them. Quinn glanced at the long turquoise ceiling beams that stood out against the muted tan walls. Native American rugs and Mexican mosaics honoring the saints hung throughout the room. The high-back booths featured dark turquoise cushions, but the heavy wooden chairs and tables were stained a dark brown with seat cushions that complemented the Saltillo tile.

Although the hostess had handed them each a menu, Suda ignored it and gazed around the room. Quinn fought the urge to babble details she knew about the restaurant and kept her eyes focused on her dinner choices. There were several great stories she could tell, but if Suda no longer cared about Route 66 history, she wouldn't subject her to any more of Aunt Maura's information.

She knew she'd order the prime rib. It was her favorite. She imagined Suda was pleased to see a vegetarian offering that was much more than various vegetables dropped onto a plate. The waiter came by for drink orders, and Suda offered her a questioning look, which she ignored.

"I'll have a vodka martini," she said.

"Then I'll have a glass of cabernet," Suda said.

The waiter left and Suda's gaze returned to her menu. Quinn knew it was an act. Suda would have the Killer Vegetable Platter, but she was avoiding conversation for as long as she could. Two more minutes of silence passed until the drinks arrived and they placed their order. Quinn covered a smile when Suda ordered the vegetarian dish. With the menus gone there was nothing to do except look at each other.

She was working up her courage to confront her, when Suda said, "I refuse to keep playing games. I can't do it in such a beautiful and perfect setting. Why are you upset with me?"

"I'm not upset." The reply came automatically as it did whenever one of her family asked her the same question.

Suda glared at her. "Stop. Playing. Games. We don't do that. What happened to our pact about honesty?"

Quinn's face darkened. "I could ask you the same question."

"What do you mean?"

"Who's C?"

At first Suda looked puzzled but then she inhaled sharply. When she exhaled, it was a groan. "Cearra is my ex. We've been on and off again many times. Now, we're off for good."

Quinn sipped her martini. It was a much more generous pour than her father would have tolerated. "I don't think you and Cearra are on the same page." She deliberately said Cearra's name incorrectly just to see if Suda would respond. She didn't and Quinn slugged down more of her martini before she added, "While you were in the bathroom at the skydome, she texted. She seems to think you're just a text away from getting back together."

Suda looked as if she was pondering her response. "I'll admit that I've not been as direct with her as I should have been."

Quinn snorted and finished her martini. The waiter appeared again and she ordered another one. Suda frowned but didn't comment. "Is that why you said nothing would ever develop from our coffee date? I mean I really appreciate you looking out for my feelings, makin' sure I knew we'd be nothin' but a quick shag." She paused. She could hear her mother's Irish brogue. It always happened when she'd been drinking. Her friend Disney called it an early warning detection device. A drunk Quinn wasn't pleasant. Her brothers and sisters became uproariously funny, but she turned into a pompous ass.

Suda dabbed her eyes, took a breath and met her stare. "That's not what you are."

"Really? Then what am I?"

Suda opened her mouth but couldn't reply. Fortunately Quinn's next martini arrived quickly and she focused on the superb drink. The vodka lubricated her mouth and she thought her tongue might fall out—but not before she provoked a fight.

"Aren't you so saintly. Or what do they call nearly perfect people in Buddhism, Buddha Buddies?" She cackled at her own joke and Suda closed her eyes. She wasn't taking the bait.

Their dinners arrived and gave their mouths something else to do. The prime rib was exceptional but it wasn't helping Quinn's hurt heart. So she ordered another martini. There was something nagging her, something they needed to do after dinner, but she couldn't remember what it was. All she knew was that Suda didn't care about her. She obviously cared more about C…whatever her name was. She couldn't remember it now. Chris? Chloe? No, it was an odd spelling to a regular name. One that normal people wouldn't spell with a C. What was it? Carbara? No. Ciffany? No. Cennifer? No, but that seemed closer. Chelsea? Chelsea Handler? Was Suda dating Chelsea Handler?

"Quinn, are you okay?" Suda asked.

She looked up, wondering what kind of expression she wore. "What?"

"You don't look like yourself."

She shrugged and returned to sawing her prime rib. The greatest thing about eating steak was the nearly cavewoman-like activity of cutting the meat.

"I'm sorry I didn't tell you about Cearra."

Cearra! That was it.

"We tried to make it work—a few times." She took a deep breath. "And in the spirit of honesty, I'll disclose that I told you a lie."

Quinn frowned and Suda took another deep breath.

"I told you we broke up because she used drugs. That's not true. We broke up because I couldn't tell my family about her, and she couldn't stand it."

"Smart lady." Quinn drained her glass and scowled. "If that was your issue, why the hell did you keep gettin' back together? That's not negotiable, at least not to me. I'd never stand for it." She waved her glass until the waiter came and took it. "It would be understandable if it were something simple," she continued.

She searched her pickled brain for something in her own past. "Like if you'd had a ridiculous fight over which way the toilet paper roll goes on. Normal people know the tail always faces in."

Suda shook her head. "It does not. If it faces forward, it's easier to rip off the piece you want."

"No," Quinn disagreed as the waiter set another martini in front of her and took away their plates. She couldn't remember ordering a fourth martini, but she'd certainly drink it. "It depends on your holder," she continued. "If you have one of those fancy holders with the little metal dowel that sort of hangs in the air, then maybe you're right. But if you have an old holder, like one that's built into your vanity, it's easier if it's away from you."

Somehow her hands had wound up in midair. She dropped them by her side and pointed her toothpick of olives at Suda, who crossed her arms, refusing to continue the discussion. As Quinn chewed on the olives, she realized it was a ridiculous discussion. Perhaps eating the olives would activate a few of her sloshed brain cells. *There's something happening after we eat. I know it.*

"We need to get going," Suda said, pointing to her watch. "It's almost seven. Are you able to walk or should we drive the tenth of a mile to the Winslow Theater?"

Quinn cocked her head to the side. "Why are we going there?"

Suda sighed and shook her head. She leaned across the table and said slowly, "We're going to get your Aunt Maura's ashes back. Remember Aunt Maura?"

Quinn nodded and downed the rest of the martini. "Let's go."

She stood abruptly and nearly took everything on the table with her. Fortunately, Suda pressed her hands on the white linen before the first glass reached the edge. The waiter appeared in a flash and several guests gasped. Quinn looked down and saw the end of the tablecloth stuck in her pants.

"I guess you're not staying for dessert?" the waiter asked with a forced smile.

"No," Suda replied. "We need to go. Do we owe you anything?"

"Oh, no. Maura took care of the bill and my tip as well." He started to clear the table and said, "Enjoy your evening."

Quinn waved good-bye as Suda took her arm and propelled her forward. She wasn't sure her feet were actually touching the ground. Perhaps she was dead like Aunt Maura and walking on a cloud. She looked at the Saltillo tile and her sneakers slapping the floor. *Definitely not on a cloud.*

They wandered through the gift shop, and as Quinn reached for a small drawing on a table, Suda grabbed her hand and kept her moving forward. "Hey!" she cried, "I wanted to see that!"

"We are not tourists," Suda said through gritted teeth. "We are here for a specific purpose."

Again, Quinn couldn't remember what that purpose was, but she thought it was rude of Suda to treat her like a child. They went out the front doors and through the garden. Coming toward them was Rain, carrying a few plastic bags from a market. Her smile disintegrated when she greeted them.

"Hi, Rain!" Quinn said. She threw her arms around Rain and gave her a sizzling kiss.

Rain pushed them apart, her eyes wide. "Quinn, how much have you had to drink?"

"Four martinis," Suda answered. "She's completely plastered."

"Yes, I am!" For once she and Suda were on the same page.

"Where are you going?"

"To see Aunt Maura," Quinn replied.

"To retrieve Aunt Maura," Suda corrected. "Someone stole her urn from the car yesterday."

Quinn listened as Suda told Rain about the note and the theater. Some of it was coming back to her but not quickly.

"Let me go with you," Rain offered. Suda protested mildly but Rain insisted. "I'll just be a moment to put this stuff in the office."

"Is that for our big night together?" Quinn asked seductively. She looked closely at the plastic bag Rain had looped through her arm and saw whipped cream. She giggled. "Another round of Quinn Everest?" She turned to Suda and explained. "All we need is a can of whipped cream, my boobs and Rain's face!"

"I'll just be a moment," Rain said in an exasperated tone.

Quinn looked at Suda. Her face was like stone. "What's wrong? Are you okay?"

Suda slowly turned and faced her. There was a tear rolling down her face. "No, Quinn, I'm not. Here's what we're going to do." She led Quinn to a bench near a fountain. "You sit here. Rain will be out in a minute. She'll take you to the theater and help you get Aunt Maura's urn back."

Quinn heard the strength of her voice. She sounded like a doctor. "Aren't you coming with us?"

"No." With one hand on each of Quinn's shoulders, she pushed her into a sitting position. "Good-bye, Quinn," she said softly, in a much less assured tone.

Quinn watched her walk away, unable to take her eyes from the gentle sway of her hips and her great ass. Rain met Suda at the front. Suda pointed at the bench and Rain glanced at Quinn. Suda talked and Rain nodded before she disappeared inside.

"I guess we're on our own," Rain said when she reached the bench. She held out a traveling cup. "Drink this."

Quinn took a sip and made a face. It tasted like rubbing alcohol and peppermint. "What is this?"

"It will help you sober up." Quinn drank it quickly while Rain stared at the front door. She rubbed her jaw and asked, "I know you're drunk right now, but when you were sober, were you and Suda…"

She waited for Rain to finish her question, but Rain just gazed at her. Quinn's gaze flitted from Rain to the French doors where Suda had disappeared. She opened her mouth to explain and realized she couldn't. She didn't know where to start. She swallowed and looked up helplessly at Rain.

"It's okay. You've said enough."

CHAPTER TWENTY-TWO

The Winslow Theater was the only theater in town. It showed one movie each week at seven p.m. daily. Quinn only tripped over herself a few times during the short walk, but Rain was there to grab her before she face-planted on the sidewalk. She'd tried to briefly explain why the guy in the FJ Cruiser had stolen the urn, but judging from Rain's quizzical looks, she knew the story wasn't coherent, but she couldn't fix it in her current state.

"Where is the real manuscript?" Rain asked.

She shook her head once and realized the motion made her nauseous. "No idea. I don't have it and I don't know where it is. Zeke doesn't know either."

"Who's Zeke?"

"Her attorney in Flagstaff. He has a really cool last name. It's like Oh-wa-me-oh-way-oh-wa-way-ah-scooby-doo. Something like that." She glanced back at the La Posada property. "Why isn't Suda coming?"

"She didn't want to," Rain said plainly.

"Why not? I thought she was into this adventure."

Rain's lips formed a tight seam, as if she were trying to keep her response locked up.

"Go ahead and tell me," Quinn prodded. "I can take it."

Rain halted and grabbed her hand. "Because you're a mean drunk. You turn into a callous no-good bitch."

"Well, don't hold back," she said dryly. "Tell me what you really think."

Rain pushed up her black cowboy hat and got in her face. "I think you really like her and somehow she hurt you. Now you're making sure she won't ever like you again."

Quinn's face crumpled and she thought she might cry. Rain threw an arm around her shoulder. "Come on."

They stood in front of the theater, a white two-story brick job that shared the space with a yoga studio above it. Playing that night was Matt Damon's latest movie, but Quinn had already seen it. Everything arrived in Winslow about two weeks after it was released in the big cities. But they weren't there to enjoy the movie.

Rain saw the marquee and her face lit up. "I wanted to see this!"

"Well, I'm not sure how much we'll really see," Quinn warned. She blinked and wiped her hand over her face. She felt tingles throughout her body. Rain's concoction was definitely having some sort of an effect.

They went in and were greeted by the single employee doing triple duty as ticket seller, concessions worker and projectionist. His name was Earl. Quinn remembered Aunt Maura had introduced them the first time they traveled to Winslow. He was the only heir to the family that owned the theater. Although he was about Quinn's age, he was prematurely bald and looked much older. He smiled and welcomed them to the theater. He seemed perfectly happy to spend the rest of his life bringing Winslownians their weekly movie offering.

She was grateful he didn't recognize her as he handed them their ticket stubs. Rain insisted on purchasing some popcorn for her dinner, and once they were loaded up, they headed into the theater. A few dozen moviegoers were sprinkled across the two hundred seats.

"Where were you supposed to leave the manuscript?" Rain asked.

She couldn't remember. She checked her pockets and withdrew a scrap of paper.

"Under seat D-fifteen."

Rain reached into a backpack Quinn hadn't noticed and pulled out a thick manila envelope. "Well, I brought a decoy. Jackie, the front desk clerk, allowed me to borrow a ream of paper and an envelope. If nothing else, we'll look like we brought a manuscript."

"Good thinking," Quinn agreed.

"Let's go," Rain whispered.

They strolled down to aisle D and found seat fifteen. An envelope was taped to the bottom of the seat.

"What's that?" Quinn asked.

Rain opened the thin envelope and found a piece of paper. *Leave the manuscript here. Aunt Maura will be returned to you promptly.*

"That's bullshit!" Quinn cried, gaining the attention of everyone in the theater.

"Hush," Rain said. "Whoever took the urn could still be here. He could be watching us right now."

Quinn scanned the patrons and her gaze settled on the only man sitting by himself. In the inky lighting she could tell he was middle-aged, white, and mustached. He wore a dark Windbreaker and stared at them. She glanced at the manila envelope and back at the man. She blinked. She could feel the vodka bleeding out of her brain, and she foresaw a killer headache in the morning. But she was also thinking clearly again.

"I have an idea. Put the envelope under the seat. We're leaving."

"What about—"

"Trust me."

"Okay," Rain said hesitantly.

She stuck the envelope under the seat and Quinn noted many of the moviegoers were watching them as if they were a preview. They hustled out of the theater with a wave to Earl, who was heading up to the projection room to start the film.

Outside on the sidewalk Quinn wrapped her arms around her middle. She'd forgotten a coat and nights were still chilly. Rain slipped off her jean jacket and wrapped it around Quinn. She had a down vest over her western shirt so Quinn didn't protest.

"Thanks," she murmured.

"You're welcome," Rain whispered.

The kiss was inevitable. Quinn had forgotten how soft and full Rain's lips were—and how talented her tongue was. A shiver traveled the length of her body.

Rain pulled away and asked, "Are you still cold?"

"Not that way."

Her brown eyes darkened and her face filled with lust. "Enough of that for now," she said. "What's your plan?"

She pulled out Aunt Maura's keys and searched until she found an ordinary gold key and an old skeleton key. "These are the keys to the theater's back door and deadbolt. For some reason, Earl's father gave them to Aunt Maura. Now that everyone has watched us leave, we can sneak back in and see who takes that envelope."

Rain nodded and followed her to the back door. They quietly inched through the darkness on the stage, the enormous screen lit up as the overture and credits rolled for the film. Quinn hugged the back wall, wishing she could use her phone's flashlight. She had no idea what Earl stored on the stage, and every time the film's lighting dimmed, she struggled to see a foot in front of her. Rain stayed close by, holding her hand. By the time they reached the front of the stage, the movie credits were over and Matt Damon had already survived a huge car crash.

Quinn turned and whispered in Rain's ear. "There's a night sex scene coming up. Let's wait for it and then we'll creep out the side and hunker down by row A."

"Is it hot?"

"What?"

"The sex scene. Is the woman hot?"

"Yes," she admitted.

"Do we have to be on the move then?" Rain whined.

"Yes," she snapped.

Rain munched on her tub of popcorn while they watched the next ten minutes of the movie before Matt Damon finally bedded his female co-star. While the audience sat riveted through the love scene, Quinn and Rain snuck down the short staircase. They plopped next to the fire exit just as the background music ended the scene.

"Shit," Rain said. "We didn't see anything good."

On all fours, they crawled up the side aisle to row D. When the next daytime scene flashed onscreen, they could still see the envelope right where they'd left it.

"I guess we wait," Quinn said.

"That's fine," Rain said, her mouth full of popcorn.

She shoved the tub toward Quinn who grabbed a handful and leaned back. While Rain became engrossed in the film, Quinn's eyes flitted back and forth between the action on the screen and the audience. Everyone seemed to be engrossed just as Rain was, including the middle-aged man sitting alone. He no longer looked suspicious, just alone.

Quinn felt bad for him. She'd never gone to the movies by herself. She didn't enjoy doing things alone. Perhaps that was because her entire family was nearby. If she wasn't working on an apartment, she was doing something for one of them. Her evenings were always full, so it never bothered her when she didn't have a girlfriend. She thought about never seeing Suda again. That felt like a loss. She wouldn't have enjoyed this adventure nearly as much if the only thing to keep her company were an urn. She looked up to the ceiling. "Sorry, Aunt Maura," she whispered.

Just then, movement caught her eye. Earl strolled down the center aisle like any good manager would do. Quinn tapped Rain on the arm and slid into the nearest seat. Rain slowly joined her, never letting her gaze drift from the screen. Suddenly Earl detoured into row D. Quinn shook Rain's arm, spilling some of the popcorn out of her hand.

"Hey," Rain exclaimed.

"It's Earl," Quinn whispered. "Look." He bent over and picked up the envelope before scurrying up the aisle and back to the lobby. "C'mon, I'll tell you what happens."

She heard Rain's protests as the movie edged closer to another car chase. Earl raced through the lobby door and light washed over the back rows of the theater until the door closed again. When Rain and Quinn barreled into the lobby, Earl was nowhere to be found.

"Where did he go?" Quinn asked. Rain shook her head, her mouth stuffed with popcorn. Quinn grabbed the tub and set it on the counter. "Can you leave this for now until we get Aunt Maura back?"

"Sorry," Rain said apologetically. "I was really hungry. Maybe he's out front?"

They went out to Kinsley Avenue but the street was empty. Most of Winslow had gone home for the evening or were sitting in the theater. Quinn exhaled and shook her head. She didn't know what to make of the situation. Perhaps the FJ Cruiser hadn't been following them. If Earl had been the person who stole the urn in Hackberry, he'd certainly done a good job staying out of sight. Quinn was positive she'd never seen him when she and Suda had stopped.

"Maybe he went up to the projection booth?" Rain suggested. "There aren't a lot of places for him to go."

"You're right. C'mon."

They headed back to the lobby—just as Earl opened the projection booth door. When he saw them, he gasped and closed it. By the time they reached for the knob, he'd locked it. Quinn yanked Aunt Maura's keys from her pocket hoping one of them opened the booth door.

"Come out of there, Earl!" Quinn shouted as she tried to jam keys into the lock. "I only want to talk to you."

Earl said nothing and Quinn doubted he was waiting on the other side. The same key that opened the back door also worked on the projection room door, but Earl was not in the stairwell. They raced up the stairs, but he wasn't in the projection booth either.

"Where'd he go?" Rain asked.

Quinn scanned the small booth and saw another door behind the lighting board. "There."

Quinn threw it open and found the theater's catwalks. She suddenly remembered Maura's Mention about the theater in *Mother Road Travels*. Before the Winslow Theater had been acquired by the Rialto Company to show movies, it had been a playhouse, complete with lighting catwalks that formed a square above the audience. She stepped onto the planks and crouched, just in time to see Earl step off the catwalk closest to the stage and disappear into darkness. She blinked, convincing herself she was sober enough to cross.

"Follow me," she instructed, but Rain grabbed her bicep.

"I can't go out there, Quinn. I hate heights."

She whirled around, unable to believe what she was hearing. She was Quinn the Mighty, but Rain was fearless, or so she thought. "What are you talking about? You'll go anywhere and do anything. You were the one who talked me into sneaking inside the abandoned copper mine. And what about the time we rode those wild horses?"

"Well, in the interest of full disclosure, they weren't that wild," Rain admitted. "I only told you that so you'd sleep with me. And when you have time to review all of our escapades, and now is not the time since we're in the middle of a chase, you'll realize none of them involved anything off the ground."

Quinn narrowed her eyes. "Are you just bullshitting me so you can go watch the movie?"

Rain looked offended. "No." She pointed toward the stage. "Now get going and I'll meet you on the ground." She grabbed the collar of the jean jacket she'd loaned to Quinn and pulled them together for a quick kiss. "Go."

Quinn started across the catwalk carefully, paying close attention to her casted arm. She glanced down at the audience. They were mesmerized by the twelfth car chase of the movie. She carefully passed a bank of old theater lights that were only used when a company rented the facility for a presentation. She saw another door at the end of the catwalk, Earl's exit point. She wasn't surprised to see it opened to a postage stamp-sized landing and two ladders: one going down to the stage and the other leading up to the roof.

She sighed. Someone with a broken arm shouldn't be on a ladder but she had no choice. "Up or down?" she pondered. "Up," she decided.

Since Rain was covering the stage area, she'd check the roof. She climbed into darkness. Her anxiety increased after she'd ascended fifteen rungs. Where was the exit? Suddenly the ladder stopped and her head bumped the ceiling. She reached up and found a knob. After a simple twist, she thought she heard a click over the booms of an oilrig exploding on the screen. A hatch opened and moonlight flooded the darkness. She stuck her head up like a gopher and searched for Earl. He was heading toward the building's edge, carrying the urn.

"Earl!" she shouted as she pulled herself onto the roof. "Earl, stop!"

He turned around as she rushed toward him. "What are you doing?"

"You didn't keep our deal, Quinn. You didn't bring me the manuscript."

She threw out her arms in supplication. "I can't, Earl. I don't know where it is. Believe me, I'd give it to you if I had it." She looked at the vase he cradled against his chest. But please give me Aunt Maura."

"No. You had your chance and you failed."

She froze and cocked her head to the side. His words didn't ring true. It was like he was reading from a script. She thought about the ransom note and the silly chase through the theater. Something wasn't right.

"Earl," she said, as she slowly advanced toward him. "Earl, give me Aunt Maura."

He mumbled something and stepped back. He was closer to the edge than he realized. As he lost his balance and a look of horror crossed his face, Quinn rushed to him. The vase slipped through his fingers. It seemed to bounce off the brick ledge before it sailed over the side. She grabbed his arm and pulled him toward her as their legs and feet tangled. They fell over, and for the first time in her life, Quinn had a man lying on top of her.

"Get off!" she cried, pushing him away. She stood and ran to the edge, expecting to the see the beautiful Hopi vase smashed to bits after a three-story drop. But when she peered over the side, all she saw was a clear sidewalk.

"What?" she gasped.

She scanned the building's exterior as best she could in the night's shadows, searching for a precipice or ledge, anything that might have interfered with the vase's descent. But there was nothing. She stepped away from the ledge and blinked. After four martinis, maybe she imagined it. She looked around the roof and saw nothing—except Earl. He'd wrapped himself into a ball.

She hovered over him with her hands on her hips. "Earl, where's my aunt?"

He said nothing. He just shook his head. All she could see was the moon reflecting off his bald dome. She thought he was crying. She wanted to kick him, but she thrust her one good fist into a pocket of the jean jacket.

"Look at me, Earl," she commanded.

He slowly raised his head and she realized he wasn't afraid or sad. He looked completely dazed. It was as if throwing Aunt Maura over the side of the building had had no effect on him at all. He was stunned because he'd almost gone over himself.

"What happened to the vase? Where did it go?" He shook his head, his jaw slack. "Why did you take Aunt Maura, Earl?"

He swallowed hard and managed to say, "She was downgrading the theater in the next edition. I wanted to change it." He scratched his head, still avoiding her gaze. "I'm sorry, Quinn."

"Do you have any idea where she went?"

He threw his chin toward the edge. "Unfortunately, she's on the ground. In smithereens."

Quinn took a deep breath and headed back the way she came. When she didn't see Rain in the lobby, she scowled and threw open one of the theater doors. Rain sat in the back row, watching the final love scene and shoving popcorn in her mouth. She poked Rain's shoulder and she jumped.

"Great help you are," Quinn snapped.

Rain stumbled out of the chair and followed her back to the lobby. "Hey, I checked everywhere I was supposed to check, and I didn't see Earl or the vase. So I decided to get something for my five bucks."

Quinn crossed her arms. "Well, while you were stuffing your face and watching heterosexual sex, Earl and I nearly fell off the roof." Rain's eyes grew wide. "Quinn. I'm so sorry. I had no idea—"

"And Aunt Maura's vase *did* fall off the roof and now it's disappeared."

"What?"

She bolted out the front doors and looked around. Rain followed, her asking questions. "Are you sure she went over the edge?"

"Yes! I saw it happen. I don't think he meant for it to happen, but he lost his footing. She sorta bounced off the roof ledge before she went over the side."

Rain looked up at the building. "There's no way she got stuck in an awning or on a windowsill..."

Quinn threw up her hands. "I can't believe this has happened."

They spent another thirty minutes circling the building and scouring the interior of the theater. The movie had ended and the customers had dispersed into the night. Rain went looking for Earl who had mysteriously vanished, and Quinn went back on the roof. They both returned to the sidewalk with nothing.

"Earl's gone," Rain said.

"I don't know what to do," Quinn said.

"Maybe she'll turn up," Rain said. "This is really weird."

Quinn rubbed the back of her neck and winced. "It's more than weird."

"What's wrong?" Rain asked as she slid her hands over Quinn's shoulders. "Anything I can help with?"

Quinn closed her eyes. The question sounded innocent, but she knew Rain's intentions were lascivious. Still she couldn't believe how good it felt to have a woman touch her, a woman who really wanted her. She turned and kissed her passionately. Rain held her neck, melding their lips, their tongues teasing each other with a familiarity established long ago.

Rain broke the connection and rested her forehead on Quinn's. "I think another night in the Amelia Earhart room is in order."

"I think you're right, but…"

"But what?"

"I feel horrible not knowing what happened to Aunt Maura."

Rain offered a soft kiss but at the last moment, her teeth gently tugged on Quinn's lower lip before releasing it. "I'll help you look tomorrow. There's nothing else to be done tonight."

Quinn nodded and they walked back to La Posada. The streets were deserted, the lights of the shops dimmed. In the quiet of the night, her fingers entwined in Rain's warm hand, she replayed the bizarre evening. She wished Suda had joined them. Something was bothering Quinn about the evening at the theater but it was a detail. As a doctor, Suda noticed the miniscule. If she'd been with them, she would've already commented on it, whatever *it* was. A train whistle sounded, interfering further with her thoughts.

She replayed the evening's events once more before they reached the hotel's entrance. Just as they crossed the threshold, she thought of it. When they'd arrived at the theater, Earl had behaved as if he didn't know her. Yet after he dropped the vase, he'd said, "I'm sorry, Quinn."

CHAPTER TWENTY-THREE

Let's talk about the ghosts along Route 66. There are several known spirits haunting the Mother Road. I have encountered two of them, but I won't bother you with the stories. Nothing kills cynicism faster than something that goes bump in the night. Travel the Mother Road long enough, and you're bound to meet one of them at least once.

-Mother Road Travels

As Suda watched Quinn and Rain depart for the theater arm in arm, she almost called out, asking them to wait so she could catch up. She hated losing the adventure. The past thirty-six hours had been fascinating, and she felt as if she knew Maura even though they had never met. Maura couldn't have known fate and a zip line accident would result in Suda meeting Quinn, but a notion tickled her brain and told her Maura was somehow involved in their connection.

Yet, as she watched Quinn cross Second Street with another woman, she felt that connection break. A couple mumbled an "Excuse us," and she realized she was standing in the middle of the sidewalk. She needed privacy for a good cry. She gazed up at La Posada's inviting front and realized she was in the right place for exactly that.

She hadn't yet explored the south side of the hotel and the original entrance. She headed back through the lobby and out the doors where the trains had dropped off guests every day. She immediately understood why Fred Harvey had literally made the back of the place into the front. A sprawling lawn and gorgeous flowered walkway greeted those arriving by train. A wraparound porch with sturdy white benches allowed guests to watch the trains pull in. She imagined an arriving locomotive fascinated people of yesteryear, in the same way that people on the docks loved watching the departure of cruise ships.

She slid onto one of the benches, picturing herself in the mid-twentieth century. She certainly wouldn't have been a doctor. She doubted she would've been admitted to America at all. Her place and station in life would've been fixed, and as much as her mother bragged about her daughter the doctor, given that Suda hadn't returned to India or married a man, Suda guessed Nima would gladly trade her for a more compliant version. She'd wanted a feminist daughter, but not one that was *too* feminist.

"And the lesbian part clearly took her over the edge," Suda chuckled.

She realized she wasn't crying anymore. Thoughts of the past had transported her from her own sadness. She decided to explore more of the hotel. She climbed a short staircase to the gallery of Tina Mion. The large, square room was dark, save for the display lights that illuminated each individual canvas. Collectively they provided enough of a glow for the room to be eerie. She hesitated before she crossed the threshold. Whereas the other public rooms had felt serene and warm, the gallery gave her a chill and she reflexively hugged herself. There was no one else admiring the paintings and she heard nothing from the floors below or from guests in the adjoining third-floor wing. It reminded her of the Grand Canyon Caverns and she suddenly wished Quinn were with her.

The feeling passed and she shook her head. She was being silly. She ventured through the arch and turned to the left. Having toured the smaller gallery before dinner, she was prepared for Mion's bizarre but creative perspective. Many of the paintings were commentaries on American life, most notably an entire collection devoted to the presidents. She recognized George W. Bush as the Cowardly Lion in a takeoff of *The Wizard of Oz*. Another showed the face of Nancy Reagan with a periwinkle background. She strolled past many portraits and landscapes, not lingering too long at any particular one.

Toward the back was a picture of a room in black. A rocking chair sat on top of a rug in front of the painting. The chill she felt intensified. She blinked. It was the oddest feeling she'd ever experienced.

She'd seen three-dimensional art before, so in deference to the work, she stepped around the rug as she moved on to the next painting, a picture of a woman on a horse with an umbrella. She studied it closely until she heard a creaking sound, as if someone had gotten up from an old chair. She slowly turned around. She was still alone and no one was in the rocking chair. But slightly, ever so slightly, it rocked.

She gasped.

A passageway to the third-floor wing loomed ahead, and she darted out of the gallery. She flew past several doors and didn't stop until she nearly plowed into a gentleman coming out of his room. He gave her a concerned look and she smiled. She realized her heart was pounding. She needed to sit down but she didn't want to collapse in the hallway. She followed the man, keeping enough distance so she didn't look like a stalker who should be reported to security. Eventually the corridor led to a sitting area that overlooked the old lobby. She fell onto a love seat and took some deep breaths. A carafe of water and cups sat nearby on a buffet. She filled a cup with shaky hands and downed cup after cup until she came to terms with what she couldn't explain.

She had been the only person in the gallery. Of this she was certain. A fan wasn't blowing. She didn't step on anything unusual that would've activated the rocking chair or caused the creaking sound. She didn't accidentally bump into it. Yet she heard the creak and saw the chair rock.

She thought back to Quinn's comments about the ghosts on Route 66. Aunt Maura believed they were real. Suda wondered if she'd ever seen the rocking chair move. Her scientific doctor brain offered several possible scenarios that the rest of her brain immediately discarded. Usually doctor brain won every argument she'd ever had with herself, but it couldn't win this one. She could go back and examine the rocking chair. *Not going to happen.*

She'd felt that sense of dread before she went into the gallery. It was a warning sign she'd ignored. Her veins had felt like ice—another sign. Suda knew better than to ignore signs. It was one of the few things upon which she and her mother agreed. Read the signs. Trust your gut. She'd learned to do that when it came to medicine. Machines could only prognosticate so far. She'd learned to trust her instincts.

She lost track of time, but she felt no urge to go back to her room, nor did she wish to explore La Posada further. There was one more garden to see, but she'd do that some other time. Perhaps she'd return to La Posada someday when she needed to recharge. *But I'll avoid the third-floor gallery.*

For now, she didn't know what to do about Quinn. She should confront her, but given the fright she'd just endured, if Quinn magically appeared, she undoubtedly wouldn't say a word about her horribly disrespectful behavior and drunkenness. Suda was emotionally drained. She grabbed a fashion magazine lying on the nearby table and skimmed it, her eyes flitting between the women's designs and the people in the lobby. It was nearly ten thirty, and groups of guests who'd been out to dinner were returning. Two teenage boys recounted a scene from a movie, and she guessed the film at the Winslow Theater had also ended. She set aside the magazine, curious to know if Quinn had retrieved Maura's ashes. She pulled out her phone and debated whether or not to call her. She pictured Aunt Maura's friendly face on the jacket cover of *Mother Road Travels* and tapped Quinn's contact. Suddenly she heard Parikrama, the Indian band they'd discussed at Mr. D'z. Quinn had made their hit song Suda's ringtone.

Suda's heart flipped when Quinn and Rain walked across the lobby with Rain carrying the familiar grocery bag from earlier that afternoon, the one that contained their necessities for the romantic evening Rain had planned and the Quinn Everest game. Neither of them held an urn, but they held hands. Quinn fished her phone from her pocket as Suda's ringtone filled the lobby. Suda leaned against the rail, willing Quinn to answer her call. Then Rain pulled her into a smoking kiss while the Parikrama's violinist serenaded them. Although their lips parted, their arms remained entangled as they headed down the hallway toward the Amelia Earhart room. Quinn held up her phone and hit the button on the side, sending Suda's call to voice mail.

Follow the signs.

She almost disconnected, but instead she listened to Quinn's cheery greeting. When the beep sounded, she suddenly didn't know what to say. She mumbled, "I can't do this," before she hung up.

CHAPTER TWENTY-FOUR

Rain straddled Quinn and waved the can of whipped cream in front of Quinn's face before she squirted some into her own mouth. She followed it with a shooter of whiskey.

"Give it to me," Quinn slurred, reaching for the can. "I want another shot."

Rain slapped her hand away. "There's only one way you're getting any of this," she teased. She sat back on her haunches and shook the can. "Where?"

Quinn's gaze traveled from Rain's small, but perfect breasts down her flat belly to her shaved crotch. Her glistening clit poked out from the tender folds. When Quinn raised her head eagerly, Rain squirted a dollop between her legs.

She cupped Rain's buttocks and slowly licked the whipped cream, enjoying Rain's soft moans almost as much as the tantalizing snack. Somewhere between licks, Rain yanked her head back roughly and fed her another shot of whiskey. Was it her third or her fourth? She'd lost count. She wanted to protest but it was her own fault. After she'd rejected Suda's call, she'd gone into a funk. Rain had called her on it and threatened to leave. She didn't want that either. The whiskey had been the answer.

The sweet taste of whipped cream and the spice of the whiskey were nothing compared to Rain's natural juices.

"Yes, yes," Rain whimpered. "Don't stop, baby."

She laced her fingers behind Quinn's head and pushed her further into loveliness. Quinn slid her hands up Rain's torso and found her hardened nipples. She gave each one a gentle tug. Rain's hips moved back and forth as she came closer to the edge.

"Pinch them," she ordered.

Quinn obliged and Rain's cries turned to guttural moans. One more pinch and she went over the edge.

When Quinn awoke, pincushions had replaced her eyes. Each time she attempted to open them—even a sliver—a sharp, gouging pain traveled to her brain and she instantly closed them. It was late morning and Rain was gone. No doubt she'd headed to work, probably without the slightest bit of pain. Alcohol didn't affect her. It was as if she had a special storage area in her stomach just for liquor.

Quinn could only wish for such a metabolism. It felt as if an oriental rug had been stuffed in her mouth, and someone had drilled a hole in the back of her head and was attempting to pull the rug through her brain and out the hole. She never should've slogged down those martinis and following them with the whiskey shooters—bad idea. About the only thing that didn't hurt was her arm. She held up the cast and immediately thought of Suda.

She needed to apologize. Rain had called her a rude drunk. That was true. She couldn't recollect exactly what she'd said to Suda, but she knew for certain Suda had said good-bye when she'd walked away the night before. She grabbed her phone. She had four messages. The most recent were from Fiona, one from Ronan, and her breath caught when she saw that Suda had called around ten thirty the night before. She searched her brain, trying to remember if she'd heard the phone ring. Then it hit her. Aunt Maura was still missing. She played back her voice mails while she massaged her temples, trying to push all of her synapses back where they belonged.

Fiona had hung up five times, but in her first message she said, "Quinn, call me."

Ronan just wanted to check in, and Suda's message was difficult to understand. It was like she was standing in a mall. But Quinn managed to make out the words, "I can't do this," before she hung up.

She called her back and got no answer. She wasn't surprised. She couldn't recall their conversation after the martinis took her brain out for a spin. She fumbled through a text, sending it with several auto-correct errors. She waited three minutes, staring at her phone and pleading with Suda to answer her.

"Crap," she said, hurrying out of bed. She ran to the shower and turned on the water. She stared at her cast and gritted her teeth. If there was a saw handy… After another spritz-down, she threw on her clothes and headed to the Mary Pickford room. Her heart sank when she saw the cleaning cart in front of the door. She ran inside and frightened the maid. "Sorry," she said, before she headed downstairs to the front desk.

Rain was there chatting up the young clerk. When she saw Quinn's troubled look she said, "Hey, what's wrong?"

"I think Suda left." She turned to the clerk. "Did Dr. Singh leave? She was staying in the Mary Pickford room."

The clerk offered a serious look and glanced at Rain, who nodded. With her approval, the clerk said, "Dr. Singh came down very early. About six. She asked for a lift to Flagstaff. I told her a taxi wouldn't be available for another few hours. She said she desperately needed to get there. One of the cooks overheard us. She arranged a ride with one of the delivery people based in Flagstaff. The bread guy, I think."

"Suda went back to Flagstaff in a bread delivery truck?" Quinn confirmed.

"Wow, that is desperate," Rain said.

Quinn scowled and scratched her head. She didn't know what to do. Rain called to her but she shuffled out the front door and wandered through the garden. She found a bench next to a burst of desert flowers and hung her head. She was a failure. Not only had she chased Suda away, she'd lost Aunt Maura's urn. She couldn't see the point of finishing the adventure. She propped her chin on her upturned palm and gazed at the flowers. She heard Rain calling her name but she didn't bother to answer. She knew everything was her fault, but she was upset with Rain too.

Her phone rang again. Fiona. She sighed. If she didn't answer, Fiona would call every half hour until she did. "Hey Fi," she said.

"What's wrong?"

"Nothing. What's up?"

"Something's wrong," Fiona declared, "but I have my own bag of trouble to deal with today, so I don't have time to play caring sister. Tomorrow looks good."

"I'll keep that in mind," Quinn replied. A small smile tugged at her lips. For as much as Fiona drove her nuts, she was one of the few people who could always make Quinn smile. "If you're so busy, why are you calling? What's up?"

"Steven went out to your complex, and you're not going to believe what he found."

Quinn sat up straight. She'd asked Steven to drive by her job site each day to check on things. "Tell me."

"He found a group of workers hanging oven doors on the wall by the laundry room. Oven doors!" she cried. "That's an awful practical joke and what a waste of time."

Quinn sighed. "Fi, I asked them to hang the oven doors. Those are the originals from when the complex was built. It's like a modern art display."

"Oven doors are art? Next, you'll be tellin' me that you're building a playground out of old TVs."

"Hmm. That's an idea." Fiona gasped and Quinn explained further. "It's retro, Fi. We want people to be proud of the complex's roots."

"I don't understand," she snapped. "Hold on." Quinn immediately pulled the phone away from her ear. She knew what was coming.

Fiona shouted, "Boys! If you don't get down here in the next five seconds, you'll be enjoying the dog's kibble for breakfast!"

Quinn shook her head. She knew Fiona wouldn't serve her children dog food… Or would she?

"Well," Fiona said, returning to the conversation, "If you're not worried, I'm not worried. But I'll enjoy saying 'I told you so' when everybody laughs at those ridiculous oven doors."

"Okay," Quinn said.

"How's the trip?"

Quinn gazed toward the entrance, hoping she'd see Suda walk through the archway. "Well, it's at a standstill. Suda went back to Flagstaff, and I'm guessing she's at the airport catching a plane for Phoenix."

Fiona gasped. "She stranded you there? Seriously?"

"Don't be mad at her, Fi. I was a jackass."

"Oh, well that explains it. You got snogged, didn't you?"

"Yup."

"Damn it, Quinn. So what about Aunt Maura? What about the adventure?"

Quinn scratched her head. "Actually, Aunt Maura is missing."

"What?"

"Someone stole her urn while we were in the Hackberry General Store. I've been trying to get it back ever since. I almost had it last night, but it went off the side of the Winslow Theater and disappeared."

"What?" Fiona cried. "How does an urn disappear?"

Although she was asking questions, Quinn heard the sharpness in her tone. "I don't know, Fi. I have no idea how to get it back." Fiona made some guttural sounds while Quinn heard her nephews laughing in the background. "I'm speechless," Fiona admitted.

"It's okay. I can't believe it myself. I'll figure out what to do."

"Of course you will, Quinn the Mighty. And I'll think about it too."

She hung up and Quinn leaned back, enjoying the garden view.

"There you are," Rain said, plopping down on the bench beside her. She rubbed her back softly and Quinn closed her eyes. "Are you okay?"

Quinn sat up and faced her. "No, I'm not okay. My favorite relative in the world is dead. I turned thirty and my parents think I should end my career as a flipper because it really isn't a career in their opinion. I break my arm, which requires me to be at everyone's mercy. I meet an amazing woman who really doesn't want me—at least not in a relationship. Why? Because she's still involved with someone else *and* she won't come out to her parents. And to top it all off, I lose my aunt's urn! So, no, I'm not okay."

Rain offered a sympathetic smile. "But you still have me?"

Quinn sighed. "I know." She threw up her hands. "What am I supposed to do? Suda was driving me to Tucumcari to finish the adventure. Now I don't have a way to get there!"

Rain slipped an arm around her. "Actually, Quinn, I'm supposed to be your driver from this point on."

Quinn shook her head. "Huh?"

Rain looked almost sheepish. "No offense to Suda, and if she hadn't left, she could've joined. But Aunt Maura had planned on us finishing the adventure together. The clue you're supposed to get at La Posada is me."

CHAPTER TWENTY-FIVE

Suda realized the ride in the bread truck was its own adventure. Truck was an overstated description for the huge metal canister on wheels. There were no side doors, and her gaze constantly flitted between the asphalt zipping past them at eighty miles an hour and her fastened seat belt that ensured she remained in the cab.

Hennessy, the self-proclaimed "Bread King of Arizona," made his last two stops east of Winslow on the Hopi reservation before heading back to Flagstaff. He barely fit on the truck's bucket seat, his wide middle and huge thighs draping over the cushion. His large hands smothered the steering wheel and the close-cropped buzz cut was the only hair on his round face, which seemed ageless, for he didn't have a single wrinkle. He might've been twenty-five or fifty-five. She wasn't sure and she didn't think it proper to ask. She could tell he'd lost several teeth, including two in the front. And judging from his questions, he had a slew of medical issues.

"What do you think this is?" he asked, pointing to a dark mole on his cheek. "It wasn't there a month ago."

She leaned toward him and studied it. "It looks like a mole."

"Is it cancer?"

"I doubt it, but it's probably a good idea to have it checked."

"What about this?" He held out his right arm and revealed a circular, purplish area.

"I think that's a bruise. Did you bump into something recently?"

He tilted his head to the side. "Maybe. What about this?"

He pulled up his shirt and swiveled toward her. He'd recently been tattooed, but she couldn't make out the design as it was hidden underneath a roll of flesh—and an enormous pocket of pus. She turned away before she almost barfed.

"Does that hurt?"

"Hmm, yeah."

"I thought so. Mr. Hennessy, that is an infected tattoo. You need to finish your deliveries and we need to get you to a hospital."

He shook his head. "Aw, no, there's no need for a hospital. I'll go see my grandma, or maybe you could take a look since I'm giving you a ride?"

The request stopped her short, but she knew bartering was a standard way of life in this part of Arizona.

"I'd be happy to," Suda said, "however, I wouldn't feel comfortable lancing that wound in anything but sterile conditions. You could get sepsis and that could lead to all kinds of nasty complications."

His shoulders sagged, or at least she thought they did since it was hard to tell. "Okay. The hospital is expensive, though. What if we went to an infirmary? Would that be clean enough?"

"Possibly. Where is this infirmary located?"

"At the vet's office. My cousin works there. If I have extra rolls, I drop them off for her."

Suda blinked. "That would be fine."

He turned and smiled with the teeth he had. "Thanks."

At the very least, she felt safe. They stopped at two small stores, and he easily spoke the Hopi language when the storeowners stepped out to greet him. She was shocked by the pervasive poverty of the surrounding communities. Laundry hung on sagging clotheslines and car parts rested against the stucco walls of dilapidated structures that looked as if they couldn't bear the weight.

Hennessy seemed to move in slow motion. He took his time unloading the racks of white, French, and wheat bread. He talked to the storeowners for several minutes, and while Suda couldn't understand them, their body language conveyed friendship and community. When they finally headed toward Flagstaff, his truck was almost empty.

"I give all of my day-old bread to those stores. They really need it," he explained.

Suda gazed at him and realized beneath his numerous medical problems was a true heart of gold. "Where is the vet's office again?"

"It's in Flagstaff," he said. "Not far from the airport either."

"Great." She turned in her seat to face him and to avoid looking at the highway just a few feet under her actual feet. "How did you become a bread delivery person?"

"Oh, I don't just deliver the bread. I make it too. I'm the baker."

"Really?"

Leaving one giant paw on the wheel, he reached behind him and handed her a bag of rolls from a plastic container. "Try one."

She withdrew a roll and took a bite. It was perfect. Not too chewy. Not too hard. Not too doughy. "Delicious," she said between bites.

He smiled and told her the story of how he came to make the bread his grandmother used to make, how he bought a small shop with an inheritance, and why he continued to travel nearly a hundred miles each day to take bread to the reservation. By the time they arrived at the vet's office, Suda was enthusiastic about helping him, realizing how important he was to the community.

His cousin, Destinee, showed them into a surgical area and found the instruments Suda needed. The room appeared clean and somewhat sterile, reminding her of the ER rooms at Desert Banner. What was painstakingly different was the noise level. There was no point in trying to talk with Hennessy during the procedure. The surgery sat next to the dog kennels. At one point, an energetic golden retriever burst through the doors, Destinee chasing after him with a collar. He thought it was a game and ran around the tables. Suda stepped away from her task and set down the scalpel right before the retriever jumped up and put his paws on her shoulders. His eyes pleaded with her to save him from whatever nastiness awaited him. She laughed and scratched him behind the ears, giving Destinee the chance to leash him.

After they left, Hennessy said, "I wasn't sure you could smile."

She gave an exasperated look. "Of course. I just take my work seriously." She continued the procedure and focused on the task.

"You looked pretty upset at La Posada."

"Well, I took a chance on something and it didn't work out," she summarized. "It happens," she said contritely.

"Huh," he said. "It wouldn't have anything to do with Quinn, would it?"

She looked up. "How did you know?"

"I saw you get some stuff out of her car, Cousin It."

"Do you know her?"

He chuckled and scratched his chin with a meaty hand. "Ever since she was about ten. Never could sit still. Always doin' something crazy with Maura." He glanced at her and added, "And Maura was quite the teacher. She loved to invent games and tell stories."

She nodded. "I've heard that. Quinn said they spent a day up in wild horse country pretending to be rustlers. They almost wound up in a stampede."

Hennessy laughed heartily. "Oh, gosh, yes. That was hysterical." He waved his hand. "Not that they almost got killed, but that they got as close to the horses as they did."

"This might hurt a little," she said.

"That's okay," he said. "I can take it."

"What else do you know about Quinn?" she asked casually.

"I know she hangs with Rain a lot. They have some sort of a strange relationship. Maura thought they were in love but just didn't know it."

Suda took a deep breath and ordered herself not to cry. She needed to change the subject. She thought about her unusual experience in the gallery the night before. "Mr. Hennessy—"

"No, it's just Hennessy," he corrected. "That's my English first name."

"Oh, I didn't realize…"

"My Native American name is much harder to pronounce. I got Hennessy from the Cognac. Have you ever tried it?"

"Um, no. I haven't." She disinfected the wound and applied the dressing. "I know this will sound like a weird question, but have you ever seen—or heard—a ghost at La Posada?"

He chuckled. "You felt the presence of a spirit."

"I heard it when I visited the art gallery."

"Not surprising," he laughed. "Tina's artwork can really get you going."

"Yes," she agreed. "So, do you believe in spirits?"

"Of course." He looked up at her and said, "My grandmother had a theory about spirits."

"Which was?"

"They come to a person when they sense great emotion, whether it be joy or despair. She believed their souls yearned to feel again." He eyed her shrewdly and said, "Have you felt any strong emotions lately?"

The flight back to Phoenix was uneventful, but Suda couldn't shake the feeling that she'd missed out on something great, like a cheap plane ticket to Europe or a chance to meet one of her heroes. As the plane taxied to the gate, she looked out the window, toward the east. She'd walked away from Quinn. Now she'd never know what happened to Aunt Maura's urn. Or who was following them in the FJ Cruiser.

Her eyes filled with tears when she thought of Quinn. She'd enjoyed her company. She cracked a smile remembering the underwear on her head and her singing to "Louie, Louie" in the car. Quinn loved life. She loved life in a way Suda had never experienced. She was her own person. She didn't give in to her parents. And Suda wasn't Quinn's only admirer. When she'd watched Quinn and Rain saunter through the lobby the night before, and the casual way Quinn dismissed Suda's phone call, she knew there was something special between them. She'd had a huge realization just before she'd fallen asleep in the marvelous Mary Pickford room: Aunt Maura intended for Quinn to meet up with Rain. It hadn't been an accident. Perhaps they belonged together.

She turned on her phone and saw several texts from her mother and two from Dr. Nightingale, aka Nightynight because he worked swing shift. Ignoring her mother's text thread, she tapped on Nightynight's. The first one sought her opinion about a young man's intestinal disorder, and the other simply said, *Don't go home.*

She cocked her head to the side. What did that mean? The plane had arrived at the gate, and she didn't have time to compose answers to either question. And her mother's texts would just have to wait until she got home and poured a glass of merlot. Probably the expensive bottle. She'd felt as if her mother was on the trip with her.

As she had no baggage, she tapped her phone and alerted her favorite Uber driver that she needed a ride. Five seconds later, Nestle replied she was on her way. During their first Uber ride together, Suda had learned Nestle was a handle and not her real name. She'd chosen it because she wanted people to remember her sweet ride—a luxurious Mercedes sedan. Her mother had called and Nestle got to listen to the awkward conversation. She'd offered Suda some sage advice about a trivial matter that was incredibly important to Nima. Nestle's advice solved the problem. Since then, Suda only rode with her. She'd realized the conversations with Nestle were the ones she couldn't have with her mother. Once in a while she'd call Nestle for a ride— just to drive around and get advice.

As she dropped her phone back in her purse, she saw the sexy underwear she'd hoped to wear for Quinn. That idea had died. She closed her eyes, doing her best to slough off the weekend. But she couldn't shake the image of Quinn walking across the lobby with Rain cuddled against her while she dismissed Suda's call. She needed to get back to work. She'd text the supervising doctor when she got home. If she took a nap for a few hours, she'd be ready for her night shift. Diving right back into work would undoubtedly erase the memory of Quinn and their adventure.

She told Nestle as much once she was lounging in the back seat, sipping a sparkling water.

Nestle glanced at her in the rearview mirror with her radiant blue eyes. She was a retired bank officer from New York City. She loved meeting the people—and wearing a hat. Today she'd chosen a pink fedora.

"The way I see it," she began, "is that you need to reconnect with this woman. She's obviously special to you."

"But what if she doesn't want me?"

"Her loss. But I don't think that's the way this will go down. Look, Suda, you're a catch. You're a fuckin' doctor." She paused and held a hand up in the air. "Wait. We have a swearing is okay clause between us, right?"

"We do," Suda said. "Proceed."

"Good. Anyway, like I said, you're a fuckin' doctor. You're a hot broad who's intelligent, charming, and caring."

She stared at the green Perrier bottle. "Thank you." Then she remembered Nightynight's second text, *Don't go home.*

"Nestle, can you do me a favor and turn down Fifth Avenue, please?"

"Sure. Are we takin' a back way or something?"

"Um, I got a weird text from a doctor friend of mine. He said I shouldn't go home."

Nestle swiveled her head and glanced at Suda. "Why not?"

"He didn't say. Go right on Granada and we'll pull up to the opposite curb."

"Will do."

She wanted to get close to her house without passing it. Perhaps there was another problem with her neighbor, Mr. Wells. He had terrible xenophobia and thought Suda was recruiting ISIS members. He'd never had the guts to say it to her directly, but she had to privately reassure her neighbors at the last annual Labor Day barbeque that her homemade hummus wasn't poisoned, as he'd suggested.

They approached Third Avenue and Suda leaned forward and saw her house just beyond the cross street. "Stop!" she exclaimed.

Nestle slammed on her brakes in the middle of the residential street. She peered through the windshield. "Who are those people?"

Suda sighed. Standing in her driveway were her parents and her brother. The Singhs had arrived in Arizona.

CHAPTER TWENTY-SIX

Route 66 isn't a straight line. There are diversions, cutouts, dead-ends, and treacherous climbs. Kinda like life. The actual road changed many times in several places during its heyday, and parts of it are no longer navigable. A short side trip includes Tijeras, New Mexico. It runs through the Sandia Mountains. Take the aerial tramway for a relaxing change of pace. This is just one of many splendiferous side trips, guaranteed to make your journey down the Mother Road memorable and exciting.

-Mother Road Travels

Quinn and Rain headed east toward the Arizona border in Rain's Tundra. Rain wouldn't say exactly where they were headed, but she guaranteed Quinn would be surprised. While Rain seemed enthusiastic about joining the adventure, Quinn's enthusiasm was waning. She guessed it was a mixture of losing both the urn and Suda. Although she felt irresponsible for losing the urn, she knew Aunt Maura wouldn't be upset with her. She'd make a joke about being reduced to a pile of ashes and then enjoy whatever new adventure awaited her—until she got dumped in the Phoenix Canal. Quinn knew she wouldn't like that.

Still, losing Suda hurt more. It bothered Quinn that they were no longer traveling together, and instead, they were traveling in opposite directions. And Quinn's anxiety increased with every passing mile. She peppered Rain with various questions, much to Rain's amusement and her annoyance.

"Are we staying on the route?" she asked.

"Most of the time."

"What about Cousin It?"

"Got it covered," Rain assured her. "Don't worry. It's in long-term parking."

"How many more clues are there until Tucumcari?"

"I couldn't tell you that," Rain said. "What? Are you in a hurry for this to end?"

She shrugged and stared out the windshield at the flatland of western New Mexico.

Rain shifted in her seat and put an arm around her. "Hey, are you okay?"

"Yeah," she said, but she could tell Rain wasn't convinced.

They'd known each other for over a decade, and Rain had been her first. Maura had introduced them just a few days after Quinn's eighteenth birthday, and Rain had given her a memorable night as a present. She was six years older but far wiser than Quinn. Maura thought of Rain as the daughter she never had. She'd met her at a rest area outside Gallup, New Mexico. She'd run away from an incestuous situation with her father. Maura had driven her to Winslow and found her a job at La Posada. She'd been there ever since.

While Quinn and Rain never discussed a future together, they'd always made a point to see each other at least once a year, sometimes enjoying dinner with Maura in tow. Usually the evening ended in the Amelia Earhart room, unless one of them had a girlfriend of the moment. It was casual and consistent and had worked for a long time. *But is that what I want now?*

She glanced over at Rain—cowboy hat perched on the back of her head, her hand lazily draped over the steering wheel. She massaged Quinn's neck with her fingertips and for a moment, a memory of those fingertips exploring her softest places sent a rush of heat through her. She stretched out her legs and Rain chuckled.

"I know what you're thinking, Quinnie."

No one else except Fiona and Maura got to call her Quinnie. She knew her cheeks were red. Rain had that effect on her.

"How much further?" Quinn asked, checking her watch. It was nearly noon, and they'd been driving for over two hours.

"Well, we still have a ways to go, but how about we stop for lunch in Albuquerque?"

"Sounds good," Quinn said.

Rain offered a long gaze. "Have anything in mind?"

"How about the Route 66 Diner?"

"Okay, maybe if I get you fueled up with one of their excellent chocolate malts you'll be more lively."

Quinn shook her head. "My bad. I'm sorry. I'm still suffering from a hangover, I can't believe I lost the urn, and I'm worried about Suda."

"Why are you worried about her?"

"I know I hurt her. But she won't take my calls."

Rain stroked her cheek and gently turned her chin toward her. "Hey. You need to leave it alone for now."

She gazed at her wise blue eyes and nodded. When they were together, Rain was always the adult, her protector and the voice of reason. With everyone else, Quinn felt she had to be in charge, but with Rain, she didn't. She wasn't sure if either role was a good one to have in a true relationship. She'd always had an image of someone walking at her side, not in front or behind her. *Is that why Suda appeals to me?*

When Rain yawned, Quinn asked, "Do you need me to drive?"

"No, I'm good, but I think I'd benefit from a little stimulation."

Quinn laughed and slid across the bench seat. She cuddled against Rain and massaged her thigh, gradually increasing the pressure with each stroke. Rain slid her legs apart, welcoming Quinn's hand.

Rain sighed. "Just what I need."

Food helped Quinn's mood and the promised chocolate malt banished her hangover for good. The Route 66 Diner was an old fifties-style diner with Formica tables and large red booths. She and Maura always sat at the counter when they visited any diner, as it gave Maura a ringside seat to the kitchen and the waitstaff. Sometimes Quinn had to remind herself that going out to eat was actually Maura's job.

Once they were back on the road, Rain studied Quinn. "It's good to see you smile. I'd told myself that I wasn't going to tell you where we were going until I got a smile."

Quinn laughed and pecked her on the cheek. "Okay, where are we going?"

"You'll see."

"Tease."

They barely reached the outskirts of Albuquerque and Rain turned north onto Tramway. Then Quinn knew their destination. Rain glanced at her and she laughed. In nine miles they would reach the Sandia Tramway, the longest aerial tramway in the US. The tram glided over the Sandia Mountains, including Domingo Baca Canyon, where a TWA crash had occurred in the fifties. Over the years, tourists claimed to have seen pieces of the wreckage during a ride on the tram, although Maura never made such a claim. Quinn had ridden the tram three times—twice with Maura and once with Rain. And she and Rain hadn't spent the fifteen-minute ride looking at the scenery. Quinn stared at Rain, who wore a lecherous grin. Apparently Rain hoped for a repeat performance.

Quinn wondered if Suda had arrived home. Did she wish she'd never gone on the adventure? Quinn had apologized profusely in her last three texts, but Suda hadn't responded. She closed her eyes and chastised herself. Why was she hung up on this woman who wasn't emotionally prepared for a true relationship? She understood strong family ties. She understood cultural pulls toward tradition. It was the same for her. *Or was it?* She stared out the passenger window at the Sandia Mountains, knowing she was on the verge of an epiphany.

"What ya thinkin' about, Quinnie?" Rain asked, trying to imitate Maura's Irish brogue.

"Huh?" she replied, turning to face her.

Rain's shoulders sank. "You looked deep in thought. Were you remembering the last time we came up the tramway?"

Quinn cracked a smile. "It was memorable."

Rain turned in to the parking area. "Yes, it was."

They bypassed the ticket counter and information center and headed straight for tram loading. A tall Native American man with long gray hair waved at them. He wore a denim shirt with the tram logo. The word SUPERVISOR was stitched in red underneath the logo.

"It's great to see you, Jason," Rain said as she pulled him into a hug.

"You too."

He offered Quinn a sad smile. "I'm so sorry," he whispered. "Me too."

He looked at her cast. "What happened? Bear attack?"

She laughed but he looked serious. Jason had the driest humor of anyone she'd ever met.

He crossed his arms and leaned toward her. "If you've got time, we could have some fun with the tourists." He pointed at her cast. "I could whip up quite a yarn about your arm."

They all laughed, thinking back to some of the practical jokes they'd played on the more boorish tourists. Maura had always felt that visitors to a new place had a responsibility to defer to regional customs and treat fellow travelers with kindness and courtesy. She'd included several hints and reminders in *Mother Road Travels*, especially regarding various Native American cultures since Route 66 crossed tribal land.

"Actually, we're on a schedule," Rain said. "Quinn's travel arrangements shifted, and we've got to get to Tucumcari by late afternoon."

"Gotcha," Jason said.

He led them through a side entrance and onto the boarding platform. No one was waiting for a tram at the moment. April was a slower time, so she didn't feel as though she was cutting in line. A tram quickly appeared and they boarded. The cold hit her immediately. It was always drastically cooler on the tram especially when they had the large compartment all to themselves.

"Happy travels," Jason said with a wink and a wave. "Your clue's at the top, and you'll want to be mindful of the ground beneath your feet," he said cryptically.

The tram left the station and began its ascent. Quinn knew they would climb four thousand feet in the next fifteen minutes. The view at the top would include all of Albuquerque and eleven thousand square miles of New Mexico.

"I wonder what the clue will be?" Quinn mused as she gazed through the window.

Rain moved behind her and pressed into her back "We'll know soon," she whispered in her ear. "But for now, I want you to free your mind. This is like flying. We're as one."

Rain slipped off Quinn's jacket, trailing her hands over Quinn's breasts and down her belly. "You're cold," she murmured. Quinn groaned. Her nipples stood at attention. She stared out at the vast expanse of country. It was so big and she felt insignificant. She was floating over the land, as if she were in her own personal cloud. It made perfect sense when Rain unbuttoned her shirt and squeezed her breasts. The lighting in the car and the sun's current position allowed her to see her reflection and Rain's hard work.

Her bra was soon around her neck. "I love your tits," Rain said as she lovingly caressed them and stared at their reflection through the glass. Quinn's areolaes turned crimson from Rain's constant attention. If Rain didn't do something about the wetness between her legs soon, she'd yank Rain's hands off her boobs and put them where they belonged.

As if sensing her growing impatience, Rain dragged her fingers southward, caressing Quinn's belly, teasing her with gentle touches. Each stroke seared her passion. Her mouth dropped open with sounds of ecstasy. She was ready. Rain knew it. She popped the button on her jeans and slid them down her thighs.

"Do you want me?" Rain teased.

"I do," Quinn panted.

"Do you want me?" Rain repeated, hooking her fingers on both sides of Quinn's bikini briefs.

"Yes," Quinn begged.

"Only me," Rain pressed.

The answer caught in her throat. "Yes."

She gazed at their reflection. Somehow she'd wrapped her arms behind Rain's head, stretching herself, supplicating herself as an offering. Rain's hands remained frozen at her hips, staring at her.

"Please," she moaned.

In the distance, a tram headed toward them. In a hundred yards, the occupants would get a free show.

Rain yanked her briefs down. She gasped as her most private parts met the chilly air in the tram. Rain warmed her hands on Quinn's buttocks, kneading them, gently slapping them, and rocking them to a sensual rhythm.

"The tram," she managed in a haggard voice.

"Then you need to find your rhythm fast, baby," Rain advised.

Quinn's hips complied. She thrust her chest forward and Rain couldn't help herself. She spun Quinn around and buried her face in Quinn's cleavage. She nicked each nipple with her teeth as her leg parted Quinn's quivering thighs. Rain's mouth met hers in a long, warm kiss. Their tongues joined the rhythm. It was all Quinn could feel. Completely freed of all thought, she cried out again and again until she fell against Rain's strong arms. Rain pulled her mostly naked body away from any gawking eyes and yanked up her pants as the other tram came close enough to see inside. Rain lifted her chin and stared at her. "You're beautiful and I love you."

Still a bundle of nerves, Quinn couldn't form the words. Suddenly her phone rang. A violin warbled. Rain looked puzzled—only for an instant.

"I have to…" Quinn managed to say, sliding out of Rain's embrace.

She hunted through her bag for her phone. She glanced at Rain, who stood at the window, staring out at New Mexico. Quinn answered the call while she readjusted her bra.

"Suda?"

"Quinn, I don't know what to do."

A voice in the background said, "I'm telling you, it's time to face it, Suda."

"Who's that?" Quinn asked.

Suda sighed. "It's my Uber driver, Nestle."

"Like the candy company?"

"Yes. My parents are standing in my driveway."

"What?"

Quinn's reply was so dramatic that Rain turned and glanced at her. They gazed at each other for only a second, but Quinn knew in that moment she'd just answered Rain's proclamation of love. She'd also missed several sentences of Suda's explanation.

"I don't know what to do," Suda continued. "It's one thing when I go to India and play their fiction, but this is my reality. I can't fake my reality. My mother will know in an instant."

"Just tell them!" Nestle shouted. "You better tell 'em, Suda, or I'm only giving you three stars."

Quinn shook her head. "It's your decision. I can't tell you what to do. And neither can your Uber driver. No one can. But I'll tell you this: until other people stop running your life, it's never truly your own."

"Is that the advice you're giving yourself?" Suda asked.

Quinn held her breath and her temper. "Yeah, maybe." She shivered and wrapped her arms around herself. "I have to go."

She hung up, wishing she weren't thousands of feet in the air. She dressed quickly and joined Rain at the window. She looked at her and opened her mouth to start the conversation.

"This is about the best view in the world, isn't it?" Rain said with a broad smile.

Quinn knew that smile. It was the one that symbolized friendship and camaraderie. She'd stepped back over to the friendship side of the fence.

"It is," Quinn agreed.

CHAPTER TWENTY-SEVEN

"I'm tellin' you, Suda, it's time."

"Just let me think!"

Nestle turned around with a huge sigh. She had parked her Mercedes behind a large green van while Suda debated what to do. The obvious choice was to say nothing. Just go on with her life. They were probably just passing through Phoenix on their way to Vegas. *But why is Pilar here?*

She closed her eyes and thought about Quinn. She'd sounded out of breath, and Suda could guess what she'd been doing with Rain. Most likely they were having a very different adventure. But if she just focused on what Quinn had said... Was her life truly her own? She hung her head and thought about how many decisions she hadn't made. It wasn't what she'd done. It was what she hadn't done. Her head shot up. There was a fire inside her now.

"Take me to my house, Nestle."

"Now we're talking!"

They circled through the one-way streets once more. As her house came into view, she saw Mr. Wells talking to her parents. He was holding his little Chihuahua's leash.

"Great," she mumbled.

"What's wrong?" Nestle asked.

"That's my xenophobic neighbor. He can only make things worse."

"Ha, don't worry. I got this."

Nestle barreled across the intersection and screeched her brakes to a stop as a horrified Mr. Wells jumped onto the curb, pulling his little dog into his arms. While Suda exited with her few bags to greet her family, Nestle rolled down her window and accepted Mr. Wells' wrath. Suda gave her parents a kiss on the cheek and pulled Pilar into a hug. They headed inside while Mr. Wells continued his tirade. Suda tapped on her phone and sent Nestle a sizeable tip.

Her parents wandered through her house while she stayed in the kitchen with Pilar. "Why are they here?" she whispered.

"Don't hate me."

"What are you talking about?" she asked warily.

"Just remember I was caught in the middle—"

"Pilar!" she whisper-shouted. "Tell me what the hell is going on."

"Mom had you followed."

Suda's eyes widened. "What?"

"She said you'd sounded strange on the phone a few days ago, so she hired someone in Phoenix to follow you."

Suda was mortified. She couldn't believe it. Then a thought occurred to her. "When was this?"

"Thursday, maybe?"

She shook her head. The FJ Cruiser. He hadn't been following Quinn at all. She rubbed her temples. "I can't believe it."

He cleared his throat. "Well, apparently it's not the first time."

She looked at her brother, dumbstruck. She could only imagine what private details of her life had been shared with her mother, the woman who had threatened to disown her if she continued her lesbian lifestyle. A few minutes later her parents reappeared in front of her, their expressions blank.

"Small," her mother said. "Clean, but small."

"It's nice," her father said encouragingly.

She smiled. She couldn't imagine life without him, and she couldn't imagine dealing with her mother without him as a buffer. She turned to Nima and took a breath as she prepared to do battle. "Mama, why did you have me followed?"

Nima gave Pilar a sharp look. "You?"

"I'm not lying to my sister, Mama."

Nima shot her gaze toward Suda again. "You lied."

"About what?"

"Not working. I called."

"I took a trip with a friend."

"Who?" Nima's trademark stoic expression slightly shifted as she asked, "Horace? The man from the bus? Are you dating a janitor?"

Suda rolled her eyes. "No, Mama. I'm not dating Horace, and he's not a janitor."

"Why lie?"

Suda threw up her hands and glanced at Pilar, who shook his head slightly. He would be no help to her. She couldn't blame him. Nima would show up at his door every day if he sided with Suda.

She looked at her mother with sincerity. "Mama, I'm an adult. I have a personal life."

"Why lie to me?" she said firmly.

"Nima," her father said.

Her mother's gaze dropped to the floor. Although she was a strong woman, she was a traditionalist. When her husband spoke, she listened.

He offered Suda a sad smile. "Your mother worries. About everything. It's because you are so far away."

"I'm not coming back to India, Papa. And I understand that she—that both of you—worry about me. But I'm fine."

"But there are things you won't share with us."

His statement opened the door for her, and his stare ripped away the walls she'd built—the lies, the convoluted stories about past boyfriends, and everything she'd chosen not to say or share with them. She'd seen wonderful places her mother wanted to visit, heard music she knew her father would love, and had funny experiences that would make them both laugh. Yet, it had been easier to deny any of it had ever occurred. It was too difficult to extract the other women who'd shared the stories with her. It would've been like cutting someone out of a picture and trying to explain the remainder.

Her gaze flitted around the room. She couldn't look at her father. She settled for Pilar, who mouthed, *Now.*

She opened her mouth and willed her vocal cords to work. "Papa, my life here is very different. You're right. There's a part of me I haven't shared with you."

"Suda…" her mother hissed.

She held up a hand but she couldn't look at Nima. "Papa, I'm a lesbian."

She stared at him, waiting for a massive coronary to rip through his heart, watching for a tear to drip down his face… anything. But there was no reaction.

"I know," he whispered.

It was Nima who spoke first. "How long?"

He shrugged. "Years. Since Hyma."

Nima gasped. "How? You weren't there."

Her father looked puzzled, obviously knowing nothing about the afternoon Nima nearly caught Suda and Hyma in bed. He looked at Suda and said, "You did not have to tell me. I saw. When someone is in love with another, it is obvious."

He offered a little smile and Suda started to cry. It suddenly made sense. Her father was an incredibly observant man. Although he left most of the talking to Nima, he listened. He watched. Apparently very closely.

"Why did you not say?" Nima asked. "Share your suspicions?"

He turned to Suda. "I thought you would tell us when you were ready. Your mother may have her own reasons for our visit, but I came today so you could finally say the words." She could see the tears in his eyes. "Your brother is about to get married. He's found the love of his life. Life should be shared with someone. I hope the same for you."

Suda glanced at her mother's worried face. He had no idea Nima had hired the man in the FJ Cruiser. She must have already known she and Quinn had spent the night together. Suda imagined the P.I. had taken several pictures. Perhaps he captured her and Quinn kissing on top of the Hotel Beale or across from the train park in Kingman.

"Can we meet your girlfriend?" her father asked.

She shook her head and shuffled her feet. "There is no girlfriend, Papa. At least, not right now."

"But there is someone special."

It was a statement, not a question. Their gazes locked, and for the first time, Suda saw her father. He'd always been there, but her mother was the force, the communicator, the one who moved the family forward. Suda realized her father had been behind the scenes. She burst into tears and threw her arms around him.

"How did you guess?" Suda whispered to him.

"There was no guess. As I said before, when someone is in love, it is obvious."

CHAPTER TWENTY-EIGHT

MAURA'S MENTION:

If you visit Tucumcari, you'll want to consider La Cita for some true southwestern dining at reasonable prices. It's located on the south side of the main drag—the only drag, really—Tucumcari Boulevard. Look for the giant sombrero. Down the road is the Blue Swallow Motel with its great neon sign that's been glowing since 1939. After a meal with a hefty amount of beans, you'll want your lodgings—and your bathroom—close by.

-Mother Road Travels

Quinn and Rain spent the final two and a half hours of Maura's adventure doing what they enjoyed most—reminiscing and catching up on life. Quinn knew the last five minutes of their ascent to Sandia Peak on the tramway had forever cemented their relationship. They were friends and nothing more. She guessed there wouldn't be any future visits to the Amelia Earhart room. It was as if a question had been finally answered, one that had been posed every time Quinn ventured to northern Arizona. Now they knew. She realized Suda had helped them define their relationship, but now Quinn didn't know where she stood with Suda.

At the top of Sandia Peak she and Rain had found a cairn, a mound of stacked stones pointed toward Tucumcari. The words FINISH LINE had been written in chalk by the cairn. When they arrived back at the tram loading station, Jason greeted them.

"Did you find the clue?"

"Yeah, it all came together," Quinn said.

Jason let out a great sigh of relief. "Thank goodness. Do you know how many times in the last week I had to restack that damn cairn? How many times my staff has fielded questions from other tourists? If Maura wasn't Maura…" He didn't finish the sentence and suddenly his face fell as he realized what he'd said. He offered a hug and they returned to the road.

"Do you remember the time," Rain began, "when Maura pretended to be blind at that awful diner in Holbrook?"

Quinn nodded. "Oh, yeah. She wanted to see how accommodating the staff would be."

"And they weren't at all. When she salted her oatmeal instead of her eggs and asked for a new bowl—"

"But they wouldn't give it to her," Quinn finished. "They regretted that for two years, until the next edition of *Mother Road Travels* was published. They begged her to come back, which she did. And they'd made a lot of changes."

"She really influenced Route 66," Rain mused. "I wonder who'll take her place?" She pointed at Quinn, as if she were the answer.

"Oh, no, not me," she said. "I've got a business and I like it. I wouldn't be any good at traveling around and rating places."

"But you loved going on her adventures."

She nodded. "That was because of her. She could make the most boring things fun."

"That's true," Rain agreed. "Remember her Rorschach cloud game? Where you had to look at a cloud and explain whose face it looked like?"

"Yeah. That got us across the panhandle of Texas one year. Talk about a boring ride." Quinn turned and stared at her, as a thought percolated. "What about you?" Rain looked at her quizzically. "You could take Maura's place."

Rain's gaze ping-ponged between Quinn and the road. "No," she said simply.

"Why not? You traveled with her as much as I did—probably more, actually. You should think about it. I don't know anything about Maura's will, but I know my family would support the idea of you continuing *Mother Road Travels*."

"I don't know what to say. I'm flattered."

"Just think about it," Quinn said.

Rain nodded. "I will."

They fell into a lull watching the long ribbon of flat desert spread out before them. Quinn felt the stress of the last few days ooze away. Although her relationship with Rain had changed, she'd given her a mantle she could carry proudly. It seemed like a fair trade.

After twenty miles of silence, Rain asked, "Can I ask you about Suda?"

"Sure. What do you want to know?"

"Is she the one?"

Several replies burst forth, all lobbying to be articulated. She held them at bay and said, "I don't know. This was the weirdest first date ever."

Rain looked astounded. "First date? Are you serious?"

She explained how they met in the ER—twice—and all the events that led them to La Posada.

"Wow," Rain commented. "So she just happened to be covering for that doctor in the other hospital. Some would call that fate. Kismet."

"Maybe," Quinn agreed. She felt a tingle course through her body. Just the thought of Suda affected her.

"I still can't believe someone would take Maura's urn," Rain said.

"I know!" Quinn exclaimed. "Talk about low." She sighed, exasperated. "And where the hell did it go? I watched it go over the edge of the roof, but then it was gone."

"Unbelievable," Rain murmured. She patted her shoulder. "Maybe it will turn up."

"You think?"

Rain nodded. "Other than that part, has it been a fun adventure?"

"Yeah, it has."

"Was that because of Suda?"

She heard the hesitation in Rain's voice. She didn't want to hurt her feelings, and she really wasn't sure if there was anything left of her relationship with Suda. But she knew the answer to Rain's question. She glanced at Rain, her steady gaze focused on the Mother Road. "Yeah."

They hardly talked after her revelation, and Quinn wondered if her relationship with Rain would suffer because of this visit. It seemed she wasn't doing well with her interpersonal skills. She doubted Suda would talk to her again. And if her parents came all the way from India, Quinn imagined it was with one goal: take Suda home. The thought made her queasy. If Suda left, there was no hope for them, and there certainly wouldn't be an opportunity for Quinn to apologize—again.

They reached the Tucumcari city limits and Rain slowed significantly. Her phone buzzed and she pulled it from her pocket and tapped a message.

"Everything okay?" Quinn asked, her eyes half-closed.

"Yeah. It's just Nacho." Nacho was Rain's boss. "He had a quick question."

Quinn sat up and took a deep breath. La Cita was on the right. She saw the brown and gold sombrero sitting on the roof before the turquoise slump-block building came into view. They pulled into the nearly vacant parking lot—next to Maura's Airstream. Quinn grinned. They got out and she walked around it. She checked the door, but it was locked.

"Keys are inside the diner," Rain said. "C'mon."

It was midafternoon, past the lunch rush and before the dinner crowd arrived. Rain passed the hostess station, as if she knew where she was going. Quinn's suspicions heightened as she followed Rain to the back room. When she entered, a crowd yelled, "Happy birthday!"

It took her a second to realize what was happening. Her family was there. DD, Bart, Ward, Rod and the rest of the crew. Disney and her girlfriend Phillipa. Zeke and Louise. Arlo from the Hackberry store, Willow, Pearl and Mr. Wally from the caverns, and Jason from the Sandia Tramway. Even Earl from the Winslow Theater. Purple and white streamers and balloons were draped across a large table. She looked up and saw a banner. *Happy Birthday, Quinn!* This was her real thirtieth birthday party.

She didn't know where to look first. Her mother drew her into a hug. Her father was next and he started crying. She pulled away and asked, "How? How did you do this?"

"It was Maura," he said. "This was her idea and she planned the whole thing. She called me…"

He couldn't finish the words, but Quinn knew how important the phone call had been since Shane and Maura hadn't spoken for years.

At the mention of her aunt, the room went quiet. Quinn could tell everyone was choked up. Obviously Maura was supposed to attend. She wasn't supposed to die.

Zeke stepped forward and said, "After Maura's accident and her return to nature, we all decided we would carry out her plan for you, Quinn, even though we had to make several adjustments. She had hoped to have a great adventure with you and surprise you with this party. She paid to fly everyone in from Phoenix and elsewhere because we all wanted to help. She wanted something special for your thirtieth." His eyes filled with tears. He took a deep breath and turned to Earl and said, "I would say that Earl had the toughest job of all."

"You can say that again," Earl joked. "It was all an act, except for that moment when I almost fell off the roof." He seemed to turn green and reached for a chair.

Quinn pointed at him. "Wait. You didn't steal her ashes?"

"No. But it was fun having you chase me through the catwalks. I haven't had that much fun since I dropped the balloons on Kinsey Avenue during the Veteran's Day parade!"

He grinned from ear to ear, and Quinn had to laugh. She looked at Zeke. "So, who took the urn?"

Arlo held up his hand. "That would be me."

Quinn shook her head. "But why?"

"Maura wanted a real adventure," Zeke explained, "one filled with drama and suspense. I don't know what she originally planned, but we improvised." Louise raised her hand and he pointed at her. "Actually, Louise gets most of the credit for the whole thing."

Quinn looked at Zeke's expressionless paralegal. "I'm a wizard at suspense," she said in a monotone voice. She reached behind a chair and pulled up the urn. "Here, you can have this as a souvenir of your trip."

"Is this really Aunt Maura?"

"Of course not," Fiona interjected. "That would be disgraceful." She looked at her sons. "Boys, show Aunt Quinn what we brought." Goran and Ivan hustled to a corner and returned with a brass urn shaped like a Route 66 highway sign.

It brought tears to her eyes. She gestured toward the Hopi pot. "But isn't this a great artistic work from the Nampeyo family?"

Zeke shook his head. "Cheap copy. Twenty-six ninety-nine at the Jackrabbit Trading Post, but since it was for Maura, Ernestine, the owner, gave it to me for twenty bucks."

Quinn tried to piece everything together. She looked at Earl again. "What about when the pot went over the side of the roof? Where did it go?"

"That would be me," Rain said. "Remember I went back down to the front. I was waiting on the sidewalk. When I heard you and Earl on the roof, I looked up. Luckily, I was only a few feet away, and I'm a good catch."

"You're a great catch," Fiona said mysteriously.

Rain gave her a sharp look, which Quinn noticed.

"Where is Suda?" Louise asked.

Quinn took a deep breath. "That's a long story." A thought occurred to her. "What about the FJ Cruiser that was following us?" Everyone shrugged and looked puzzled. Quinn supposed it would be a mystery forever. "What happened to the Flagstaff clue?"

Zeke rolled his eyes and Louise shook her head. "We had to get rid of it. Maura had you stopping in Holbrook for three more clues, but we knew Suda didn't have the time. So I took it out."

"It was the only way," Louise said. She looked at her watch. "It's time to eat."

After everyone had filled up on Mexican food and birthday cake, the guests said their good-byes. Some went back to work, like Jason, Willow, and Mr. Wally, while others headed to the Blue Swallow Motel for the night.

"I'm heading back," Rain said, pulling Quinn into a hug. "Happy birthday."

"Are we okay?" she whispered.

Rain stepped back and cupped her cheeks. "We're more than okay." She kissed her tenderly once more before hurrying out the door.

"Hey!" Quinn shouted. When Rain turned around she said, "You need to become the new travel writer."

"We'll see," she called back.

Quinn watched her stroll to her truck, wondering if she should run after her. But as she watched Rain's taillights vanish in the dusk, a calm settled over her. She'd made the right choice. Even if nothing came from her weekend with Suda, she knew she and Rain were destined to be friends—and nothing else.

Before Zeke left, he handed Quinn the keys to the Airstream. "It's yours now." He made a face and added, "You probably should change the litter box quickly."

Soon it was just Fiona and the boys. Goran and Ivan had pulled down the streamers and wrapped themselves up like mummies, in a cleanup effort gone awry. Fiona sat with Quinn and rubbed her back.

"What happened with Suda?"

"We had a fight. She's not out to her parents, although that might've changed in the last six hours."

"Do you want it to work?"

"Maybe."

"What about Rain?"

"We're just friends."

"Oh." There was definite disappointment in Fiona's voice.

Quinn turned to her with a sharp gaze. "Is there something I should know?"

Fiona shook her head. Growling and moaning drew their attention. The boys had splattered salsa on their streamer bandages to look like blood and were walking around like zombies.

"Those were new shirts!" Fiona cried. "You two, come with me. We're going to the motel." She kissed Quinn on the cheek and hustled the boys out of the restaurant.

Quinn looked around. The party had broken up. She stared at the head of the table. Aunt Maura's real Route 66 urn sat next to the fake Hopi pottery. Zeke had confessed it was filled with sand. Quinn grabbed both and headed to the Airstream. Sure enough, the litter box needed to be changed. Maura's cats, Billy Shears, Penny Lane and Eleanor Rigby were glad to see her, and even happier when she fed them.

She spent an hour going through Maura's trailer, searching for the mysterious test results. She only cried twice as she opened drawers and poked around in cabinets, but there was nothing. She found an entire closet full of games, Maura's favorite way to pass the time. Dotting the walls was Route 66 memorabilia and dozens of photos. In many of them Quinn stood next to Maura at various ages. She'd completely forgotten some of the pictures, while others were as clear a memory as if they'd occurred yesterday.

Sitting on a shelf was the new Mac laptop. She opened it and stared at Maura's desktop. Right in the center was *Mother Road Travels*, seventh edition. She'd peruse it eventually. Maybe she could see it to print and give the proceeds to the various Route 66 historical societies. That's what Maura would've wanted.

She searched the documents folder and desktop for test results, but there was nothing. Another icon was labeled *Quinn's Birthday Movie*. Her finger hovered over the track pad. She bit her lip. She wasn't sure she wanted to know what Maura had originally planned. With hesitation, she clicked on the icon.

She froze. It wasn't Maura's face that filled the screen. It was Rain's.

She cleared her throat and stared into the camera. "Quinn, there's something I've wanted to tell you for a while now. We've always been great friends, and I share everything with you. It's like we fit. When you're around, you make me a better person. I'm not great with words like Maura, but will you marry me?"

CHAPTER TWENTY-NINE

After she found Rain's video she'd called Fiona immediately. "How much did you know?" she demanded.

Fiona came back to the Airstream and they talked until midnight. Fiona explained the entire adventure had been a backdrop for what was really the point of the trip: Rain's proposal. "Maura wanted to do something amazing for your thirtieth, and Rain had told her how she felt about you." Fiona had sighed deeply. "Then everything changed."

"So the whole running through the catwalks thing was planned?" Quinn asked incredulously.

"Of course! Maura maintained you couldn't have an adventure without some danger."

"What about the test results?"

Fiona looked at her sheepishly. "Well, she made those up too. She wasn't sure she'd be able to convince you to come up north since you're in the middle of a project, so she thought she'd play the dying card if necessary. She knew there was some Catholic guilt still swimming in your gene pool, even if you don't claim to be religious."

Quinn shook her head. "Just tell it all to me." Fiona recounted how all of the players became involved, and Quinn could almost picture Aunt Maura sitting alongside Fiona for the telling.

Quinn had wanted to call Rain immediately, but Fiona convinced her to give Rain the space she needed. "Rain needs time to heal. She'll probably be kicking herself for a while that she didn't tell you sooner." Then Fiona had cocked her head and looked at her thoughtfully before she said, "But I'm thinking you would've declined."

Quinn shrugged. "I don't know."

"Do you love Suda? You've only known her for a week."

"Sometimes that's all it takes."

* * *

When Quinn pulled the Airstream alongside the apartment complex the next day, her entire crew was waiting for her. Fiona and Steven pulled up behind her. As a seasoned veteran of manual transmissions, Steven had driven Cousin It back to Phoenix while Fiona drove the family's van.

Fiona had barely stopped the van when the side door flew open, spewing Goran and Ivan to the pavement. They were laughing hysterically.

Fiona got out in a huff and turned to DD. "Please tell me there is a cement mixer nearby. I'd like to have busts of my children created."

"Oh, like statues?" DD asked quizzically.

"No," Fiona replied, "like having their bodies permanently trapped in cement." She pointed as Goran and Ivan ducked inside the construction zone. "Someone might want to go catch them before they dig a swimming pool with your backhoe." Bart and Ward jumped up and followed them.

DD turned to Quinn. "You're not going to believe what happened this morning." He held out an envelope. "This came by special courier." Inside was a letter from *Phoenix Magazine*, congratulating Quinn O'Sullivan and the FaceLift company for revitalizing some of Phoenix's historic apartment buildings, most notably the Seymour, their last site. The letter discussed their creative ideas for making "everything old, new again."

"My gosh, Quinn," Fiona said, reading over her shoulder. "You're going to be famous!"

"I doubt that," Quinn replied.

"But I bet it will convince Dad that this flippin' thing is for real."

Quinn beamed at the thought.

"I'll betcha we'll get more contracts," DD said.

"That could happen," Quinn agreed. She smiled and high-fived DD. "Way to go, team!"

Bart and Ward reappeared with Goran and Ivan, who were covered in mud—as were Bart and Ward. "They accidentally fell," Ward said.

Fiona shook her head. "Trust me, Ward. This wasn't an *accident.*" Goran and Ivan grinned. Their white teeth contrasted sharply with the rich brown mud.

"Boys, back of the van," Steven directed. "The way back."

They groaned but followed their father after offering Quinn a wave good-bye. Fiona kissed her sister and whispered, "You'll figure it out. Who knows? Maybe things will change."

Fiona offered a mysterious smile as she climbed into the van. Quinn was about to ask her to explain, but DD said, "Boss, there's one other thing."

Quinn braced herself. "What?"

Wordlessly, DD pointed toward the gate. Quinn looked at him suspiciously, but he chuckled. And pointed again.

She grabbed her stuff and headed inside the complex. That's when she saw the first sign next to the sidewalk. It was a strip of neon yellow poster board stapled to a pine stake. It said, *Prospective girlfriend.* Ten feet later was the next one. *Might need a push.* By then, Quinn was smiling and walking much faster. She rounded the corner and was confronted by the third sign. *But she's worth the effort.* The last sign was in front of her door. *If you're not in a rush.* Her breath caught when she saw the infamous red panties, the ones she'd donned as a cap during their adventure, hanging on the doorknob. She fingered the smooth silk and inhaled traces of Suda's perfume. Her hands shook, a tingle of electricity coursed through her middle, and her legs wobbled as she went inside.

The living room was dark. The only source of light was a single candle sitting on a bookshelf outside her closed bedroom door. It smelled like cinnamon. Quinn couldn't stop the groan that escaped her lips. She dropped her bags and shed her coat. She thought she heard a giggle, and that made her smile. It was good to know Suda wasn't an expert at seduction. She didn't want an expert. They weren't good girlfriend material.

What she found as she stepped inside the doorway was exactly what she wanted to see. The lights were off and three candles formed a triangle, one on each nightstand and the third at the foot of the futon bed on Quinn's old footlocker. In the center was Suda, lying on her side, her head propped up on the palm of her right hand, her long legs crossed. She wore only the newly purchased leather jacket. It was zipped to her chin and seemed ridiculously modest since the curve of her glorious bare ass was silhouetted in the candlelight.

Quinn stared at her, imprinting the entire tableau on her brain. She wanted to remember this moment forever. Whenever they fought or their relationship hung in peril, she would summon this image.

Suda's expression shifted and Quinn sensed she was growing uncomfortable or anxious. She started to change her pose, and Quinn reached out. "No. Don't move."

"I wasn't sure—"

"Be sure."

Quinn stripped off her clothes and felt Suda's burning stare on her flesh. "I loved your signs."

As she slid onto the futon, Suda smiled and reached for her. She traced a lazy finger around her areola, down her abdomen and between her legs.

Suda turned on her back and stared at the ceiling. "Is this how you wanted me?"

"It is," Quinn managed to croak. She slowly unzipped the leather jacket until an ample amount of her cleavage was visible.

With the lightest of touches, she stroked Suda's left breast, pushing the fabric aside and exposing her nipple.

Suda shifted on the bed, a moan escaping her lips. "Quinn, stop teasing me," she whined.

"Never," Quinn whispered.

In a fluid movement she unzipped the jacket entirely and climbed on top of her. Their mouths immediately connected. Quinn offered sweet kisses, reminding herself of Suda's signs. She didn't want to go too fast. She let Suda set the pace. When Suda's fingers gripped the back of her head and pressed their lips together, she took it as permission and pushed her tongue into Suda's warm mouth for a delightful welcome.

Her hands cupped Suda's small breasts and she slid a leg between her thighs. She broke the kiss, yearning to hear Suda's sweet sounds of pleasure. She placed a kiss behind her ear, found the hollow of her neck and dragged her tongue to a waiting nipple. The smell of leather intensified her desire—and brought forth that image of Suda lying on the bed in the leather jacket.

Suda's moans grew ragged as Quinn's kisses reached her soft belly. She smelled her desire, but she gazed at her face for confirmation. She didn't want Suda to regret anything, for Quinn had every intention of spending the rest of the day in bed—if Suda agreed, and she intended to make that happen. Her eyes were closed and her mouth hung slightly open, as if she were waiting for Quinn's lips to return. She'd put one hand behind her head while the other caressed Quinn's shoulder.

"How far do you want to go?" Quinn asked between kisses. It would be incredibly difficult for her to stop, but she would muster all of her self-control if necessary.

Suda seemed unable to form words as Quinn kissed her inner thighs. There was no mistaking her want—her need. She said something incomprehensible and slid her legs farther apart. She tensed slightly when Quinn gently stroked her wet, delicate deliciousness, but she moaned when Quinn put a single finger inside. Suda undulated her hips, finding a rhythm.

It wasn't enough. Quinn wanted Suda on fire. She reached up beneath the fine leather jacket, squeezing her hardened nipples in time to the rhythm Suda desired. One finger became two. Suda gave a guttural cry like none Quinn had ever heard, and Quinn slipped another finger inside. Suda pushed herself up on her elbows. She wanted to watch Quinn make love to her.

"Now," she cried. "Please."

Quinn gazed at her pleading brown eyes before disappearing between her legs, flicking her tongue against Suda's wet center in time to the rhythm of her hips. The orgasm that ripped through her body had three short aftershocks. When it was over, she collapsed, her legs still shaking. Quinn traced the contour of her side and nestled against her.

It wasn't clear who kissed whom first, but when their lips separated and they looked into each other's eyes, Quinn knew it was love. Suda's smile told her she was right.

Bella Books, Inc.

Women. Books. Even Better Together.

P.O. Box 10543
Tallahassee, FL 32302

Phone: 800-729-4992
www.bellabooks.com